Sign up for our newsletter to hear
about new and upcoming releases.

www.ylva-publishing.com

Other Books by Georgette Kaplan

Ex-Wives of Dracula

The Scissor Link Series
Scissor Link
Face It

The Cushing-Nevada Chronicles
Easy Nevada and the Pyramid's Curse

the woman at the edge of town

Georgette Kaplan

For Zuzu. I promise we'll stop calling you that as soon as you understand words mean things.

Chapter 1

Fingers of rain tapped at the world with the quiet insistence of an unwanted question. It had rained all morning the day of Sarah Kay's twentieth birthday, and it would continue into the afternoon and evening and keep going into the night. Drizzling. Not the fun kind of puddling showers or the exciting, gothic-horror rainstorms, but an uneven, wavering rainfall that would let up just long enough to give a little hope that the sun would come out, then piddle out jerkily again from graying clouds.

It went with the gray day Sarah was having. It had started with pancakes from Eileen, her mother, which were nice, but…just enough effort to make her feel ungracious for not being more impressed. Then she'd been to work, where no one had much noticed. A dull, six-hour shift of front-facing in a supermarket, the same as any other, the same as any job she'd worked over the summers or holidays since she'd started high school.

The first box of Pop-Tarts in the stack had been taken out, leaving a little cavity, so she pulled the next one up, then the next box of cornflakes, the next box of microwave popcorn—all because it looked better when products were all lined up front and center like Tom Cruise's teeth.

Two thoughts circled each other with depressing regularity as Sarah worked. The first was that her job only existed because some consultant somewhere—who wore a suit that cost more than her internal organs—had done up a report saying that the company could increase its earnings by 0.000002% if the products were on the front edges of their shelves instead of recessed by a unit or two. Identical men in identical suits with identical millions had done similar reports for Walgreens, Target, Walmart, and all the other big-box stores Sarah had tried and failed to fit in at.

The second thought was that she could go back to college, figure out her major, graduate top of her class, and this would still be the only field that would be hiring.

After work was a birthday party at home that bored her sick. There was pizza, sure, and ice cream and…well, balloons. Perfectly fine for, like, Tuesday. But she'd rather have some *real* fun.

Instead, her mom was threatening to watch *Practical Magic* with her as if it was some kind of ritual. None of her real friends were here, except for her boyfriend Tyrese; the rest were all her mom's friends and people she was *supposed* to be friends with, and she was twenty seconds away from just bailing. It'd probably take hours for anyone to notice anyway.

There was one real perk. She'd been paying on her car for three years now, a gently used 2013 Prius that she'd gotten two thousand dollars off of because the dealer was trying to move inventory and no one else wanted a car with a purple paint job like Willy Wonka was riding around in it. So her big birthday present was that her mom had finished paying it off for her. It was so damn practical that she would bite her tongue clean through before she let herself be ungrateful.

Vanilla ice cream, though. She could be petty about that. Who got vanilla ice cream for a birthday party? It was like signing *Have a great summer* in someone's yearbook.

She soldiered through thanking everyone for their gifts—mainly gift certificates, gift cards, and some sort of amulet that was supposed to protect her from evil spirits. But if it worked and evil spirits were a real concern, who would sell something like that? Then she was finally able to bolt, with Tyrese in the passenger seat and her behind the wheel.

She put the Prius through its paces, and it seemed to accelerate just a little faster, purr just a little louder, with the pink slip all hers. They orbited town like a satellite, tires throwing up gales of puddled water.

"It's a race thing," Tyrese told her.

"What? No."

"I'm ninety-nine percent sure it is. They make a *Baby-Sitters Club* show where Kristy's a black girl. People hate it."

"That's not what it is."

"So you like Kristy being black?"

"I'm…confused why Kristy needs to be black when Jessi's black…"

"Oh, so being black is Jessi's thing?"

"Kinda. It was the nineties."

They'd been friends since elementary school, when he'd been the only boy willing to keep pulling her ponytail after she'd clobbered Billy Finch. In middle school they'd been bros, Tyrese sneaking her his dad's beer and Sarah bringing him her mom's lingerie catalogs. In high school, they'd made it official, going out to Sandra Bullock movies together and everything. There'd been some make-out sessions, she'd let him feel her up when those Sandra Bullock movies got steamy, and then at prom—

He was her first, he was her boyfriend, and she loved him. They'd even done the long-distance thing for a bit while she'd been away at college. Eventually, they'd get married, maybe start a family...

"So you think Kristy should be white?"

"You're not listening."

"Of course I'm listening. I'm spellbound by you. I'm entranced."

He plucked her right hand from the steering wheel and gave it a kiss. She snatched it back, gripping the wheel tighter. "C'mon, ten-and-two. I'm trying to drive."

"You're trying to explain why you don't like a TV show without sounding racist."

Sarah made an exasperated sound of disbelief. "They're not even babysitters anymore! They grew up, moved to the city, started a law firm, and now they *call themselves* the Baby-Sitters Club because they 'babysit'"—Here Sarah thought to do air quotes, but since she was determined to keep her hands on the wheel, she did a similar motion with her shoulders instead—"their clients. They're in their thirties now! Which, by the way, is a ridiculous age to be partners in a law firm."

"It's a reinvention. This is what they do when they grow up."

They passed a herd of cows grazing in their fenced-in enclosure, drooling cud from their chomping jaws.

"They all become attorneys? It's using a bunch of familiar names to get people to watch another generic doctor-cop-lawyer show. Not even familiar names, since now they're calling Stacey 'Simone,' so I guess thank God they finally did something about a girl being named Stacey. That was really a glaring plot hole..."

"So you just want a show about teenage girls babysitting?"

"Kinda. I mean, if it's *called* the *Baby-Sitters Club*... I just don't get how it's the *Baby-Sitters Club* if they're in a different city, with different backgrounds, different names, different jobs—when you read a story, it has a kind of a soul, and you shouldn't mess with something's soul."

"So you want the same thing over and over again?"

"I just like things the way I like them."

"Yeah…" Tyrese drawled, grabbing her hand again. "That's the way I like you too."

He began sloppily kissing her hand, bathing her knuckles in spit. She tugged, but he had a good grip and bigger biceps than her.

"Tyrese, c'mon, quit it."

"You gotta learn how to drive with one hand sometime, babe, or how are you ever gonna use your cell phone?"

"Tyrese, I'm serious." She gave him her best death glare. "It's a ten-minute drive. You can't go ten minutes without molesting—"

She happened to glance forward then and saw it so abruptly that it was like her previous view of clear, empty road had been shattered by this new sight: a car, its front end hugging the trunk of a tree, its back half protruding back onto the street and into her lane.

Sarah jerked the wheel—one-handed—and stomped on the brakes. The Prius obeyed, swerving to one side as the brakes locked, but there was no reassuring stop, just a liquid feeling of suspension—drifting, drifting, drifting on the wet pavement. Then she was thrown to the side, the car spinning out as it was ripped to a stop. She couldn't keep it on the road, heard the squealing tires give way to a meaty, pulping sound as her wheels dug into the dirt and grass of the ditch. Then, mercifully, they stopped.

For a moment, Sarah was frozen. Just breathing. No videogame reflexes, no adrenaline rush, just a prolonged wondering: *What the hell happened, what the hell happened, what the hell happened?* Her mind ticked away like a clock; she actually shook the cobwebs out. This was an emergency. She was in an emergency. She always pictured herself being cool, calm, collected—not an action hero, no, but if someone robbed the store she was working in, she'd keep a level head and open the cash register and send them on their way. Now she was one of those people who just went into hysterics.

No. Emergency. She had to make sure everything was okay. She looked at Tyrese. He was gulping air, his eyes wide, a slight tremble in his frozen face. As much in shock or whatever as she was. Maybe more so. Sarah patted his arm. "You okay?"

"What the *fuck?*"

"You're okay…"

The other car. Belatedly, Sarah realized she was still holding down the brake pedal. The Prius was still in drive. She groped for the gear shift, found it, jammed it into park. Then, just on instinct, she pressed the stop button and killed the engine. Her headlights continued to blare out, drawing a mournful beep from the car's systems. She barely heard it. Where was she? *The other car.* She undid her seatbelt, pulled herself out of the Prius. She didn't feel as if she was hurt. No broken bones or blood—probably should've checked for that before she started moving.

Her legs seemed to have developed all sorts of interesting kinks, though, threading needles through the flesh of her thighs as she staggered the few feet up to the road. The Prius looked fine; just one side had been gone over by Freddy Krueger, and— Holy shit, the driver's side mirror had been clipped off entirely. Her mom was going to *kill* her. Her gaze moved past the gouges of muddy soil where the tires had clawed over the fresh skid marks on the road.

She could see the other car's taillights, their glow rising like smoke to the branches of the slanted tree above, which had shifted aside for the darkly wheezing car bundled up against its trunk. From here, it didn't even look like a wreck, but rather some kind of bizarre taxidermy. A jackalope or something.

Sarah took a step forward, getting her feet under her, then stopped immediately, recognizing the car. Anyone in Bathory would've recognized the 2002 Vertigo Streiff, one of those cars that was halfway to being a Batmobile. In a town full of Ford trucks and electric-shaver Japanese imports, it was the only automobile that made her understand how guys could think of cars as sexy.

And it was driven by Nina fucking Rose.

She looked back at her Prius. Her modest, piddling little Prius. Tyrese was groaning, coming out of his daze with a stupefied slowness. "Call 911!" she called out to him.

"Wha?" he asked. "What happened? Everyone okay?"

"*Call 911!*" she insisted, but he was even more out of it than she was, sluggishly patting his pockets for his phone. Sarah hurried back to the car and reached inside for hers, in the sunglasses case in the roof. It wasn't really designed to be reached for by someone who wasn't in the driver's seat, and she slipped on the wet grass, driving her knees into the mud. Growling at herself, she wrenched herself up, grabbed the cell phone, and sloughed her way across the road to the wreck.

It didn't look bad. Well, what had been a gleaming model of engineering perfection was now a Christmas ornament, but it looked more like a fender bender than anything with the phrase *wrapped around* in it. Exhaust drooled out into the red atmosphere of the taillights, while something hissed out from the engine into the grass underneath the car. The headlights captured the leaves still falling from the struck tree. Sarah pulled her jacket shut around herself, suddenly registering the cold attacking her leggings and blouse.

The windows were rolled up, tinted, and Sarah could see her own glossy shadow in the driver's side one as she approached. "Hello in there? Are you okay? Ms. Rose?" She rapped her knuckles on the glass, and the sound was weirdly echo-y. In a cartoon moment of imagination, she wondered if that was because she'd broken something, picturing the whole car collapsing into dust from her tapping on it. Something tasted bitter in her mouth. Maybe she'd bitten her tongue.

There was a dull, flat roar from the car, and Sarah stumbled back, nearly tripping over her own feet before realizing it was the window. It only came down a few inches, and through it the cabin was completely dark; she couldn't even see through to the other window. What she could see were a pair of eyes.

They were dark, narrow like a cat's, and rimmed with kohl, with hazel irises flecked with deeper black trapped in them like they were amber. The pupils were totally black, so black they actually caught the light like a glossy stone and reflected little pinpricks of white. The eyebrows were manicured, each eyelash a deft brushstroke, and the look in the eyes was clear and intent, so intent it seemed to push through to something behind Sarah, staring through her with such power that she felt an urge to turn around and see what it was.

And there was blood. A scarlet strand of it, weaving from higher on the forehead down between the eyes, marking the profile of Nina Rose's straight, distinguished nose. On her pale skin, it seemed to pick up the little light seeping past the cracked window, glaring like fire, triggering a wave of guilt inside Sarah.

There was a pregnant pause; Sarah couldn't think of what to say.

"You're about the most beautiful girl I've ever seen," Nina Rose said, her voice a dreamy whisper—centered, prepossessed, and totally out of tune with the wet, dreary evening, the shuddering car wreck, the blood still halving her face.

Absurdly, Sarah felt herself blushing before she realized it was probably just the head trauma talking. "I'm going to get you out of there."

Sarah reached for the door but heard the echoing *click* of the car's locks being engaged. She pulled on the handle and, no, Nina Rose wasn't unlocking it. Sarah was locked out.

"There's no need for that." The voice had risen to a slight, breathy timbre that seemed more fitting to the smoky eyes and their cool gaze. More focused now, the eyes scoured Sarah's face. "I'm fine."

"I should still take a look at you. I've taken a first-aid course—I could do something about that cut."

"There is no need." The voice was firm, definite—the woman behind the glass had the air of someone who decided things that stayed decided.

Frustration swarmed inside Sarah. She looked down, spotted a decent-sized rock at her feet, and picked it up. There were worms underneath. *Eww.* "You might have a concussion, a spine injury, so either I can break the window, or you can let me in."

The eyes narrowed. Then, quite counterintuitively, there came a rich, deep laugh. It seemed totally incongruous to the first impression she'd just gotten, an unlearned sound like that a broken toy would make, and Sarah almost thought the woman was going into hysterics before it abruptly ended.

Sarah supposed she cut quite a figure, standing there in a Katy Perry concert T-shirt, leggings as pants, with her hair mussed up by the crash, and holding a muddy rock as if it was a lethal weapon. It wasn't as if she would've actually *done it.* She just needed to be sure no one was bleeding out or going into shock or—anything. But then she heard the sirens, turned and spotted the red lights coming like watercolors mixing in with the mist, and dropped the stone.

Tyrese must have managed to call 911 after all. And they'd had someone in the area. The benefits of living somewhere where nothing ever happened.

Eileen showed up right on the heels of the ambulance and proceeded to have a full-blown freak-out. All Sarah wanted to do was get a look at Ms. Rose, right across the road, hidden in a swirl of EMTs, but no, she had to get a lecture. Really, a double lecture, because Tyrese's grandfather showed up too and had it out with him. More of a teeth-gritted scolding than Eileen's audio offensive, but equally effective. Both of them kept their defenses half-hearted, hoping they could play dead and convince the 'rents to pass up an easy kill.

Then, to Sarah's horror, Eileen went to talk to Nina.

Sarah tried to follow her, talk her out of it, but Eileen gave her a loaded finger point and generally insinuated that the Warsaw Pact would be kaput if she didn't stay right where she was. So Sarah was left watching and listening to Tyrese's continued dressing-down, as Eileen went to apologize on her behalf.

When Eileen came back a few minutes later, Sarah winced inwardly. This must've been what criminals felt when they saw the Bat-Signal. "Well, *she* appreciates your help—"

"Oh, *she* does, does she?"

"Yes, well, she isn't your mother, and she isn't wondering why you were going so fast that you nearly ran into a car wreck instead of being able to stop in time," Eileen enunciated. "Although I suppose I should just be grateful you're still alive."

"Yes. You should always be grateful for that."

"Don't get snippy!" Eileen waved her hand at the crumpled Vertigo. "That could've been you."

"For all you know, I saved someone's life today. And maybe I already feel bad about the car, *Mom*, so you don't have to—" Sarah stumbled over not saying the F-word. If it were anyone else… "Rub it in!"

"Wow. Guilt. I didn't know you were capable. I'm sure this will make your Prius 'gently used' all over again."

"I'll get it fixed. It's not like this town doesn't have a body shop."

"And you'll pay for it how?"

"I'll figure something out."

"Because that's your strong suit," Eileen finished for her. "Figuring things out."

Sarah just bit her lip and looked away. Eileen never understood. She wasn't in any mood to battle anymore. "I'll start looking for a second job in the morning."

As she walked to her mom's car—no way in hell Eileen would be letting her drive home; she'd sooner eat the bill for a tow truck—she felt eyes on the back of her neck. Dark, hazel eyes.

Chapter 2

Eileen woke Sarah up the next morning by dropping a DVD on her pillow. Sarah was dozing lightly enough to try making sense of the slipcover instead of falling out of bed. "*Defensive Driving?* Mom, come on, it's…eleven a.m."

Eileen was merciless. "You said in the morning—"

"It's still the morning."

"If you were going to stay up half the night, you'd think you could've filled out some job applications…"

No, *now* Eileen was merciless. She'd had a little bit of mercy before; it was gone.

"I couldn't sleep. It was the adrenaline."

"And every other night? Do you go skydiving? Street racing? Well, now you're up, so I expect at least one interview scheduled by the end of the day, and you can watch the first disc of that program. And it came with a booklet, so I will be testing you."

Sarah opened the DVD case. "*The Dangers of Drunk Driving?* Mom, I wasn't drunk."

"At least a drunk person would've had an excuse. Now go and get the mail; you can have breakfast before you hit the pavement."

Sarah had slept in the hoodie and sweatpants she'd thrown on after scrubbing the mud out of the clothes she'd been wearing last night. She pulled the hood up over her ears and got out of bed. "No one hits the pavement anymore, Mom. All the applications are online."

Eileen was in hot pursuit as she trudged downstairs. "You're in trouble and you expect me to put you on the computer all day?"

"You could install Windows 8 on it." The joke was clearly lost on Eileen, who didn't respond.

Sarah stepped into some flip-flops, taking far longer than necessary to put them on because she was determined to use only her toes—Goddamn her to hell if she had to use her hands for fucking flip-flops—and then walked out to get the mail. Thankfully, the lecture stayed indoors. Eileen was even less a fan of airing dirty laundry than she was of a full sleep cycle.

Sarah took the mail out of the box—giving the old post-and-flag configuration a kick for being so damn quaint—and automatically sorted through it. Netflix, bills, birthday cards (no money), coupons for Sizzler, and… Holy shit.

An envelope with her name in the middle and Nina Rose's in the corner.

In her room, Sarah had all the lights off except for the neon *Eat at Joe's* sign that'd been a gift from her friend Beck, who'd worked at a junkyard. Its green glow served as nightlight and possible Superman deterrent while Sarah used her laptop.

The usual gang was all on Skype, except for Tyrese, whose grandfather still practiced corporal punishment: turning off the internet router until he'd done a laundry list of chores. There was Jonesy, who'd been childhood friends with Sarah until she'd moved away. They'd rediscovered each other on Facebook a few years back. In the interval, Jonesy had discovered boys and put on weight. She seemed happy, and Sarah had gotten too many maternal comments about at least getting diet soda if she was drinking sugar water to want to police how many chins Jonesy had.

Beck she'd met in high school. She was a townie like Sarah, but way straightedge, though she didn't look it: brush-cut head with what little hair was left dyed pink, nose ring, blue lipstick. Since none of them really drank, smoked, or shot up, things were civil with her, though she'd shown worrying signs of getting into veganism.

Then there was Sarah. She liked her looks. Her current ensemble was, well, "affordable," but she loved her body almost as much as pop stars said she should: the breasts that had taken approximately forever to come in, the legs that had sprung up just before high school ended, the hair that she'd stopped wearing in a ponytail so it could messily wrap around her shoulders, long and latte-colored. It had all come together pretty well. Athletic enough, thin enough, busty enough—everything "enough."

She supposed she should be more enthusiastic about it than that. It wasn't like no one ever liked her selfies. She guessed it just wasn't in her nature to proclaim herself beautiful, even mentally. Beck had her cool punkish side, Jonesy had her confidence…and Sarah just felt like…the sum of her parts.

"Hey, Sarah? We're wondering why you called us all here today?" Beck asked.

Sarah almost apologized for spacing out. Instead, she held up the envelope. Nina Rose's neat signature over the address: 101 Gothel Lane.

"Holy darn," Beck said. "Nina Rose. So we know she has hands, then?"

"She could've had someone write it for her," Sarah reasoned. "She's supposed to be a millionaire, after all."

"Who's Nina Rose?" Jonesy asked.

"Right, that was after your time," Sarah realized.

Beck took over. "She's like this hermit millionaire who moved into the old Stauffer place."

"What old Stauffer place?"

Beck huffed out an exasperated sigh. "Did you even live here, woman? It was the seventies or something and this whole family was living there, white picket fences and everything—"

Boop. Sarah got a chat message from Jonesy underneath the roulette wheel of video windows. *So what's the story with you and Ty, meow?*

What story? Same story as ever, Sarah typed back.

Beck was still going strong. "So he starts wondering who all these letters are coming from, right, so the next Tuesday he stays up all night to watch the door—"

Siriusly biutch? You tell me you're trying something new in the bedroom and then all quiet on the Sarah Kay front.

"Naturally, he gets an axe, goes to his wife's bedroom—"

Sarah flicked an annoyed glance at Beck's ranting; she'd always been one step away from one of those girls who wrote to serial killers in prison.

Then she started typing: *It was fine. We bought some lube, tried out some different positions—*

"Then, covered in blood, he takes the bodies and—"

Sarah muted the audio. What to say? What the fuck to say? She typed: *It didn't feel good. It didn't feel bad. I wasn't really expecting it to be great, not right away, but we've had plenty of practice, and I still don't feel anything. It's like my body responds, but I'm not invested in it. I don't care. I keep thinking about the condom and the lube and shit like that. All the mechanics. Then it's over and I don't feel any different. No matter how many times we do it, it's still like I don't...*

The words just flowed out of her, like her fingers were attacking the keyboard, punching and chopping and no end in sight. She deleted all of it without sending and unmuted the conversation.

"And that rookie cop who found them is still in a madhouse to this day," Beck concluded triumphantly.

"Wasn't that an episode of *Hannibal*?" Jonesy asked.

"They have to get their ideas somewhere. So what's the letter actually say?"

"Pretty much nothing." Sarah held it up to the webcam.

Ms. Sarah Kay,
You are cordially invited to the home of Nina Rose, Tuesday, 6:00 PM. Semi-formal wear acceptable. Refreshments will be served.

"Nice calligraphy," Beck noted. "She definitely pays someone to write that for her."

"Like a medieval monk or something."

"Is she suing you?"

"Are you bringing a lawyer?"

"Do you *have* a lawyer?"

"Sounds more like a party."

The screen began artifacting, her friends' faces decomposing into a collection of misplaced pixels. Sarah fought the urge to give her laptop a smack. Why did the internet in America suck so bad? She'd heard that in the Netherlands, they had free broadband as a civil right.

Purr purr, Jonesy sent via chat. Still waiting on an answer.

Sarah forced her fingers to press down. *It was great. I just don't wanna talk about it and have my private life end up in one of your weird sex tweets.*

Moments later, a reply popped up. *Now she's too good for my two million followers. *rubs paws all over your face**

Eh, most of those are bots.

"So are you going to go?" Jonesy asked, and Sarah realized it was directed at her.

"Yeah, I think so. At least it'll get me out of the job hunt for a while. Why is it that the supermarket can't give me more hours again?"

"Because then they'd have to give you health insurance," Jonesy said.

"Oh, yeah, right."

Tyrese came on then. Beck brightened instantly. "Hey, Ty."

"Hey. Anyone on Twitch?" A chorus of nos. "You gotta check this out." He sent them a link.

It was an ice rink, one big enough for the Stanley Cup finals, viewed from one of those high-up cameras you occasionally saw getting investigated by birds. The feed showed a number of people scuttling like beetles about the ice and the seating.

"What am I looking at?" Jonesy asked.

"It's the World Domino League, or something like that," Tyrese replied. He typed as he spoke, and it wasn't long before Sarah got a message in the chat box: *U OK?* She typed back, explaining about the letter as he went on. "They're building a domino knockdown with three hundred thousand dominos, going for the world record for knockdown with most tails... At least, that's what their tweet says."

"So...what am I looking at?" Jonesy asked again.

"No, it's cool," Beck said. "Something out of nothing. Thanks, Ty."

Tyrese got Sarah's message, read it rapid-fire, his lips moving a little as he parsed it. "Damn," he muttered. "So, the old Stauffer place?"

"Old Stauffer place," Sarah confirmed, feeling a little bit of pride for no real reason. Maybe just the result of being the center of attention instead of Beck's latest crusade or whatever weirdness Jonesy had uncovered in her mom's seventies romance novels.

"Wonder what it looks like on the inside. I hear Nina Rose never steps foot outside the place."

"Well, her car does," Sarah told him.

"You gotta wonder what she did on the inside, after the exterior renovations," Beck said.

"What renovations?"

"You haven't seen the renovations?" Beck asked. "I mean, sure, no one's gone inside, but there's nothing to stop you from *looking* at it."

"I thought it was on an island," Jonesy said.

"Islet," Beck corrected. "In Dutch River."

"Are you her real estate agent now?" Sarah asked.

"Hey, Jonesy moved away, fine, but I can't believe you've lived here your entire live and never checked out the haunted house of Nina Rose."

Sarah coughed. "Ditto. I can't believe I've lived here my entire life either."

"So what's it look like, then?" Jonesy asked.

"Nobody tell her," Tyrese ordered. "Sarah, go see it, take a selfie—"

"I'm not doing that."

"How do *you* even know what it looks like," Jonesy persisted, "if it's on some kind of towhead?"

"Towhead, whoa, look who moved to Mississippi," Beck sniped. "I have binoculars, Jonesy, clearly."

"You think it makes them happy?" Sarah asked. She was looking at the window she still had open to Twitch, watching all those thousands of dominos being put into place.

"What?"

"All those dominos. It must feel pretty good, looking back and seeing all the ones you've placed. And having a big—" She gestured with her hand, symbolizing a domino tipping over. "To look forward to."

"They're probably just doing it for attention," Tyrese said.

"Got a check from a deodorant company or something," Beck agreed. "They just want it to go viral, or whatever buzzword their marketing guy used."

"Yeah…" Sarah agreed hesitantly.

After they'd all signed off and she was *way* past a reasonable bedtime instead of just "up late," Sarah left her laptop on as she lay down. She was playing an audiobook to narrate her to sleep, but she was also watching the dominos be lined up. It was soothing. Had to be for them too, all those people working on it. Having a passion for something. Must be nice.

>~~~<

Sarah was sure the note could've been inviting her to be executed by firing squad and Eileen would still insist she look her best. She still had her prom dress, a beaded, one-shouldered black gown from Laundry by Shelli Segal that she'd gotten for two-fifty. She and her mom brokered a bit of a peace, with Eileen fixing up her hair in a chignon.

When Sarah checked herself out in the mirror, she deemed the look professional, but cute professional. Sequins colorfully lined the left side of the dress, which also featured a ruched detail throughout and a mid-thigh slit to break up the oppressively floor-bound length. She loved the way it didn't cling to her body like some needy, desperate Kardashian thing, but sort of got a firm grip on her physique and then gentled out into smooth, slight folds, modest and becoming. A few unambitious pieces of jewelry—she liked the simplicity of her Michelle Chang ear climbers, shaped like shooting stars—some trying-not-so-hard kitten heels, and a dark orange wool coat that she hoped went with the dress as well as it went with jeans and slacks.

Then her mom drove her to Dutch River. There was a little boathouse in a gully of the river, with a garage connected to it by a covered walkway. Sarah guessed that was where the Vertigo was stored when it wasn't hugging a tree. After all, it wasn't like Nina could drive it across the water.

"Just call when you need me to pick you up," Eileen said, putting a definite end to any cool, confident, sexy vibes Sarah might've felt.

"Sure. When's my car getting out of the shop again?"

"When you've paid for it."

Sarah gritted her teeth and reminded herself to get one of those insurance packages that offered a rental when her car needed repairs. No way she should be this dependent on her mother one day into being twenty years of age.

Sarah stepped out of the car, pulling her coat tightly around herself. The sun was high in the sky, but it was going from nippy to outright cold. She waved for her mother to drive off, stepped toward the short, squat boathouse, then waved again for her mother to drive on instead of parking there with the engine idling like a creeper. Finally, she heard the big minivan rumble as it drove off, and she was left alone with the scenery.

Dutch River spread out in front of her, wide and low, a fat, lazy thing painting itself from north to south. The current was gentle, tugging along leaves and a few branches at a stately pace, the island in the middle clearly visible. It looked like quite a few acres, shrouded by vibrant trees in the same shades of orange, gold, and red as the rest of the fall foliage. They reflected into the clear water, spreading around the island like a wreath. It looked pleasant enough.

Something was beeping. Exaggeratedly electronic beeps, like a misbehaving phone. Coming from inside the boathouse. She went to the door, with its beveled lights, and saw a phone lit up in the dim space. Abruptly, the door opened outward, and she stepped back to make way for an elderly man to come out into the light.

He was maybe sixty, full-cheeked and ruddy-nosed, wearing a pair of slacks, a comfortable-looking sweater over an amenable belly, and a flat cap atop his silvery hair. When he saw her, he put away his phone and drew up the glasses he wore on a chain around his neck, seating them on his bulbous nose.

"Oh, hello there. You must be the young lady." His voice was reedy with age but warm and friendly. "I'm Bill Shannon, the groundskeeper about here. So you don't have to worry about the cars or boats, anything this end of the river. That's all me."

Okay. Good to know. "Sarah Kay," she introduced herself. "I was, uh…invited."

"Yes. Right this way. Hope you don't get seasick!" He stepped back into the boathouse, crooking his finger to lead her on, and flicked on the light.

Inside, the place was rustic, wooden, with tools lining the walls, some replacement parts on a few stock shelves, and a plain, unadorned motorboat moored inside the cement pool the wooden structure sheltered. There was a sort of combined railing and ladder, and even with his obvious lack of finesse, Mr. Shannon was able to nimbly help himself down into the boat.

"You can feel free to leave anything you want on the shelves. I'll lock the door for you—only other way to get in here is to swim in, and brother, nobody'll do that, not when they've got any sense!"

"Yeah." Stepping carefully, Sarah lowered herself into the boat and quickly seated herself with fingers firmly wrapped around the bench underneath her. "Does this thing have seatbelts?"

"Nah!" Mr. Shannon didn't look at her, instead concerning himself with unmooring the boat. He did it with practiced ease. "Now pay attention, because a lot of this is real simple, so I'm gonna think less'a you if I have to repeat it." With a tired grunt of exertion, he cracked his back and then dropped himself into the driver's seat. Pilot's seat? The seat. While checking over the equipment, he said, "This river runs through the Partry Dam upstream; that powers your TV, your Xbox, what have you. So most of the time, these waters are nice and calm. Perfect for fishing, really… Ya mind pulling the zip start?"

"The what?"

"On the engine. Red doohickey. Just like starting a lawnmower."

Sarah looked behind herself, grabbed hold of the red grip protruding from the engine, and pulled awkwardly. The cord it was attached to came out, and the crankshaft growled but then settled back into silence.

"Give it another tug! Real hard now."

Rotating her shoulder and gritting her teeth, Sarah put all her might into ripping the cord free of the engine. The engine rattled, she let go of the cord, and an approving rumble set in, smoke puffing out of the engine in big cigar exhales.

"That'll do her!" Mr. Shannon said, words muffled by the plug of chewing tobacco he'd just popped in his mouth. It only added to the chipmunkish, cuddly-old-man vibe he exuded, and Sarah found herself quite at ease. "Got your seat?"

"Yeah," Sarah said, planting herself again, wrapping her fingers around the bench, a little less white-knuckled this time.

"Okey-dokey!" They took off at a steady clip, eating away at the distance between the shore and the island with no real appetite, the engine making quiet sounds of contentment. Sarah relaxed, reaching down to draw her hand through the water. It was cold, but not so bad.

"Hope you'll excuse the lack of a proper welcome. Thought you weren't coming; stepped inside to get out of the wind."

"That's okay, no problem."

"Ha! I love that with you young people. 'No problem'! Hope you folks hang onto that attitude."

"We'll try. So, what about the dam?"

"There's no need for foul—*oh*, oh, Partry Dam. Yeah." Mr. Shannon looked over his shoulder at her, keeping the boat on course with one hand. "Now most of the day the water comes through nice and easy, but at eight o'clock on the dot, they have to relieve the pressure or some such and they let a whole mess of it through. River gets fast, licks at the shore like no one's business, and here's the trick, now: waters are rough as hell. Before eight, you could get to where you're going in a rowboat, maybe even swim it if the water weren't so damn cold. After eight, forget it. I keep the boat nice and roped up, so whichever side you're on at eight, you best believe you're staying there for the night."

"I don't think I'll be here that long."

"Maybe yes, maybe no." Mr. Shannon checked the forward view again, killing the engine as the island loomed up to meet them. On their remaining momentum, they sidled up to a gnarled old pier. "Now, think you can tie us off?"

"Oh, I wouldn't—"

"Nothing to it," Mr. Shannon assured her. "See the rope I untied when we got on? Just take that big ol' lasso at the end, loop it around one of the pilings, and pull 'er tight. Can't barely mess it up."

Sarah tried it and was gratified when she got it on the first go. Mr. Shannon gave her an approving half-laugh, "Hee-ha," and started up the ladder built into the pier.

"So have you worked for, eh, Ms. Rose long?"

"Since she got here." With a huff, Mr. Shannon pulled himself up onto the creaking dock. He turned around to offer Sarah a hand up, but she demurred.

"So—what's she like?"

Mr. Shannon straightened, parking his hands on his hips. "Couldn't rightly say. Aloof type. Not mean-spirited or cussed or anything, just prefers her own company." He offered his hand to Sarah again as she reached the top of the ladder, but she politely ignored it. They walked side by side down the pier, to the start of a paved trail. It was somewhat overgrown with lush, fulsome weeds and grass.

"I bring her groceries, mail, anything she asks for. She likes having me about to work the boats—don't think she much cares for them, even if they don't give her any trouble. But neither of us are much for small talk. Guess that's why we've gotten along so famously. Now this way, miss. As you can see, there's not much to get yourself lost in. One trail—" He tapped his heel on the slightly cracked cement. "That takes you up to the house. You wanna leave, it takes you back down. There's some spare canoes and oars set up around here—" Mr. Shannon looked around, pointed them out well after Sarah had spotted them. They were upside-down, stowed but looking seaworthy. "And Ms. Rose has one of them inflatable rafts up in the house, so there ain't much chance of getting yourself stuck here. Just remember—whatever you do, don't try the river after eight. I'm a pretty experienced seaman, not to give myself airs, and I wouldn't try it. No disrespect meant, but I'd lay odds on you getting swept away if you even thought about it."

"Got it. Evil river. Don't piss it off."

"Not evil, no, but certainly not your friend. Now, I've got one more personage I'm transporting this afternoon, but once I've brought him over, I'll be waiting right here until you need to go back." He gestured to a patio chair set up on the rocky beach. Sarah had to laugh. It had all the essentials for a bit of fishing, rod leaned up against the armrest, and even a floppy, fly-strewn fishing hat sitting on the seat.

Mr. Shannon started back over the water-warped pier.

"Wait," Sarah called to him. "Aren't you going to walk me up? Introduce me?"

"No," Mr. Shannon demurred. "I'm not to go inside the house—I suspect she wouldn't even want me hanging about. But don't worry. You're expected."

"Well, uh—" Sarah didn't want to part from the man. She found his presence comforting, and the lack of it… "Can you give me any…Nina Rose pointers?"

Mr. Shannon paused to think about it. "Well, don't be foolish. She always struck me as the type with very little patience for fools."

Gee, thanks. "Anything else?"

Mr. Shannon scratched his sideburn. "Maybe—ask her if she wants you should take your shoes off? She may be the kind doesn't like strange shoes tromping about her carpet. Best to ask, worst to wonder, I always say."

Sarah left him to it—wincing a little when she heard the engine flare up again, rotors churning the water to take him back across the river—and started down the path. It was strewn with mats of dead leaves. The canopy had been stripped bare by autumn, browning leaves clogging the waist-high grass that extended in all directions. Moisture from an earlier gale had turned everything to shades of brown. The entire island was muted with it, even the grass beaten down by it.

Then she saw them. Splotches of pink and red, like dabs of acrylic paint on the fabric of the world, were blowing down the path. She stepped on one with the toe of her shoe, stooping to pick it up. It was a petal, though off what plant she couldn't imagine. She held it in her hand, rubbing its gossamer-soft surface between her fingers as she continued up the slight slope of the path.

She noticed other pink petals. There were more of them. A lot more, buried like treasure throughout the landscape, sticking to wet tree trunks, glistening in patches of grass, or just swirling in the air like tiny birds, never seeming to land.

Coming up the crest of the hill, she found her way laden with the petals, like roses thrown at her feet by an admiring throng, and she let out a delighted little giggle. The wind picked them up, stirring them at the hem of her dress like playful little fairies. She watched them wafting in the air, hanging in it like a perfumed mist. Then she saw the source.

It was a rhododendron, but it must've been at least a hundred years old. The shrub had grown to the size of a condo. The path circled it, expanding into a sort of driveway before cutting in toward the house, which had this gargantuan plant and its aura of feminine petals as a sort of front lawn. Sarah marveled at it, smelled the sharp scent of it, walked under its sheltering branches, and saw the sun through its multitude of leaves, held up for her like an umbrella. God, it was magnificent.

Then she emerged on the other side and saw the house. It was crazy. Queen Anne style, reminding her of the Carson Mansion but not nearly so big. Well, *big*, but not sprawling. Grand. All but the color. No grey slate, no prim white paint, no stucco brick. No, *this* house was painted in sharp, strong Day-Glo colors. Magenta, electric blue, neon green—each section of trim a new color, but all of it forming a whole, a punkish but unified scheme arising out of the chaotic mash of mad color. Sarah let out another delighted laugh. The whole damn place looked as if it was made out of bismuth, the crystal that refracted light in multiple iridescent hues.

Crunching the delicate petals under her shoes with a satisfying, fortune-cookie sound, Sarah went to the stoop and up the front steps, her fingers alighting on the black cast-iron railing as she came up the short staircase to the door. There was a brisk, unadorned floor mat, a glowing doorbell button, and—Sarah looked around—a camera in the upper corner of the recess, where most old houses had a wasp's nest. She gave the lotus-seed pod of the lens a half-hearted wave. Then she pressed the doorbell.

She was surprised when, instead of sounding a tone, it emitted a buzz like an intercom.

"Yes? Mr. Shannon?" The familiar voice of Nina Rose came, shocking in its clarity. Uncut, undiluted.

"No, ma'am. It's me? Sarah Kay?"

"Ah. Yes." Whatever drubbing Nina had taken from the accident, she was long past it now. Her voice was husky, authoritative, a lioness amused by her own hunting prowess. Sarah felt herself gulp. "Please. Turn the knob. It's unlocked."

"I was just kinda wondering what I was doing—"

She heard a click. Call over, evidently. Sarah reached for the brass knob—it was tarnished a little, worn half-smooth by time and lack of repair. She had to grind it in place a little to get it to turn before she could push her way into the house.

It was dark. The windows were drawn and shuttered, subduing what little sunlight did make its way through. She could see clearly enough, though. The house surprised her. She'd expected it—well, she'd expected some kind of Hammer Studios movie set, with cobwebs and cobblestone. Torches. But realistically, she'd thought it would be one of those modern aesthetics. Everything matchy-matchy, looking as if it was just waiting for a bunch of Gucci models to be draped across the furniture: lots of dark glass, lots of wide-open space, lots of Bond-villain opulence.

Instead, it looked almost like Sarah would've decorated it. The furniture was old, antique even, but well-made and sturdy. Largely oak or other wood, decently sized but obviously hand-me-downs or scrounged from various sales, maybe even some high-end Craigslist deals. It wasn't Early Single-Income Family like Sarah's room—no milk cartons as makeshift bookshelves—but the furniture was scarred, aged, or reupholstered at times. Some was leather, some was plush with fabric, but the dark colors and subdued patterns tended to go together. Nothing really matched, but it was on the side of eclecticism instead of being garish or clashing. It looked to Sarah like…a home. The way her house had looked before her father—

She nearly jumped, seeing the dog. It was one of those big black creatures that could double as a small horse. Since Sarah was on the short side, that put it pretty much at eye level with her even though it was sitting. She stared nervously at it, but it was so still, so quiet, that Sarah realized the darkness of the place had spooked her. It was just a statue.

"You seen the woman of the house around here?" she asked pleasantly, drawing up to the beast. "If she's in the Batcave, you don't have to tell me."

She reached out to give the statue a pat, and abruptly, it was on all fours, teeth bared, growl reverberating as if a bass guitar had been struck. Sarah felt her heart punch her breastbone. "Nice doggy…"

"I see you've met my roommate." Nina's voice seeped into Sarah's ear like honey, as slow and easy as ever, but Sarah was a bit too scared for her life to appreciate it.

"Is he vegetarian?"

"Not in the slightest. Takes after his mistress that way." Out of the corner of her eye, Sarah was aware of Nina pausing on the flight of stairs she was coming down and folding her elbows across the railing. "What do you think, Barnaby? Would she taste good?"

Barnaby barked once.

"Yes, I think so too. But oh, what about portions? There couldn't possibly be enough for both of us…"

Barnaby barked again.

"I think so too. Let's just stick with dog food. Ms. Kay, if you would be so kind as to hold out your hand?"

Sarah did, subtly positioning it to catch her heart if the damn thing succeeded in breaking out of her chest.

"Barnaby, safe."

Barnaby eagerly smelled her hand, bullet-sized nostrils pulling inward as his cold nose sniffed from the tips of her fingers to the pulse of her wrist. When he was finished, he parked his butt back on the floor.

"Good boy, Barnaby." Nina addressed Sarah next, her voice losing some but not all of its condescension. "Now that he has your scent, he won't bother you. You'll be welcome here at any time."

"Thanks," Sarah said, her voice hiding some but not all of her sarcasm. Seemingly bored of her, Barnaby the Big Black Dog turned around and padded deeper into the house.

Sarah looked up the stairs. Nina Rose didn't disappoint. The woman was dressed somewhere between exquisite and modest, somehow making Sarah feel underdressed and overdressed at the same time. She wore a wine-dark cowl blouse over a lacy camisole, hip-hugging slacks, and shoes with red bottoms. There was an elegance in the casualness of the look, sweet because it was so unexpected. Sarah had imagined some Old Hollywood thing, a glistening gown, an expanse of leg.

Her face too. Not at all what Sarah had expected. She'd pictured high cheekbones, thin lips—a chilly, aristocratic face to go with that cutting voice. David Bowie as a woman. Angelina Jolie before she stopped eating.

No. Nina Rose had a face made for noir, beautiful like an old pin-up or a decal on the side of a WWII bomber, but she was also *cute*. Adorable, even. Mouth wide and lips full, smiling with a gleam of white teeth, full cheeks fitted to that fond smile, eyebrows finely sketched, her hair cut short into a dark wreath about her scalp, exposing the neat little seashells of her ears. Seeing it, seeing her smile, Sarah felt an irresistible urge to smile back.

"Ms. Rose," she stammered out, trying to maintain eye contact. Nina was making her feel inadequate from the neck up; no need to look further. "It's a pleasure to meet you. Meet you again, I mean."

"We have met before, you know." Nina took another padding step down another creaking stair. "One of your birthday parties, when I was new in town. You were ten—as I recall. I was seventeen." She looked Sarah over, her eyes seeming to suck in all of Sarah's body. "It seems like only yesterday you weren't even as high as my boots."

Nina in boots. Sarah blushed for no reason she could figure out. "Well, I've filled out a lot—*grown* a lot," she corrected hastily. "Ms. Rose, I'm a little unsure why I'm here.…"

"For a reward, of course." Nina's voice flowed into Sarah's own words like wine filling a crystalline glass. She took another step, the tap of her heels muted on the carpeted steps, then the uncomplaining creak of it taking her weight.

"Reward?"

"For the other night. You saved my life," Nina said. "Do you prefer Sarah or Ms. Kay?"

"Whatever you like is fine, Ms. Rose."

"I prefer Nina. And that would make you Sarah." Nina descended to the landing with a little exaggerated flourish. "There. Now we're on even footing."

Lame joke. Sarah laughed, not falsely.

"Say it," Nina said.

Sarah was momentarily confused, but those dark eyes pressed in on her, and then she just knew: "Nina."

Something seemed to pass through Nina. Her eyes opened a little wider.

"I didn't save your life," Sarah continued. "It was really just…"

"It's really just my money," Nina said. "I'll decide how to spend it. And who on."

"Money?" Sarah repeated.

"This is a big house, but I've never noticed an echo in it before."

Sarah flushed. "Sorry."

"Don't be. Just…improve." Nina reached into her pocket and took out an envelope. "One thousand dollars. If that isn't enough to cover repairs to your vehicle, I'll have to assume your mechanic is cheating you, and that's really your problem. I assume a check is okay?"

One thousand… "A check is very okay."

"I am sorry about your car."

"My car?"

Nina smiled, seeing Sarah realize she'd repeated herself again. "I heard that you ran it off the road to avoid hitting me. Since you don't seem to think you saved my life, you'll at least let me thank you for not killing me. Come. There is one other thing, since you've come all this way," she said, and led Sarah further inside.

She turned on the lights as she went through each room but only dimly. Sticking to Nina's heels—practically walking in her footsteps—Sarah decided the place felt cozy more than anything else. There was something surprisingly light about Nina's presence. It drained all the intimidation out of the house.

They came to a sort of breakfast nook built into a bay window, offering a view over the river. The table was brief and circular, its top inscribed with a checkerboard pattern. Instead of chess pieces or checkers, though, there was a bottle of Perrier and two glasses on top.

Nina sat down on one end of the wrap-around booth. "Given that we met so briefly, I wouldn't presume to guess at your tastes, but it's water, so if you don't like it, you're probably going to die."

"Water's fine," Sarah said, still standing. But at Nina's slightly admonishing head tilt, she sat. "I'm just not very thirsty."

"Then I'll give you not very much to drink. But just so you know, at a job interview you should always accept refreshments. It makes you seem more accommodating."

Sarah cleared her throat. "Wait, this is a job interview?"

"You're not looking for work?" Nina asked. She wound the cap off the bottle. "And I was really hoping to snatch you away from the grocery store. They must've bought your loyalty quite thoroughly. What was it? 401(k)? Dental?"

"It's not that I wouldn't like a better job, it's just…"

Nina poured for her first. "Just? I should think, having been invited to a strange woman's house in the middle of nowhere for no earthly reason, there should be quite a lot of reservations on your end."

Sarah smiled, almost more to herself than for Nina. It was like Nina kept throwing down the gauntlet, seeing if Sarah would respond in sarcastic kind.

She picked up her glass. "And a woman of your wallet never has to bother with reservations."

"I wouldn't, no, but then, the local Olive Garden doesn't have much of a waiting list."

"Don't knock it. I'd love to work there. Hear you get free breadsticks." Sarah sipped. The bubbles rushed in faster than she was ready for, tickling the roof of her mouth; the taste hit her tongue comparatively gently.

"Not bad?" Nina asked.

"I could get used to it."

"A lot of people like it." Nina played with her own glass a moment, tilting it this way and that to watch it catch the light, then set it down and poured for herself. Her eyes stayed locked on the flowing water, all business. "It so happens that my estate's gardener retired last spring, and I'm ashamed to say that the vines and such have gotten a little out of hand. I could really use someone with a strong back to come by twice a week and help out. And I've heard your family has a green thumb. I paid the old gardener forty dollars an hour, and I see no reason to pay you any less."

"My mom runs the flower shop, not me."

"Then you wouldn't know how to care for the tree in front of the house?"

"Rhododendrons aren't trees; they're shrubs," Sarah said automatically. When Nina stared at her with approval, she felt an overwhelming urge to bite her hair like a little kid. "A very old, very big shrub… And it would need to be lightly watered, fertilized infrequently, a top dressing in early spring; and in the winter, you'd want to knock the snow off the branches with a broom handle so they don't get overburdened and snap off."

"That hardly sounds arduous. I'm not expecting you to work yourself to death, just to get a little sweaty." Nina looked in Sarah's eyes at the last word.

Although Sarah wanted to look away, she didn't.

"You or whoever your business sends, that is."

Sarah laughed disbelievingly.

Nina set the bottle down and swiped up her glass. "Did I tell a good joke? I do hope you let me know what it is."

Sarah spoke apologetically. "Not that I get into a lot of car accidents, but I have the feeling not a bunch of them end with job interviews."

Nina pursed her lips musingly. "I recognized something in you."

Sarah poked at the cliché as if it was a cut on her lip. "Yourself, when I was your age?"

"Would you like that?"

"Of course. You're accomplished, successful. Why wouldn't I?"

"At the moment, I can't think of a reason."

Sarah cleared her throat. Something about the way Nina had said that. More than sincere, it'd been…aching. "Your offer's very intriguing…"

"Oh, I haven't begun to be intriguing."

Sarah grinned. "I would have to check with my mom. She's very— She wouldn't like me making a decision like this without her."

"Take out your phone," Nina said simply.

Sarah did. No bars.

"Shame. I guess we'll have to leave things in suspense. Do feel free to look around, get a feel for the place, then go back to your mother and discuss it. If you're here tomorrow, I'll assume you've taken the job. Until then…Sarah."

Sarah's stomach was a balloon animal as she walked away from the house, feeling those hazel eyes on her again. When she looked back, Nina gave her a wave through one of the upstairs windows. She waved back, feeling lightheaded, dizzy enough to tuck her head down and focus on one foot, then the other.

She heard the trill of the motorboat running as she came down to the pier, then saw it as Mr. Shannon idled the engine and used an outstretched arm to hold close to the dock. There was another man in the boat—tall, handsome in a way, gym shirt, gym pants. He pulled himself up onto the pier, eying Sarah as she came down.

"Hey," she said cautiously. "I'm Sarah."

Still he eyed her. "How many passengers does this ride seat, anyway?" he asked, inclining his head slightly to Mr. Shannon, but directing the comment nowhere in particular. Then, hoisting a duffel bag, he walked past her.

Sarah took a last, lingering look as he walked off. The woozy feeling was gone; he'd jarred her out of it. After the quick warmth of Nina's den, he'd felt cold and grating.

"Who was that?" she asked, accepting Mr. Shannon's hand to come down into the boat.

"Marshall something," he replied. "I think one of Ms. Rose's business associates. He comes by about once a week."

"He always that much of an asshole?"

"Can't say I would put it in that language, but yeah."

Sarah seated herself for the trip back. Nina was so kind and understanding and considerate. She didn't deserve to have to deal with an oaf like that.

He was unworthy of her.

Chapter 3

"Absolutely not," Eileen said, the moment she caught sight of the check. "I forbid it."

"You forbid it?" Sarah asked, pursuing her mother through the kitchen as she fixed dinner. She could almost hear Nina in her head, saying "echo." "What are you even talking about? It's free money."

"Nina Rose's money."

"So?"

"She feels bad about your father, she thinks this will make it right, and it's not something we're going to take advantage of." After taking the towel off her risen dough, Eileen started slotting it into bread pans. "What do you need money for, anyway? You're not in school. You live here rent-free."

"I want to get my car fixed and then maybe pay off some of our debts."

"We don't have—"

"We do!" Sarah interrupted. "We're behind on the mortgage. You think I don't notice this stuff, but why do you think I stopped going to college?"

Eileen stared at her. "You're rewriting history."

"And you're not? You make it sound like dad's accident was her fault somehow."

"I did not—!" Eileen began shrilly, then settled. "I never said that. But we don't need her charity."

"Don't we?" Sarah took a deep breath.

Eileen turned away. She probably thought the argument was settled. Like after she said what she said, that was that.

Sarah tried a different tack. "It's not charity if I earn the money. She wants us to do her gardening."

"Now we're gardeners?"

"We do it every Tuesday and Thursday for three blocks. You close down the flower shop. What do you call that?"

"They're in the area," Eileen argued. "We can't drive all the way out to Nina Rose's every week. You saw how far it is. It'd take up the whole day."

"Not the whole—I'll go. I can handle the place myself. She wants me to come twice a week. And she's offering to pay forty bucks an hour."

"And your other job?"

"I can work it in around my schedule at the store. They're not giving me full-time anyway. And they only pay minimum wage. The only place I can go from here is up."

Now Eileen seemed past the point of sighing, in some weirdly tranquil place. "Sarah, what do you remember about Nina Rose? Really?"

"She was one of dad's students. He tutored her, she made a bundle—so she's grateful, so what?"

"I don't think you appreciate how complicated things are."

"It doesn't matter to me," Sarah said. "It's a second job. You wanted me to get one. And I'm not asking for your permission, I'm asking for your blessing."

Eileen still didn't look pleased, but she said, "I'm not giving you my blessing. I'm giving you my permission. I hope you appreciate the difference when the time comes."

>~~~<

"Guys, you sound like my mom," Sarah told her webcam.

The Skype screens registered identical expressions of exasperated disappointment.

"C'mon, Kay!" Jonesy demanded. "What's her deal? Is she all *Sling Blade*?"

"She's my *boss*," Sarah stressed. "I'm not going to gossip about my new boss. It's really cool of her to give me this opportunity—I'm making forty bucks an hour. I had to agree to start paying rent before Eileen would let me take the job, so half of it's going to the mortgage, but still, that fucks the supermarket up the ass."

"Can you just take a few pictures?" Beck asked. "I mean, she's fine with Google Earth taking pictures—you'd just be closer."

Tyrese barely looked up from the mail he was opening. "C'mon, lay off her. She's got a good thing going here. Speaking as one of her other good things, I appreciate she doesn't want to screw that up."

"Thanks, babe."

"You two are boring ever since you hooked up," Beck said. "At least tell us if Nina's a vampire?"

"Of course not."

"So you've seen her in direct sunlight?"

Sarah sighed. "Jonesy, what's new with you?"

"Yeah, have *you* seen any vampires?" Tyrese asked, as Sarah got a chat from him: *4real, what was she like?*

Sarah rolled her eyes and punched some keys. She could think of a lot of things to say about that woman.

The kind of person I wish I had met at college. Maybe one of the teachers. She could have gone all Dead Poets Society on me.

Sarah deleted that, instead writing: *She's intense, smart, friendly...lonely. Very lonely.*

The next morning, Eileen gave Sarah pancakes for breakfast, and then she hitched a ride with Beck to the boathouse. Once more, she got to enjoy the house porn of Nina's manor. The grounds were overgrown, but it wasn't a jungle. All the weeds and wildflowers made it look like the Garden of Eden.

Sarah had always figured Eden wouldn't be an orderly garden. It'd be wild and free.

On the long walk up the path, Sarah groomed herself a little, gathering up her hair into a ponytail, adjusting her stockings, and even putting on both straps of her backpack. All of a sudden, she wanted to look her best for Nina. Maybe it was just the house, so intimidating in its near perfection. Even it couldn't live up to Nina's impeccable fashion sense and general elegance, but it did throw her into stark relief. She was like the crown jewel of her own life.

Sarah wanted to be, like, one of the other jewels. Maybe that orb thing royals had, with the cross on top? She buzzed the intercom. No one answered. The pause was long, jarring—a wrench in the gears. Sarah stood there long enough not to feel awkward about hitting the intercom again. Still nothing. Panic fringed her thoughts; ridiculous as it was, she worried this was all some elaborate prank, that Nina was fucking with her, laughing at her...

The door flew open. Nina stood there in a sort of kimono, its glossy, green fabric leafed loosely over her body. She was dripping wet, bare-bodied except for the robe, hair falling in wet straits past her ears, tickling at the nape of her neck. Sarah could hear a shower still running in the background. And she could see Nina in quite a lot more detail than she'd expected: her womanly hips pushing out the confines of the kimono, the way it flowed over her hourglass figure, the generous breasts, pendulous but firm, well holding their own against gravity… Nina pulled the kimono tighter around herself, hiding most of her skin but for her wet feet, her sculpted calves.

"Sarah…you're here early."

"Yeah." Sarah's mind was still off on an odd tangent, picturing Nina as a lounge singer in some old TCM movie with Rita Hayworth. All she needed was a glimmering red dress and an old-fashioned microphone to croon into. The woman looked made for black-and-white—Sarah found herself mentally dressing Nina in a gray silk robe instead, befitting her fine skin, and… *What the hell is wrong with you, Sarah Kay?*

"Yeah," Sarah said again. "I thought I'd get an early start. For my first day and all. I didn't mean to disturb you—"

"No, no trouble at all. I was just wrapping up." Nina smiled at her own pun as she adjusted her robe, slender fingers neatly working the dangling belt halves. They were little silk ribbons, whispering through the air as Nina deftly tied them. "Have you eaten?"

"Yeah, I had pancakes."

"Oh, poor dear," Nina cooed with mock sympathy, and Sarah laughed. "Come in, but give me a moment to throw something on. Just because I work from home is no reason to dress like it."

Sarah followed her, Keds squeaking on the wet footprints Nina left on the tile, trying not to notice the wiggle of Nina's ass in the tightened kimono. That was just how she imagined Nina would sway her hips while she performed in some elegant nightclub—not vulgarly, but just enough so that every man in tuxedo and tails would be fantasizing about what else those hips could do.

Nina disappeared upstairs, coming back a few moments later in a baggy white T-shirt and boot-cut jeans with the right knee wearing thin. Dressing down did nothing to make her less attractive. The looseness of her shirt only made the ample swell of her breasts more prominent, pushing as they did against the folds of the fabric. And while her jeans weren't tight, the way she moved was interesting enough with just a hint of her figure showing. She came down doing up her belt, and Sarah fought the urge to look away as she pulled the leather taut.

"Laundry day," she said.

Nina wasn't much of a tour guide. There were shelves and shelves of books, odd curios lining shelves and dressers, a big hand-painted Victorian globe in one corner—Nina didn't stop for any of it. "Mr. Shannon informed you of the river situation, yes?"

"Yeah."

"Good man. So if I have business in town, I could very well be stuck there overnight." Sarah was about to volunteer the guest room of her house when Nina said, "Obviously, I'm not above slumming it in a Four Seasons, but I'm a bit anal about my house. I'm one of those people who can't relax if she thinks she's left the oven on. So, while you're in my home, just in case I'm called away suddenly and unable to return, don't leave any electrical appliances on while you're not using them. No doors left open. Windows closed if you're not in the room. Exterior doors preferably locked."

"Yeah. Of course. I mean, I probably won't—won't be around enough for it to be an issue, but—"

Nina continued leading Sarah about, hitting a bathroom, the kitchen, a guestroom. "I'm not a slave driver. The reason I pay you is so I don't have to worry about the garden, thus it only makes sense that I don't worry about you either. You strike me as a fairly hard worker, and I rarely miss my guess about people. As long as the work is done, I don't mind you going at your own pace, or relaxing a little. If you're tired, take a nap. If you're dirty, use the shower. If you're hungry, help yourself. You might want to bring a change of clothes: this can be a dirty job."

"But someone's got to do it," Sarah leapt in.

Nina smiled at her. "Quite. I can't imagine you being too curious about this place—it's just a house, no different from any other—but feel free to explore. If you're looking for something in particular, it will probably be around here somewhere. No need to worry that you'll stumble across my seven previous wives or anything. One exception."

Nina showed her to a door, trying the knob for Sarah. It was locked. "This door leads to the basement. A few years back, there was something of a flood, and the water damage was particularly bad down there. The insurance company gave me a huge hassle, and I decided to hell with it, it's not like I need another room in this labyrinth. It's quite unsafe down there, so leave it alone."

"Absolutely," Sarah said, trying her best to look as if she was paying attention and diligently filing away mental notes, rather than wondering how Nina's hair could look so good fresh out of the shower.

Or why the shower was still running. She knew they weren't in a drought or anything, but still. Bad for the environment. She was about to ask Nina if maybe she should run up and turn it off when she heard the spray decisively stop, reducing itself to a dribbling, plinking echo.

Oh...

Nina escorted Sarah to the garden shed. It was in good repair from the last gardener, and Sarah quickly proved to Nina that she knew her way around the various tools. She really was good with plants; she'd helped Eileen with her business on and off, back before she'd been old enough for a real job.

"I suggest you start with the weeding," Nina said sweetly, handing Sarah an angled tool that would make it a breeze. Sarah had begged her mother for one of those, but no, doing it by hand built so much frickin' character. "And if you need anything, just let me know."

"Well, maybe…" *A glass of ice water. A power bar.* "I mean, if it's not too much trouble…"

"Yes?" Nina asked, and there was a tiny universe in how her lips wetly parted, teeth gleaming, almost feral, and in the quirks at the corner of her mouth as she waited for Sarah's reply. For what Sarah wanted.

>~~~<

Strong and insistent hands pulled Sarah in. Almost before she could feel their touch, warm lips were against her own and a tongue pushed into her mouth. It felt good but also weird. The hands slid down to crush themselves against Sarah's ass, pulling her further into their owner's reach. Her body was responding, but not in the right way. It felt as if she was short-circuiting. This was wrong somehow. She tried to push the thought away; this couldn't be wrong. She touched back, her hands groping and massaging—not as forcefully as her lover, more experimentally. It all felt so…different.

But that was nonsense, right? What was she expecting? What else would Tyrese feel like?

"We should stop," Sarah said, pulling away.

Tyrese's hands kept running over her as if he was looking for something. They were just…rough. Like they were made of sandpaper. Not like a woman's would be.

"I said *stop*!" She gave him a shove, and he broke off, immediately pouting.

"You said we *should* stop. Girls always say they should stop."

"How would you know!"

His hand slid out from under her shirt, which he'd jammed up over her belly.

She pulled it down, straightening it until the band logo on the front was unwrinkled.

"So what? Why'd you come over if you didn't want a little something-something?" Tyrese asked, trying and failing to keep his voice away from a whine.

"To talk!"

"We talked at dinner, we talked at the show—"

"So I guess I have a lot on my mind, okay?" Sarah lowered her harsh voice, softened it. "Rub my feet?"

Tyrese wasn't any more eager to fight than she was. "Sure," he said, groaning as she reoriented herself on his bed, kicking her shoes off and bringing her feet up so he could start kneading them. That always felt nice. A little clumsy, a little weird when his palms skidded temptingly up her ankles, squeezing like they were some sort of erogenous zone, but she thought it was good for them. He got to touch her, and she didn't have to try so hard to let herself be seduced.

Tyrese pressed a kiss to the side of her foot.

It tickled. Sarah forced herself not to kick.

There was a notecard sticking out of Nina's front door. Sarah pulled it free and read: *Prior engagement—the door's unlocked. Please get started, will catch up later.*

Automatically, Sarah flipped it over. The back read, in Nina's same elegant writing: *We'll have to get you a key.*

Sarah tucked the card away and tried the doorknob. Sure enough, it was unlocked. She wondered what kind of 'prior engagement' a hermit-cum-possible-vampire could have. From the few times she'd been over already, they'd started to settle into a routine. Nina liked to get in a brief greeting and serve her a snack and a drink before she got started. Nothing much, just fruits or veggies, some juice or a smoothie. And Nina would ask about what Sarah's plans for the day were, with Sarah gladly telling her.

It always felt nice, having someone ask her what was up and not expecting an essay. Eileen always grilled her at dinner, like on a daily basis she needed to make sure Sarah hadn't brought shame to the family.

There was a sudden thump from upstairs—the kind of thing that would have plaster falling in a less well-made house. Sarah stared up at the resounding ceiling. That had been Nina, right? It had to have been.

"Ms. Rose?" Sarah called. She still wasn't quite comfortable doing first names. That whole "respect your elders" thing Eileen had drilled into her ran deep.

She started up the stairs. "Nina? Are you alright?"

She could hear a mélange of sounds—muffled, meaty, rhythmic. Footsteps. Something creaking, metallic. "Nina?"

A pregnant pause. Sarah thought she could feel each individual air molecule against her skin. The noise stopped. Then Nina's voice, out of breath: "Sarah? Did you see the note?"

"Yeah, I got it... Is everything okay?"

"Everything's fine. Do you need help refamiliarizing yourself with your duties?" Nina's voice was tinged with irritation.

"No. No, it's all good."

>~~~<

Nina's backyard had six-foot-high hedges that hid it, and a goodly portion of her house, from the rest of her land. Sarah decided to tackle them today, killing anything that looked like a dandelion and stuffing it in the trash bag she dragged behind her. She was getting pretty into it, letting her mind wander.

Who had been in the shower while Nina was showing her around the house that first day? What was making those noises today? *Who* was making those noises?

Knowing there was no point in speculating, Sarah distracted herself with Barnaby, who had taken to watching her work like a prison guard in a chain-gang movie. Sarah didn't take many breaks, determined to give Nina her money's worth, but when she did, it was usually lying in the shade, petting an ecstatically grateful dog. He wasn't so bad, once you won him over with belly scratches.

She was about to go inside to see if Nina had any more ginger snaps when the woman herself came out. She wore a loose silk dressing gown, the material nearly translucent, beckoning Sarah to try to look through it. The flesh underneath was...

Sarah quickly concentrated on the next weed. God, she was perving on *her boss*. What was wrong with her?

Nina waved at her, and Sarah waved back, her hand doing a twitchy thing instead of the graceful acknowledgment Nina had perfected.

"I think it's time for my hour of sun," Nina said. Then she took her gown off, laying it ever so neatly across a patio chair. She sat down on a lounger, every inch of her stretched out for the light.

Sarah only allowed herself to look out of the corner of her eye. All Nina wore was a bikini, the two-piece covering almost nothing, like garnish on a steak. The rest of her... The school district had been too cheap to hire models for Sarah's photography class and too prudish to get them naked anyway. They'd had to make do with photographing volunteers from the class, fully clothed, which meant that Sarah had wasted far more rolls of film than posterity could justify on Kesha T-shirts and jeggings.

But Nina... God, Sarah wanted to photograph that body every which way. Low-light, blinding light, silhouette, black-and-white. Under the bleachers, against a white background, in the woods. Everywhere. She wanted a portfolio of Nina, proof to convince the harshest skeptic that a woman really could look like that.

Nina gave her neck a crack, did her fingers next, and finally picked up a pair of sunglasses off the patio's dining table. She slipped them on like the finishing touch of the picture she was making of herself.

Keeping herself very focused on her work—seemingly—Sarah craned her head just barely to the side. Her eyes took in the cute little toes on Nina's bare feet. She dared to tilt her head further, taking in Nina's legs. They seemed impossibly long with Sarah's gaze traveling up them second...by...second.

A glob of white liquid squirted onto them, and Sarah looked away hurriedly, pulling the next three weeds at record speed. When she looked back, Nina was smearing suntan lotion up and down her calves. Completely ordinary and responsible. Sarah looked away just as Nina's legs started to shine with it.

She pulled weeds and pulled weeds and pulled weeds. Quietly, efficiently—her mother would've been so proud. And when she looked back, it was practically by accident. A drop of sweat ran into her eye and stung, and as she wiped it away, she happened to look over at Nina—at those hands traveling over her breasts, up her throat, over her cheeks like the caress of a lover. Sarah had the feeling of being an intruder, stumbling upon a private moment—Nina in a moment of autoerotic pleasure. Then Nina's hands slid back down, over the tops of her breasts, applying the lotion with the lightest touch. Sarah's mouth went dry. If she'd tried, she would've found it impossible to look away.

Not that she tried.

Nina tugged her top down a little ways, exposing even more of her cleavage. The bikini top was loose-fitting, the kind of thing that might come off at a quick pull. She spread the lotion over her areolas, almost to her nipples—almost letting Sarah see them. Then she saw she'd gotten lotion on her top. Sighing, she moved to untie the knot in the middle. Sarah felt her breath hitch and couldn't imagine ever exhaling again.

Then Nina looked right at her. Her expression was impossible to make out with the black sunglasses blocking her eyes. "Oh, I'm sorry, Sarah. I forgot you were there."

"No, it's…okay. Don't mind me." Sarah tried to force a chuckle, but all that came out was a very hoarse cough.

Nina smiled graciously. "I know it's just us girls, but we don't know each other that well."

"But how are we going to get to know each other better if we don't…" Don't what? Don't see each other naked? Sarah wasn't sure if she was joking with Nina or trying to defuse the tension, or what that tension even *was*.

Nina turned over with her top held to her chest. "I think I'd better do my back anyway."

And what a back it was. Supple muscles, slender waist, and…a feature men were fans of and the appeal of which Sarah could very well understand. Nina's bikini bottoms could've been mistaken for body paint at first glance.

And it all needed suntan lotion.

"I could—" Sarah started, her words coming out as a squeak. She cleared her throat, but before she could start again, he came out, straightening his clothes. The man from the boat. He held a single glass of water clogged with ice.

"Your drink, madam." He set it on the ground under Nina's lounger. "Need someone to get your back?"

"Mmm. Desperately. Sarah?" Nina called out.

Sarah felt as if she was going to pass out. "Uh, y-yeah?"

"Would you like a drink?" Nina offered.

"No thanks." Sarah finally caught her breath. "I'm just gonna do the rest of the yard."

On the other side of the hedge, Sarah dropped flat on her face and just breathed. God. Shit, shit, shit. What was she doing? Nina was good-looking, but she wasn't *that* good-looking. Okay, she was, but Sarah didn't *care*. She was straight. She had a boyfriend. She had posters of Chris Hemsworth. So Nina was getting a tan? Good for her. It was probably just to stop her from getting Alzheimer's or something, not so she could give her gardener (her *female* employee) wet dreams. Fuck!

"Nice workout today," the man said, sounding exactly the way Sarah imagined an internet comment section would.

"You weren't so bad yourself, Marshall. Do you mind if I remove my top?" Nina asked, the question drifting distantly through the leaves of the hedge.

Sarah felt her head shoot up like a prairie dog's, despite the split-second realization that Nina wasn't talking to her.

"Sure thing," Marshall said. "And my guy is sending you the sample. You can look over it, tell me if you're interested."

"Wonderful." Nina sighed.

Sarah's eyes darted to the hedge. She could just make out Nina, quivering under Marshall's hairy-backed hands as he lathered the suntan lotion onto her shoulders. "And get my sides too, if you don't mind…"

Sarah felt herself being pulled to the hedge as if her head had a magnet in it. And the leaves were magnets too. She nearly shoved her face in it as Nina leaned up, her breasts swaying under her, Marshall's grubby fingers running down the sides of her body. They barely touched Nina…there. Sarah suddenly developed a keen appreciation of Marshall's self-control. How could you *not* want to touch those? They were just so…and they were really…and then there was just how *round* they were!

"That feels good," Nina cooed. "But…just a little lower. You missed a spot."

Sarah knew what Nina was talking about. So did Marshall. His hands traveled back up Nina's ribs, toward her—

Sarah pulled herself away so hard she nearly gave herself whiplash. This was so wrong. The man was just helping Nina put on some suntan lotion, and Sarah was using simple skin-cancer prevention like an issue of *Maxim*! What, had she been a teenage boy in a previous life? Gross. She'd helped her friends put on lotion plenty of times and there'd never been anything sexual about it. It was just something you did at the beach.

"And my lower back now?" Nina asked.

Sarah forced herself not to listen. There was work to do. Nina had given her a great job. She should be doing it, not…*whatever* that had been. Almost viciously, Sarah returned to tearing out weeds.

"God, you must have magic fingers, Marshall."

"Thanks."

"Oh, I should be thanking you. Just work your magic on my thighs, and I'll be absolutely *beholden*."

Sarah heard herself groan. Okay. Just this once. Gently, her hands actually shaking a little, she spread the branches of the hedge and eased her head down to look through the hole she'd made.

Marshall was on his knees between Nina's legs (they were spread, Jesus Christ), those oily fingers "working their magic" just below Nina's ass. His hands moved with firm strokes; if he was nervous about touching Nina, he didn't show it. Maybe he had a lot of experience with it.

Sarah felt another groan make its way up her throat.

"Between my thighs too, Marshall," Nina said, her voice just barely carrying to Sarah, thanks to the wind. "I'd hate to get a burn there."

His hands moved up Nina's thighs and then down between them, as if he was spreading Nina's legs. Sarah could've sworn that Nina raised her ass a bit but couldn't be sure from this distance. She involuntarily arched forward for a better look, but it did no good. She could just make out Nina's mouth. It seemed to be opening and closing. In pleasure, or was she just breathing…?

Did she hear Nina hiss in a breath, like she'd just been touched somewhere sensitive, or was that just her imagination?

Sarah didn't notice she was leaning too far forward until she lost her balance and crashed through the hedge, displaying all the grace of a Bigfoot sighting.

>~~~<

"So you said you tripped?" It being IRL, there were no connection issues to spare Sarah an iota of Beck's sarcasm. "And they bought it?"

"Why wouldn't they buy it? Why would they think I was spying on Nina Rose putting on suntan lotion? Why would *I* think I was spying on Nina Rose putting on suntan lotion? You don't think I was spying on Nina Rose putting on suntan lotion, do you?"

Beck gave the sidewalk a kick, propelling her skateboard a few more feet. Sarah hastened a little, walking her bike a smidge faster to keep up. When they were side by side again, Beck looked over and pretended to notice her again.

"No, no, you were just…enjoying the show. Lots of girls enjoy spending time with older women. They're called lesbians."

Another, stronger kick took Beck's skateboard out of comfortable conversing range, and Sarah broke into a jog to keep pace.

"Very funny. So you don't think I should change my name and move to Bulgaria?"

"Well, everyone should do that once in their life, but at least wait until your car's out of the shop."

Sarah was about to mount her bike when Beck slowed down to check the storefronts they were passing. "Is this it?"

"No, it's up against a Victoria's Secret, for some reason."

"Why wouldn't a Half-Price Books be next to a Victoria's Secret?"

"I don't know." They passed the park where the statue of Sarah's father sat, which she pretended not to notice. "You looking for anything in particular? Tell me now. I don't want you to bitch me out later because I didn't help you find a Brazilian translation of *The Fault in Our Stars*."

"Anything by Guy N. Smith. I've got five of the Crab books, so—one to go."

"Why do you read those things? They're not even scary."

"No, they're not scary, they're *awesome*."

"Here we are," Sarah said. The bookstore had spinner racks of ninety-cent paperbacks out under the awning. She gave one a spin, like the appetizer before the meal. Cheesy old Harlequin romances were currently tickling her fancy, and in her experience, ones about bare-chested Scotsmen were the Velveeta-iest. Easy to find too. You just had to look for the kilts.

Beck stopped, stepping on the tail of her skateboard to flip its front end up to her hand as she perused the other spinner rack. "Also, I'll take anything about anyone fighting a war on crime."

"Like detective stories?"

"No, like the Executioner. He's pretty much the Punisher, only he runs out of criminals to kill, so he just starts fighting the Cold War. It's amazing."

Sarah knew for a fact that Beck had every Ryan Gosling movie where he wasn't killing someone on DVD. It always struck her as odd that Beck could be into shopping and sewing and One Direction and basically every stereotype of the X-chromosome, but then also proudly display the cover to a splatterpunk horror paperback and declare triumphantly that it featured the killer bashing a victim's head against the wall so hard that her eye popped out, into his mouth, and he ate it.

Still, it made Beck easy to shop for. While the woman disdained internet shopping for herself—she preferred the thrill of the hunt—she was happy to accept treasured old paperbacks as gifts, no questions asked. Anyone who looked at Sarah's eBay bids around Christmas would be liable to suspect psychopathic inclinations.

Sarah plucked out a Dean Koontz book with a suitably lurid cover—she knew, she knew, but needs must—and was about to show it to Beck when she caught sight of him.

"Holy shit! That's the guy?"

"The guy?" Beck asked, following Sarah's line of sight.

"The fucking guy!"

"Oh, the Fucking guy," Beck said, pronouncing the capital letter.

Sarah gave her a look, setting the Koontz book atop the rack. "I'm following him."

"C'mon, I left my good stalking shoes at home."

Sarah pushed her bike into Beck's arms. "Watch my stuff."

"I'm already—" But Sarah was off. Beck groaned, called "Hey!", and tossed Sarah her skateboard. Sarah caught it.

Marshall was across the thoroughfare of the shopping center, obscured by rows of parked cars and their sunlight-throwing windshields, but it was him, Sarah was sure of it. From the sidewalk opposite his, she kept pace, clutching Beck's skateboard like a shield. She wasn't sure why. In case he spotted her and went into a berserker rage, she would bludgeon him with it? Hold it up in front of her face so he wouldn't recognize her? Sarah hung back, lingering behind the pillars that held up the 'covered' part of the walkway, dashing from one to the other but keeping mostly out of sight.

It didn't take long for Marshall to turn into one of the shopping center's storefronts. Sarah came out of hiding, crossing the street in just a little disbelief. It was a goddamn dojo. Gym mats, punching bags, katana stands, and samurai armor on display for that decorative flair. A class of students was working out under a young red belt. The sounds of sparring hit Sarah's memory like a freight train. Last time, she'd heard it through floorboards…

Marshall emerged from a backroom, now wearing a black-belted gi instead of his street clothes. So she stepped inside, ringing the bell attached to the door, drawing Marshall's attention as he looked out over the practicing students. He walked to her, bare feet slapping over exercise mats. "Kay, right?"

"Sarah," she half corrected, half confirmed. "How's it going?"

"I have class, so—busy." And he started turning away.

"Nina and I were talking about you the other day!" Sarah bluffed quickly. "She said you were a really good teacher."

"Did she now?" Marshall asked, crossing his arms.

"Yeah. She doesn't want to presume too much, but she thinks she's making really good progress with your lessons."

"Well, she's a hard worker," Marshall said, and Sarah felt a goddamn hot-air balloon in her guts as the realization hit her. He was her fucking *guru*. "And I'm a pretty good teacher. Would you like to sit in on a class? You'd be surprised how much you can pick up in just forty-five minutes."

"No, no," Sarah demurred, trying hard to hide her smile. "I've gotta get gone. But good talking to you!"

"Yeah, you too. Tell Ms. Rose I said hi."

Sarah nodded agreeably and headed out, feeling a bizarre urge to dance.

Beck pulled up next to her, riding Sarah's bicycle, all wobbly. "God, this thing is so wack. Do all these fuckers have seats like this? …What are you so happy about?"

Sarah tossed her skateboard back. "To him, she's 'Ms. Rose'."

Chapter 4

Mercifully, Nina didn't mention the natural disaster of Sarah's crash through the hedges the next time they saw each other. But it was hard not to notice that she never again tanned when Sarah was over. Sarah had mixed feelings about that. In the coming weeks, she pruned the hedges, revved up Nina's riding lawnmower, and trimmed back the roses.

Cultivated to Nina's exacting specifications, the estate became more imposing. And yet, the more Sarah was there, the more familiar it was. Maybe she was becoming a vampire herself. Coming to call the twilight at Castle Nina home.

Today, the weather was all fog and drizzle, not at all like the sunshine she'd gotten used to working in. Before she even got to the house, the tank top Sarah usually worked in was damp enough to have her shivering, and she was already griping in her head about spending an afternoon rooting around in the mud. But splashing closer to the front door, she saw that Nina had left it open. A much-abused welcome mat had been added to the austere porch. Sarah wiped her shoes off, as an army might've done before her.

Nina appeared as if a switch had been flipped, carrying a towel that she threw around Sarah without a syllable of greeting. "We're having such awful weather. I would've understood if you hadn't come by."

Nina looked as she always did, so tasteful and buttoned-down, and all the more tempting for how she wasn't trying to be. In her own body-rocking outfit—tight jeans and abbreviated shirt—Sarah felt crass. She wished she could pull off the suits Nina wore. Not butch, not effeminate, but somehow perfectly poised. A total knowledge of her place in the world and how she should look to fill it.

"Neither rain, nor sleet, nor snow," Sarah quoted. "It's fine. I've had worse jobs. At least it's not retail." She shut up as Nina wiped off her wet face and bundled her up in the cloth.

"I admire your work ethic, Sarah. But I have something altogether different in mind for today."

The memory of Nina, next to nude and glistening with tanning lotion, blew into Sarah's mind like a summer storm. *My usual masseuse is out sick. You don't mind, do you?* Stupid. And Nina was a woman. God!

"Marshall said he saw you the other day."

"Oh, yeah, I ran into him."

"He made it sound as if you were trying to be run into. Interested in learning self-defense?"

"Who would I have to defend myself against?"

"Quite." Nina pulled the towel away so fast, Sarah wondered for a split-second if she'd be naked underneath, like a magic trick. She wasn't. "Come with me."

Sarah's tennis shoes squeaked on the floor as they walked, leaving wet marks. She felt like a little girl tracking in mud. She would've given anything to make Nina see her as a woman.

They passed many windows, and the sound of the rain striking them lulled Sarah out of her doubts. She slung the towel over her shoulder and found her eyes pulled to the muscles of Nina's back, working under the tight cloth of her Oxford shirt. It was a more casual ensemble than Sarah had ever seen her in.

Sarah was thrown out of her musings by the creak of Nina opening a door for her. They were deep in the west wing of the manor.

"Welcome to my library," Nina said, crooking her finger to usher Sarah inward. Sarah didn't hesitate, following Nina to a table and sitting down in the chair Nina pulled out for her without question. "Let's call today a holiday. Your 'work' will simply be giving me the pleasure of your company." She nodded to the books. "Feel free to enjoy yourself. You seem like a very literate girl. I'm sure you can find something to your tastes."

Sarah picked up a hardcover from a stack on the table and flipped through it. "Good God…you must have a million books in here."

"Five thousand and sixty-eight," Nina said, obviously relishing her precision. "But who's counting?"

"Wow." Sarah looked around. The bookshelves towered like skyscrapers. Intimidating but welcoming. "You must spend a lot of time on the can. Reading, I mean."

Nina took a moment to blink. "Actually, I have a Barcelona I prefer."

"I probably would too."

Nina's hand dropped to Sarah's shoulder. "But I did get the joke." Her fingers played at Sarah's skin, flowing through the strap of her tank top. If a cat was trying to decide whether to undress someone or not, Sarah could imagine its touch being like that. Not that Nina would ever take so much as a stitch off her. "Excuse me a moment now." She stepped away, her hand the last to go. Sarah tried not to read anything into that.

She opened the book she'd picked up and stared fixedly at the first page, though her mind was entirely focused on Nina. Sarah heard her taking a cell phone out of her pocket, thumbing it on with an electronic trill, and then the little pulses of selection as she manipulated it. Deft, sure sounds, the kind that would come from Nina's hands. Then Sarah heard Nina's weight shift, settling into the posture of a woman making a phone call—the ringtone, the ringtone, the ringtone. Plenty of time for Sarah to wonder *who* she was calling. Was it Marshall? And if so, *why* was she calling Marshall? Just because he was her sensei or something didn't mean they weren't…groiny.

"Mr. Shannon," Nina said with the pleasant confidence of someone experienced at broadcasting over the phone. Sarah couldn't set a doctor's appointment without feeling as if she was running a marathon. "I've noticed the poor weather we're having and was wondering if you'd like to come up to the house. I'll be starting a fire, and presently I'll be making a little something to eat." She paused a moment. With her ears straining, Sarah could hear Nina's breath move between her lips like a ribbon of silk. "Really? Very well. Let me know if you change your mind." She ended the call and turned around to regard Sarah. "That book cannot be very engaging if a mundane phone call like mine can grab your attention away."

Sarah set the book down. "I guess he couldn't make it?"

Nina shrugged. "His shack has a space heater, he has a stack of magazines, and he just sat down."

"It's just…" *Don't say anything, you little idiot*, Sarah's mind shouted, with translations available in all the Romance languages, but with Nina looking at her as if she was, Sarah didn't think she could hold anything back. "It's just I was wondering why you invited him."

"It's raining. I thought he might not be comfortable out there in the cold."

"I get that." Sarah stood, feeling suddenly vulnerable sitting down with her back to Nina, and paced a few steps. "It's just he said he never comes up to your house, so…why start now?"

Nina matched Sarah's movements, mirroring them, strolling along the perimeter of the bookshelves as Sarah walked around the long table. "I invited you. It would be rude not to extend him the same courtesy."

"But would it be so bad?" *Shut up, shut up, shut up!* "It just being us girls, I mean?" Sarah could feel her brain tendering a letter of resignation. Now she'd have to watch *Floribama Shore*.

"You want to have a girls' night?" Nina asked, seeming amused at the idea, or maybe just at Sarah.

"I, uhh…" Sarah bumped into something. She'd walked past the reading table and managed to plot a collision course with another object. Not a table, precisely. It was a Hi Phile record cabinet like Sarah would find in a record store if she was a hipster. There had to be hundreds of LPs. Jogged by her impact, the album sleeves in the compartment in front of her shuffled forward like dominos falling. Sarah stopped the first one, but the rest kept piling up against it, their covers flashing images at her in kaleidoscopic sequence.

Nina came over and gave her a hand, swiping albums back into their resting places.

"I didn't figure you for such an audiophile."

"Please. I'm more of a snobby elitist," Nina said. "I hold the very unfair position that if you can't listen to it on LP, it's not worth hearing." She flicked through a few of the albums, stopping at one with a cover that was a simple picture of an unpretentiously pretty woman, photographed as if in an unthinking moment of stillness. "Judee Sill. I think you'd like her."

"You're giving me this?" Sarah asked, disbelieving.

Nina gave her a look. "Do you have a record player? No, but we can play it on mine if you like."

Crumpled newspaper flared orange, blackened, and crinkled into ashes. Before it did, the fire spread upward, starting in on the logs. Nina touched the fireplace match to a few more places along the wads of newspaper, then tossed the whole thing into the fire.

"How's the record player treating you?" she asked.

Sarah lowered the needle onto the rotating platter. "I can't find the aux cord," she joked.

A song started playing, sounding to Sarah like Tori Amos a generation early, a gentle, undemanding, yet plaintive singing voice, the lyrics soft but strong… *relieved*, she thought. Like the work of someone who had known real pain.

"'Jesus Was A Cross Maker,'" Nina's voice issued forth from the minibar. "The first single by the first artist David Geffen signed to his first label. She ODed on heroin before she was thirty-five, came from a broken home, went to prison, drugs, health problems…and she still sang like this. I suppose it doesn't make it okay that she went through all that—but at least it didn't all disappear. So many people, when they're done, they just disappear, with all they've gone through, all they've sacrificed. She stayed. I think a lot of her got to stay."

Sarah didn't know what to say to that. She just kept listening as the record kept spinning, the needle in its groove. There were two chairs by the fireplace, and Sarah sat down in one of them, laying her stocking feet on the brickwork of the fireplace. The flickering heat was like putting on socks fresh out of the dryer.

Nina came away from the minibar bearing two glasses and a bottle of wine. "I mean, you hear how…jaunty it is, don't you? That's not happiness, not exactly. That's joy. It's a kind of determination to be content. I've always thought so, anyway."

She leaned down in front of Sarah, setting the glass on the carpet within Sarah's reach, then relaxed back into the opposite chair. The bottle went into a wine cooler, placed incongruously by the fireplace. She'd already poured herself a drink.

"*Salut*," she said, and sipped.

Barnaby trotted into the room, circling around the furnishings and sniffing at both women for pats.

Sarah looked down at the wine glass by her side. "I can't drink this."

"Nonsense. It's a perfectly good Albariño."

"I mean, I'm only twenty."

"Is that too young to drink alcohol?"

"Yes."

Barnaby gave Sarah one more sniff, then had himself a big doggie yawn and shuffled in front of the fire to lie down. He turned over onto his back and wiggled around, inviting someone to pet his belly. Sarah reached out with her foot and rubbed it around on his ribs.

Nina swirled her drink. "I thought you could drink at eighteen, and then at twenty-one you could join the Army and get blown up someplace no one should be fighting over anyway."

"It's the other way around."

"I like my way better." Nina made a sweeping gesture toward Sarah. "Go on. It's not even real wine; it's white wine."

Sarah picked up the glass—cold in her hand—and took a sip. "It's bitter."

"Most things are, when you get right down to it."

"Profound."

"No, holding wine just makes me look sophisticated. You should see me smoke a cigar." Nina waited for Sarah to take another sip and then followed suit. "I hate drinking alone. And yet I own a wine cellar. Explain that."

"The duality of man."

"Just so. May I ask you a personal question?"

In the next millisecond, Sarah had a dozen nightmares of being asked about the tanning lotion. "Sure."

Barnaby tired of Sarah and got up to sniff at Nina, then laid down at her feet.

"You seem like a very bright girl. Good work ethic. I can't imagine you doing poorly at school…"

"So why am I here and not pledging Delta Theta Psi?"

Nina studied Sarah, eyes prying at the neutral expression on her face. "Should I not ask? I'm interested in you. I want to know what's inside your head."

"Well, I'm interested in you," Sarah fairly burst out. "But you don't see me asking questions—"

"You're interested in me?"

Sarah shut her eyes. Tension built between her eyebrows. "I think the wine's going to my head."

"Nonsense. It's white wine. It only goes to your bladder."

"I don't mean 'interested' in, like, a creepy way…a gossipy way…"

"If you have questions, you can always ask me. Provided it's all right I get to ask about you."

"That's fair." Sarah took a lazy sip. It really wasn't bad, once you got used to it. "Why don't you ever go into town?"

"I do, occasionally."

"Yeah, but not to get Burger King or anything. I don't think I'd ever seen you out before that car accident."

"Your loss," Nina said, cavalier.

"Really. How come?"

Nina's eyebrows jogged as she took a slow sip. "I suppose I make people uncomfortable. It just seems better not to…task them that way."

"You don't make me uncomfortable."

"No? Not even a little?"

Sarah took a drink, holding the gulp in her mouth a long moment before swallowing, feeling her tongue tingle like it'd touched raw sugar. "No. Not even a little."

"I must be losing my touch. Why aren't you in college? I'd heard you were being educated at a very nice school."

Sarah snorted. "We're going from 'why don't you get Burger King' to 'why'd you drop out of school'?"

Nina ran her finger around the rim of her wine glass. The sound splayed itself through the room. "We can't help what we're curious about, Sarah. It calls to us."

The needle escaped the loop, skipping over the record with a jagged sound, and Nina got up and went to it. Barnaby immediately jumped up to follow, leaving Sarah staring at the fire—coils of flame coming off ember-red logs. It popped and hissed, sending sparks to sting her socks. She pulled her feet back a little.

Nina raised the needle. The scratching sound stopped. Sarah heard a switch clicking, the record player slowly winding down. She stared at her reflection in the wine glass as she spoke.

"I wanted to go pre-law. But then I saw a life where I spent seven years at school, then eight years as an associate—fifteen years before I could enjoy being alive—and all so I could help people with millions keep from losing thousands to people with hundreds. And that's a career. That's a goal. I'm supposed to accept that? I'm supposed to *want* that?"

"I don't think that's every lawyer on the planet," Nina said, coming back, Barnaby still at her heels.

"It is when they have student loans. I mean, if I were passionate about being a public defender, I'd do it—I'd sleep four hours a night until I'm in my thirties. But that's not what I want… I just want something that *I want,* you know? Not my mom, not my dad, not…Ronald McDonald. Something *I want*, for me, that I can hold on to because it's mine. Fuck," Sarah finished, realizing how much she'd said. She looked up at Nina, standing over her in the light of the fire. "What about you? What do you do for a living?"

"What your father taught me to do." Nina swirled her drink. "Mathematics, algorithms—what do you remember about him?"

"Math. Lots of math. That was his job, right? To be boring?" She sobered. "Distance. It was like I was throwing a ball to him and he was out of range. It'd come down, roll across the ground, and he'd have to wake up and take a few steps to pick it up and throw it back to me. I'd catch it, throw it back, and he'd be too far away again. Why? What do you remember?"

"A very wise man," Nina said after a moment, sitting back down. "He seemed to know everything. Even now, I don't feel like I've learned all that he was trying to teach me."

"Did he ever talk about me? Or my mom?"

"We…weren't like that. I was his student, so it was all patterns, rhythms. I knew he went home to someone, was someone's father, but I could never picture it. He was only ever the taskmaster with me."

"Well. I guess that's what he was like when he paid attention to someone."

"You don't think he paid attention to you?"

Now I've put my foot in it. "I guess that's what my mom thinks more than what I think."

"So what do you think?"

"I think you were his passion—his *job*," Sarah corrected herself. "And we were his family." She thrust a consoling hand at Nina. "Which isn't your fault. You were younger than I am. You couldn't tell him to go back home and read me a bedtime story."

"Did you need a bedtime story?" Nina finished off her wine and let the glass loll about in her loose grip a moment.

Sarah bit her lip. "It's rude of you to ask a question without answering mine."

"Oh, you mean the money." Nina shrugged. "The government comes to me on occasion with word problems, I offer them solutions, they pay me for my efforts. And I've made some investments. It's all boring, really. And anyway, you don't have the security clearance."

"Was that a joke?"

"Yes, it was, but you still don't have security clearance. Anyway, now I'm… comfortable. I mostly spend my time on my own projects. I listen to stockbrokers telling me how rich I am, and I listen to philanthropists telling me how thankful they are, and I paint. Badly."

"Oh!" Sarah realized. "The house!"

"Yes." Nina blinked. "You think the house is badly painted?"

"No, I just… It's very artistic."

Nina smiled, nodded. "The ancestral home. They can make me live here, but they can't make me keep it looking like a mortuary."

She sat back down. Sarah stared at her. The fire was in Nina's eyes—when Nina looked at her, did she see the little pinpricks of flame in Sarah's eyes too? The two of them reflecting back at each other, on and on, into infinity.

"What do you mean, 'they can make me live here'?"

"Where else would I go?" Nina asked, pouring more wine for herself. "I suppose if I wanted to surf, I'd go to Hawaii. Or if I wanted to climb mountains, I'd go to the Rockies. But everything I want to do, I can do here, so…why leave?"

"To get away from it all?"

"Is that what happened when you went to college? Or did it follow you?"

Sarah held up her glass. "I'm empty."

Nina topped her off. "Does being here remind you of your father? Is that why you stay?"

"Is it why you do?"

Nina grew quiet; from looking at her, Sarah would've believed even her heart was beating more silently. "I lost more than him in the crash."

"Of course," Sarah said apologetically.

"It was a long time ago," Nina said, apologizing for making Sarah apologetic.

"No, it wasn't."

"No—it wasn't," Nina agreed. "I guess I've never been much good at knowing when to change the subject."

Sarah took a quick sip of her drink. "What do you think of the new season of *Making a Murderer*?"

"They made a new one?"

"New season or new murderer?"

They talked for what felt like hours—so long that Nina had to get up and throw more logs on the fire. Sarah felt…*delved into*, as if Nina was examining her piece by piece, layer by layer. She didn't mind it. She'd never felt worthy of such attention before, but suddenly she, Sarah Kay, was fascinating and intriguing and important. Why else would a woman like Nina be so interested in her?

Sarah cut herself off after the second glass of wine, content to play with the empty glass. Nina put on another record, this one by Portishead. *Dummy*. The music drifted into Sarah's ears, soft and supple, as Nina went on a lengthy, impassioned digression about the band, like there was a reservoir inside her and some of the water was finally being called upon.

The needle slipped again, turning the album into rickety scratching. Nina stopped herself, as close to abashed as Sarah had ever seen her, and looked at her Cartier watch. "Well. I think you've served your sentence for today."

Sarah stood, was suddenly dizzy, and tripped forward. She stopped herself against the fireplace, her forearm clanking against the mantel, the empty wineglass slipping from her fingers. It shattered on the hearth, sending glass shards slashing out into the carpet beyond.

Sarah was still in her socks. "Oh, uh, shit," she concluded.

"Quite all right," Nina said, standing alongside Sarah. "I have far more glasses than I have people to drink with anyway."

"I think if I…" Sarah lifted one foot, figuring that if she made as wide a step as possible, she could carry herself over all the shards. It wouldn't be huge on dignity, but at least it would be small on stitches.

Nina didn't give her the chance; she simply seized Sarah, putting one hand on her shoulder and lowering her back until she could place her other arm under Sarah's legs and lift her up, holding Sarah in both arms like…like a sack of flour. *Yeah, a sack of flour in a wedding gown, maybe.*

Nina carried her away from the fireplace as if this were a perfectly natural thing to be doing, while Sarah tried not to make it any more awkward than it was—not that it felt awkward. It felt a lot of things, but not awkward.

"I'm sorry about your glass," she said, needing to say *something*, and that being the only something that presented itself.

"As I said, it's fine."

"I think you can put me down now. I don't think the glass spread this far."

Nina looked at her. Then she bent her head down and sniffed Sarah's hair. And all of a sudden, Sarah had no idea what she was feeling. It was as if every single thought she had was locked in a vault inside her, and she couldn't open the lock in a million years.

"You're smelling a little rank," Nina teased. "Maybe I should take you down to the river and give you a bath!"

Sarah smiled, and Nina smiled back, showing teeth. When she set Sarah down, the tile floor felt as cold as ice beneath her feet, sobering her instantly.

"I think the wine went to my head a bit," Sarah said. "I'm not a big drinker."

"Of course not. You're a petite drinker."

Sarah giggled.

Nina watched her closely, then took her to the kitchen and fed her a cup of hot coffee before she was satisfied that Sarah was okay to drive.

Her shoes were in the hallway, and Sarah sat down on the first step of the staircase to pull them on. With Nina standing there, over her, she felt something tingling between them—an awareness that just a few feet away, Nina was warm flesh and firm muscle, not just some…picture that couldn't be touched.

Her fingers were numb as she tied her shoelaces.

"Look at that," Nina said, staring at the transom window above the door. "The rain's stopped."

Sarah's knot fell apart, and she scrambled to retie the laces. "Guess I'll be mowing next time."

"I could play a record for you," Nina offered. "While you work. A little music always helps me when I paint."

"Yeah, but you don't paint so well," Sarah replied.

"Hard to find a good subject." Nina watched as Sarah tightened the knot into a tiny fist. When Sarah was done, she offered her hand. "Well, I had a very enjoyable girls' night out. Even if we didn't go anywhere."

Sarah let herself be pulled to her feet. Then, as if she'd dozed off and slept through hours of her own thinking, questioning doubt, she surged up and kissed Nina's cheek. The skin was warm and soft, burning her lips, leaving a whiff of something sweet that Sarah couldn't place as she rocked back on her heels and thought only of licking her lips, of biting them, of doing something that would stop them from tingling like they were…incomplete.

Nina stared at her. Then, very gently, she bent to Sarah like a tree bowing under the wind and kissed her forehead. Sarah didn't know what it was, but it felt like a dismissal, as if she should go, and with her hands stiffly fisted at her sides, she went out the front door and tried not to look back.

Chapter 5

Sarah lay on her bed, laptop straddling her chest, obsessively refreshing her Facebook page, watching updates slowly spool in. The trending section had *Kanye West smiles at paparazzi* as a lead story. Slow news day all around.

She got a Skype call. Declined it. She didn't want to talk. Didn't want to think. What she wanted was to leech away the memories in her head, all the confusing sensations that had felt so right and muddled everything. She wasn't gay, wasn't into girls—so why was she into Nina?

She knew the feel of Nina's flesh now. It invaded her thoughts, colonizing old memories. She'd never gone on spring break, but in another life, she could've told her mother she was going to Cancun and then just stayed at Nina's place. Watching old movies and drinking wine. Maybe Nina could tell her how to kiss Tyrese. She always felt as if she was doing something wrong.

She refreshed again, like a corpse's death twitch. Her stopped-up timeline finally flowed: a new photo post, of Tyrese, kissing her. She clicked on it. She didn't remember him taking that picture. Then Nina dropped out of her mind; she came awake in a plunge like you'd get on a roller coaster. It wasn't her he was kissing. It was *Beck*.

Reflexively, she pressed F5, trying to place the photo. Maybe it'd been before they were dating. No, no, he had the dreadlocks he'd started cultivating five months ago. They'd teased each other about it. He'd asked her if she wanted her own dreads.

She got another Skype call, texts on her phone, then the sustained vibration of an honest-to-God call. She tossed the phone away from her, letting it hum into a pile of unfolded clothes. Her fingers were clumsy, numb, as she refreshed the page again, as if that would change what she was seeing. But she was fooling herself. There was no room for uncertainty, no need to double-check. He was cheating on her, with her *best friend*, and she'd had to find out about it from some gaffe—a pointless tech glitch had upended her world.

She forced the laptop shut and it went into sleep mode, hard drive no longer whirring. The phone purred into the fabric, where it was nestled a second more, then went silent. It had gotten dark outside. She'd lain around for so long that the comfortable lighting of afternoon had turned into an eye-straining evening haze. Her phone started buzzing yet again. Suddenly, she couldn't take it.

Downstairs. The clay dish she'd made in elementary school holding the family keys. She drove, her car smelling perversely fresh after its recent repairs. It was raining again. Big fat gobs of rain spat down on the windshield, barely streaked away by the wipers before more came, plonking on the roof, hands clapping against the entire exterior of the Prius.

Something stung her eyes. Tears. And just like that she was sobbing, deep, howling cries cutting their way out of her throat. She was hacking them up, vomiting them out.

At the boathouse, she punched the code into the lock and went through untying the boat just as Mr. Shannon had showed her. Ingrained caution made her check her watch. 7:50. Fuck it. She could make it. Besides, how bad could the waters get? She wouldn't come this far just to turn back now, with Nina right there on the other shore.

Two convictions grew in her as the waves hit when she was halfway across. That she'd made a mistake, and that she couldn't turn back. The waters were rougher than she was used to, lumpy like an old mattress, hard shocks of water hitting the bow and sloshing into the cabin with her. She just concentrated on pressing forward, even as bracingly cold water gathered at her heels and slapped against her body, penetrating deeper and harder than the rain could. She started shivering, caught a glimpse of frost-ridden exhale issuing out of her mouth.

Something seemed to ram her—a hard wave making the motorboat twist to the side, nearly dumping her in the water, the boat almost vertical for what seemed like a small eternity before it settled down to the instability that passed for evenness. Then another burst from a broken wave, splattering her all over. She screamed and the rain screamed back, gales of it now, the river roaring, the rain coming down in volleys, and the sound of the motor small, pathetic.

She wiped the rain out of her eyes, storm clearing, water smoothing, and saw the island rising in front of her. She killed the engine and skewed the wheel, but still ran ashore in a shuddering haul, the sandbank crushing down on her keel as she bludgeoned through it. Sarah pitched forward, hitting her head against the rim of the windshield—a sharply biting pain that blurred out everything else. She winced and cursed herself and thought for a second that she'd merely given herself a bitch of a headache before she touched her forehead and felt an alien warmth in the chill of the rain and river water. Blood.

Cursing louder, she got herself down from the boat. It looked pretty soundly embedded in the shore, but she grabbed the rope anyway, binding it around an outcropping before pulling herself up the grassy embankment. It was steeper than she would've thought, and with the rain making everything slick and her fingers numb, she tumbled back down a few feet before she reached the top. Blood ran into her ears; there was a pounding pain inside her scalp. She redoubled her efforts, clawing her way up to firm footing. She was in luck. She could see the manor nearby, an upstairs window blazing away like a second moon. Pressing the heel of her hand into the bitter gash, she stumbled forward. Faster. Always faster.

She got there with lungs burning and legs made of molten lead, but she felt as if she could keep running forever. Out of this goddamn town, away from crappy boyfriends and crappy friends and crappy mothers. Oxygen flooded into her body the moment she stopped. She felt lightheaded, as if she might just float away, if it weren't for the thought of Nina tethering her.

Sarah knocked at the door, but no one answered. Nina had to be there—she was a fucking hermit, after all. Sarah wanted to pound on the door, knock it down, throw herself through a window into the safe place. Tears burned in her eyes. Desperate, she used her key; the door swung open freely, and Sarah nearly fell inside. Quickly righting herself, she pushed the door closed behind her.

Just being inside the manor was comforting. Everything was so stylish and sophisticated.

"Nina!" she called. Her voice echoed back to her, all cracks and heartbreak. She fell silent, but Barnaby came scrabbling to find her, nails clicking on the tiles. He trailed after her as she looked for Nina, trying to comfort her, or maybe just hoping for snacks.

The last room she checked was the bedroom. Nina wasn't in any of the others, and Sarah half-expected to find her in there with a man, someone as charming and beautiful as she was. It was that kind of day.

She tried the door. It swung open. Nina was in bed, propped up on pillows and reading a newspaper. She even had a fashionable pair of glasses on. And all that hid her from Sarah was a filmy nightgown.

"Sarah?" Nina folded her newspaper up. "What are you doing here?" Her gaze moved to Sarah's still-bleeding forehead. "Jesus, *what happened*?"

It was more than Sarah could take. She was crying and sobbing and cursing, and all she could hear through her own grief was Nina's voice.

"Sarah, come here. *Come here.*"

Like a master ordering around a dog, expecting to be obeyed. And yet Sarah felt her legs carrying her forward, betraying her to Nina; she madly thought Nina would slap her or hit her for her foolishness. Because she was a foolish, foolish little girl, thinking she could trust Beck, thinking Tyrese loved her. Thinking Nina could love her. She braced herself, but Nina opened her arms. Like a ship caught in a whirlpool, Sarah was sucked down. She felt herself hit Nina's impenetrable exterior and be embedded in it, given all the protection of it, strong arms wrapping around her and holding her tight. Everything melted away until there was only the softness of Nina's gown and the warmth of her skin. The tightness of her embrace.

"You came across the river? At this time of night? You could've been killed, you little fool—"

"I'm sorry, I'm sorry…" Sarah kept repeating it over and over. She felt like she'd offended something, some great force, and all she wanted was for it to stop hurting her. "Sorry—sorry…"

"Out of those wet clothes. Now. You'll catch your death." Nina gave her a last clenching squeeze, then sat her down on the bed. She hurried to get her dressing gown, a thick, woolly robe, and no sooner had Sarah removed the offending garments than Nina had her wrapped up in it. It soaked up the wetness on her skin, restoring her to something like warmth. "How'd you get that cut on your forehead? Did someone—" Nina's voice flashed with rage.

"No, no, I…kinda ran the boat aground. Hit my head on the windshield."

"Ah." Nina opened a drawer in the dresser and brought out a first-aid kit. "I see you're working your way through all the methods of transportation. I wouldn't buy any plane tickets if I were you."

Sarah let out a shrill laugh.

Nina shoved the kit into her arms. "You know what I'll need?"

"Iodine and bandages and sterile pads—"

"Sutures," Nina corrected. "It's been a while since I've had to deal with any lacerations."

She was going to the fireplace now—Nina's bedroom had a *fireplace*—taking logs from the holder, tossing them onto the andiron. "Newspaper," Nina said firmly, and Sarah handed it to her. She wadded up sheaves of it, stuffing them under the andiron, then rose to grab a fireplace lighter from the mantelpiece, knelt again, lit the newspaper—and had the whole mess burning red and rosy in seconds.

"Come," Nina said now, gesturing Sarah over. Faithfully carrying the first-aid kit, Sarah joined her, kneeling by the warm, glowing fire.

Nina took the kit, ripped a moist towelette free of its packaging, and efficiently cleaned the wound. "You're lucky. It's a very shallow cut. You could've concussed yourself. Here." She shined a flashlight in Sarah's face, moving it from eye to eye. "Look *straight* ahead." Then she handed the light to Sarah, guiding her hand to direct it at the cut. Sarah held it there as Nina assessed the wound.

"I know it hurts," Nina said. "I've seen that look enough times before. But be brave just a few moments longer. Let me take care of this. Then you can cry. Then you can be broken."

And Sarah forced herself to. Because Nina had said. Because more than anything, she knew that if she did as Nina said, everything would be all right.

It didn't take long to sew up. Just three sutures. Then Nina put a plaster over it. The fire had dried Sarah out, burned the chill out of her. She felt human again. The sadness still welled inside her, but less intractable and oppressive. Now it was something she could wash off.

Nina gently checked the bandage, making sure it was correctly applied in much the same way Sarah imagined someone would cut a diamond. Then her swift, efficient touch became a soft stroke of Sarah's cheek, a permissive caress, a fond one.

"What's wrong?" Nina asked, whispering even though they were alone.

Sarah fell into Nina's arms, and the warmth of her body made the fire seem cold. She told the whole lurid story, even as it ran together in her mind. She stayed in Nina's arms, slowly getting comfortable, gently being rocked, pulling her arms and legs closer to Nina, her body into Nina's lap. Telling Nina about how she'd met Tyrese, about their first date, about how she'd thought he'd be her husband.

"He was your first, wasn't he?" Nina asked, giving Sarah a little squeeze. Letting her know it would be all right either way.

"Yes. I was so sure. Not the first time, or the second time, but I was so sure it would come if I just kept…if I loved him hard enough… And Beck. She's supposed to be my best friend."

"It's not your fault." Nina unwound an arm from Sarah's back, only to bring her hand to Sarah's hair, gently running her fingers through it as she murmured, "You did nothing wrong. It's very hard to find someone who understands you as completely as you deserve. Who you can share yourself with, who you can give all that you have to offer. You're a precious gem, Sarah. As beautiful as you are rare. You will find someone who truly values you. It will just take patience."

"It doesn't feel that way. It feels like no one even sees me."

"I see you, Sarah." Nina twisted a lock of Sarah's hair around her finger, lightening the mood somehow. "Do you know what's happening to your body right now?"

"My heart's breaking in two?"

Nina lowered her voice sympathetically. "Besides that." She rubbed her hand between Sarah's shoulder blades. "Right now, your brain isn't releasing enough serotonin. There's too much stress on your body for it to keep up. Not without help."

"You mean…wine?"

"No. I don't mean wine. You see, just being held by me, being touched by me, is releasing beta-endorphins, reversing all that. And you'll feel even better after a good night's rest, when your brain has time to normalize. So I want you to lie here, close your eyes, and try to get some sleep."

"And you'll keep touching me?" Sarah asked. She was so tired that it took her a moment to realize what she'd said.

"If you like. Or should I stop?"

Sarah was silent. She didn't know what to say.

Nina traced Sarah's hair down to her back, which Sarah felt right through the robe. "Would you like to take that off? Get comfortable?"

Sarah consented before thinking of what she was wearing—or rather, *not* wearing—underneath. She hesitated with one arm out of its sleeve. Nina just smiled. She gently took the robe's soft fur and tugged until it was off. Now the darkness was all Sarah wore. After a moment, Nina reached to a nearby chair and pulled a quilt from its back. She draped it over both of them, and Sarah exhaled—relieved, disappointed, to be covered again. She felt safe now, but part of her didn't want to feel safe.

Under Nina's gaze, Sarah lowered herself back to rest against Nina's body. Nina's hands pressed flat, possessive, along Sarah's spine. Sarah grew used to the weight of them in only a second. Then they started moving up and down, rolling over Sarah's back like the tide. It wasn't like when Nina had held her before. Her touch was more daring now, more intense.

"You're a very trusting soul," Nina whispered, her breath barely stirring Sarah's hair. "Coming for comfort to a stranger's home."

"You're not a stranger."

"Aren't I?"

"No. You're, like...my best friend."

"Please. I don't even have a Twitter; I'm like the Crypt Keeper. You must have other friends your own age besides this Beck."

"*Please*," Sarah mimicked. "If I asked them to get into bed with me and rub me down, they'd call me a dyke."

"And what's so bad about being a dyke?" Nina asked, her voice sweetly sinuous.

Sarah's chest tightened around her heart until she could feel its beat pounding against her skin like a caged animal. Was one of Nina's loved ones a d—homosexual?

She didn't even like that word; it was the others who used it.

"I don't know," she stammered. "I've never tried it."

Nina gave Sarah a little pat and pulled the quilt higher up around their bodies, tucking it under their weight. It helped. Sarah felt less exposed, cuddled up like this. Snug as a bug in a rug.

Under the quilt, Nina's hands were as subtle as shadows; Sarah couldn't hear or see them. She just felt them, on the back of her neck now, leisurely stroking from her throat to her shoulders like Nina had all the time in the world...to explore. When they met in the middle, at the nape of Sarah's neck, it felt like her head was being tilted toward a kiss that never came.

Nina's hand came to Sarah's cheek. It was shockingly intimate, the touch. Nina had never gotten so close...to her lips.

Sarah lay still while Nina's fingers, sly and insinuating, ran over her cheekbones. Touched her lips. Breezed over them like a breath of air. Stopped in the middle, as if seeking admittance, but Sarah was too stunned to even breathe. And then the fingers descended, off her chin, down her neck. Turning her sideways now, Nina's hand moved in circles on Sarah's sternum, just shy of Sarah's breasts, then returned almost to her lips.

Sarah shivered. She fought to keep her voice steady. "I don't think you're sleeping with Marshall, but I think maybe you wanted me to think that."

Nina laughed warmly. Her hand dropped down. To Sarah's belly, brushing it with her knuckles, almost tickling. "Oh?"

"I think what you really like is...people like me. Girly people."

"Girls, even, one might say."

Sarah froze. "I can't believe you told me that. This isn't…college! People would care."

"I trust you," Nina said, raising her hand again. She ran the side of her finger down Sarah's spine, her fingernail making a faint noise on Sarah's skin. "We have something in common."

Sarah didn't dare ask what it was, not thinking, only feeling as Nina's finger followed her tired bones like a cat with a string.

"You have such beautiful skin. Such a beautiful body. I wish I had your body," Nina said, her voice low. Just for Sarah. "It's getting late. Get in the bed. I'll call your mother. Try to explain—most of this."

Everything was warm and blurry, like a pleasant dream. Like none of this was real. It was all just a bedtime story. She'd never seen Beck and Ty's betrayal. She'd never even dated Tyrese. She'd always been with Nina, here, now, touching her and being touched by her.

"Thank you," Sarah breathed. It didn't sound like her voice, but that was okay. She liked this new, strange voice. "But I think my feet fell asleep."

"Oh, I'll take care of that. Put your arms around me, dear. Let's see if the personal trainer has earned his keep."

"Yes, ma'am." Sarah giggled as she put her arms around Nina's neck. She was liking this new voice more and more. It was like another person was speaking for her. Someone fun and adventurous and exciting. Someone who never got cheated on or grounded and who always knew what to say.

Nina pulled away for a moment, reorienting herself into a kneel beside the quilt, the fire through her gauzy nightgown brilliantly playing at her body. Suddenly, Sarah could see all of Nina again, and the sight was enough to take her breath away. Nina was a vision, a goddess—

Then she was lifting Sarah up, blanket and all, carrying her like a blushing bride to the bed. She'd left the sheets pulled back on her side of the gargantuan mattress, and after she'd set Sarah down, it was a simple matter to pull them back up over her. Sarah moaned—as the cool silk touched her body, she suddenly felt overheated.

Nina came down over her, checking the bandage one last time. She lowered her lips almost to Sarah's but not quite, and Sarah didn't have the energy to lift herself even that one little centimeter to Nina's wet, open lips.

"You must sleep now." The feel of Nina's breath against her lips was torture. "You need your rest."

"I need you," Sarah begged, the words barely more than mouthed.

"I'll be right outside the door."

Sarah couldn't fight anymore. She lost herself in the endless, loving balm of the bed…still warm from Nina's body.

"Sweet dreams."

Sleep took her at last.

>~~~<

When Sarah woke up, she felt so well-rested that Beck's betrayal and Ty's cheating could've been a hundred years ago. There wasn't much to see by the soft yellow dawn that filled the room like water, but it was obvious Nina was gone. Sarah was alone. At some point in the night, Nina had hung up a nightgown on the chair near the fire, presumably for Sarah to wear while her clothes were washed. Sarah smiled to herself at the woman's thoughtfulness.

She got up for the nightgown, and that was when the door opened. Sarah hurled herself back under the covers as Nina came in, bearing a tray of breakfast. She wasn't able to get the blanket over herself, just the sheet, which felt as thin as a tissue.

Nina wore a gauzy white robe, translucent except for tattoos of butterflies along it. It was tied with a silk ribbon, but underneath Sarah could see Nina's bra and panties. They were modest, more than what she'd worn while tanning—the black panties came up to her waist and the bra barely let her jiggle. It wasn't the sight of Nina that struck Sarah so much as the energy she radiated. Sarah knew the feel of her, and not just that, but the receptiveness, how accepting she could be. It made Sarah feel as if she was standing on a high-dive board, far above the swimming pool, and all it would take was one bounce and then she would dive.

"I thought you might feel better if you ate something," Nina said. The tray had little legs that let her set it over Sarah's lap, trapping her under a prison of fried eggs, short-stack pancakes, grapefruit, orange juice, buttered toast, and a bowl of cornflakes. "Eat. I'll take whatever you don't want."

Sarah picked up a piece of toast and nibbled on it. Nina was looking at her. Sarah pushed the cereal bowl toward her; obliging, Nina sat down beside her on the bed and began to eat.

"I feel so embarrassed," Sarah said.

"There's nothing to be ashamed of. People feel things. It's what they do. And there are far worse ways to handle it than having a good cry."

"Like breaking and entering?" Sarah asked.

"You had a key. We're friends, after all."

"Is that all you are?"

Nina busied herself eating cereal. After a moment, she said, "Mr. Shannon rescued the boat. You can go home when you wish. Your clothes are in the dryer—"

Sarah chewed her toast, wondering if Nina wanted her to leave, or if she was just afraid of Sarah asking to go. Maybe they could just keep eating, and neither one of them would have to say anything. Was that why Nina had made so much food?

She reached for the glass of orange juice but didn't drink. Her lips twitched. She remembered feeling the bone of Nina's sharp jawline as she'd kissed her cheek. Had Nina turned away? No. As she'd pulled back, Nina had shifted toward her, almost a twitch, and if Sarah had just kissed her cheek again, once or twice, she would've found Nina's lips under hers.

"Nina," she asked, dry-mouthed, "do you want me?"

Nina looked away. "That's not what you want to know."

"Do you?"

Nina picked up the breakfast tray and set it down on the floor. Suddenly Sarah realized just how closely the sheet clung to her naked body, outlining the curve of her hips, the swell of her breasts. And Nina—it felt as if she could see right through it.

Sarah didn't feel embarrassed, though. She felt a guilty flush between her thighs, and her toes curled, hidden under the covers where Nina could see them and not see them.

"You want to know if you're a lesbian," Nina said, "and in my experience, people who ask *that* question don't tend to be straight."

"And do you? Ask that question?"

Nina shook her head. "I don't anymore. You know what I am, Sarah. But you've never asked, and I've never kept it secret. Either you are or you aren't. Either way, that's not what is important."

Sarah was getting tired of double-talk. Maybe Nina thought she was giving her a taste of her own medicine, playing hard to get, but Sarah had never… She hadn't *known*.

"What *is* important?" she insisted.

"What you want, of course," Nina said. She set her hands on her knees, and all Sarah could think was that if they'd been touching her, they would've been irresistible.

"I don't know what I want," Sarah admitted, which was at least half a lie. She knew a lot of what she wanted. She wanted Nina to kiss her. She wanted to stop looking at Nina and thinking about kissing her. She wanted this electricity going through her to stop. She wanted it to never end.

No, she didn't know what she wanted. Sarah knew what she *needed*, and it was a million different things, and she couldn't tell if any of them were good for her.

Nina was looking at her. Sarah wanted to meet her eyes. She wanted to stop feeling Nina's eyes on her.

"That's why you're here," Nina said. "Because you don't know what you want. That's what draws you to me—finding someone who does know, who knows *you*, knows what you want, how to give it to you."

The way some of those words felt in her ears, Sarah couldn't admit in a thousand years. "And what do *you* want?" she retorted, suddenly angry.

"That doesn't matter," Nina said sagely.

"Yes, it does!" Sarah insisted. "Because what I really want is for you to stop pretending this is all on me! You want it too. You can be as respectful about it as you like, but you want to *fuck me*."

The crude words hung between them like smoke after a bomb had gone off, like debris sailing through the air and coming slowly crashing down, like shrapnel was embedded inside them.

Nina's voice faltered. "That's not what I want."

"Yes, it is!" Her own voice cracked too, because of course Nina looked at Sarah the same way Sarah looked at her. Of course Nina wanted from Sarah what Sarah wanted from her.

That wasn't a need or a want, that was *bone*, and it underlaid everything Sarah felt or thought she should feel.

"Sarah," Nina stood, as firm, as unshakable as a rock. "I want so much more than that."

Then she smiled, but it wasn't a reassuring smile. More like they were going on a roller coaster together and Nina was trying to share how her own nervousness and excitement were all mixed up. She set her hand down on the sheets between them. Her fingers were long and slender, and two black rings set off the red lacquer on her nails. Sarah imagined those nails on her skin, the rings' cool metal pebbling her flesh as Nina's palm ran up her leg. The hand steepled, arching the thin sheet as if about to rip through it, then bunching the fabric inside Nina's long fingers.

With the slack taken up, the top of the bedsheet traveled an inch down Sarah's body. Its movement was so much like a caress that Sarah could've gasped. She stared, disbelieving, as Nina pulled at the sheet, slowly, softly, every inch a whisper directly into Sarah's body. She felt cool air prickle the skin over her collarbone, the tops of her breasts. Then a flushing heat filled her as the blanket came off her cleavage, leaving it bare, and began to trickle over her abdomen, which clenched and contorted with subtle muscles coming to the surface. Sarah could feel Nina's gaze, heavier than the sheet had been, savoring every inch of skin she uncovered. But she didn't rush it; it was still so slow. Down her sternum, along her ribs, she could feel every little wrinkle in the sheet as it kissed her body, lower, lower, over her belly, her navel, the wisps of hair that led the way to her sex, and she felt so bare, so exposed, so vulnerable just having the sheet so close to not being *there* that she let out a low moan.

"Are you all right?" Nina asked, pausing, the length of bedsheet in her hand like a weapon.

Sarah was acutely aware of her naked breasts jogging up and down with each breath, catching Nina's eye, and she couldn't stop them moving, couldn't still their heaving or make her hardened nipples stop aching for Nina's touch. She couldn't say anything.

The sheet slipped a little from Nina's hand as her grip loosened. "Do you want to keep going? Sarah, I'm not going to keep going unless you say it's what you want."

It was like pulling teeth just forming the words in her mind, but finally, shivering, Sarah said, "I want you to stop."

Nina pulled the sheet over Sarah, hiding her again, and Sarah clasped it against herself, even as it felt so cold and she'd been so warm…

But she wasn't gay. She couldn't just *be* gay, no matter what Nina said. If she was, she was, but she wanted the chance to ask herself, instead of being so malleable that she contorted herself to the first person who showed her warmth.

"I want you to go," she forced out.

Nina left the room as if she had never been there.

Chapter 6

Back at home, she repeated the story Nina had made up about a tree that had been struck by lightning. She'd changed into her work clothes and was just starting to feel human again when the doorbell rang.

"Got it!" Sarah called to her mother.

It was Tyrese.

"Thought we'd talk," he said, terse but soft-voiced. As if he could lull her into a false sense of security.

"A picture is worth a thousand words," she replied.

He backed up from the door as if shaking off a hit, coming to lean against the side of the porch. His expression was surly. He always had been quick to pout.

"That wasn't me."

"It sure looked like you."

"That's not—" He'd raised his voice. He had to lower it again. "That's not what I meant. I mean I'm not like that."

"You were once. How many more times do you get? Before it counts?"

"You're putting words in my mouth—"

"So what are your words? Why exactly am I supposed to feel so damn sorry for you?" It was the voice she'd used last night—sarcastic, quick-witted, but cutting far deeper than it had with Nina.

When he came up out of his lean, he towered over her; she didn't bother looking up. "Because she was all over me! Sarah, she practically gift-wrapped it! She came onto me. She wanted me. There's only so much a man can take."

"Then I'll get someone who can take more!"

"Baby, you're being ridiculous. I make one mistake and that's it? After all we've been through, you're just gonna chuck it all out the window and start over? With who? Who you got that has our history? Who's been a friend to you like me, man to you like me?"

Sarah felt her hands coil, lash out, shoving against his broad chest—only able to drive him back a step or two with her thudding palms on his collarbone. "I'm not interested! Not just in you. I'm not interested in being your girlfriend anymore. I'm not interested in being that girl anymore."

"You don't want to be the girl I grew up with? You don't want to be Sarah Kay? Who else is there?"

"Someone else. Anyone else!"

"Mr. West!" Eileen spoke firmly, clearly, and when Sarah turned around, her mother was standing behind her with her arms crossed, her gaze fixed so firmly on Tyrese that she barely seemed to notice Sarah. "You've said all you came here to say, and it's time for you to leave."

Tyrese looked from mother to daughter. "Oh. Now you don't mind her living your life for you. Hey, Moms, you know your girl hates you, right? Hates you."

"*Good day*, Tyrese."

He left, exaggerating his strut into a dance, trying to make it seem as if he cared less than zero.

Eileen graciously closed the door before she put her arm around Sarah.

Sarah let herself be hugged.

"How about a movie this weekend?" Eileen asked. "A spa? Maybe just anything with not a lot of talking required?"

"Yeah. That'd be nice."

There was no escape from what Sarah had seen. It felt like she'd taken a drug. Cool metal felt as cold as the Arctic, and sunbaked concrete was the Gobi Desert. Looking at a wall had her imagining Nina pinning her against it. Work was at least a distraction.

She walked the aisles of the supermarket like some ghost stuck in a living death pattern, trying to think of nothing but making every row of product straight and smooth. She went from aisle one to aisle seven; there were thirteen more aisles, but those were other employees' purview. Yes, they hired more than one person for the job.

And still she thought of Nina. Of herself. When Nina actually appeared, she could've been summoned right out of Sarah's imagining.

"Do you want to talk?"

Sarah stopped, holding a box of Captain Crunch like it contained the secrets of the universe along with a sheaf of temporary tattoos.

Nina was there, standing close but not too close. Dressed so elegantly yet so simply: black turtleneck, white slacks, hair neatly combed. Everything buttoned down, covered up. But Sarah could see it in her eyes. Right there past all the mascara. That wildness she'd let blaze as she prepared to savage Sarah. It was still there, had always been there.

The sight of Nina, the hermit, the ghost, standing in the middle of a store as if she needed to pick up Pop-Tarts crashed right into Sarah, refused to be broken down into thoughts. For a moment, everything had the peculiar resonance of a waking dream. The thing was so strange that it wasn't strange, like seeing a tiger in the street or the moon at midday. She had to work to believe her eyes.

Sarah felt herself start to turn, start to go to her, and then she was putting the Captain Crunch neatly in the front of the shelf space it occupied. That was the most important thing in the world for her just at that moment.

"I'm working," Sarah said.

"You weren't yesterday. I thought that was when you were scheduled to tend the grounds."

"I felt sick. I sent you an e-mail."

"And now you're feeling better."

"No such thing as sick days on minimum wage."

Nina nodded. "Do you get breaks?"

"Under six hours, I get fifteen minutes. Over six hours, I get half an hour. I don't think I can spend fifteen minutes listening to you."

"Then should I assume you don't wish to work for me any longer? Of course, that's your decision. I'll understand if you stop coming by—"

"I didn't *say that*," Sarah stressed.

"Do you want to work for me or don't you?"

"That's not even what you want to know!"

"Ah." Nina held herself very still as Sarah moved on. There was a box of Cocoa Pebbles that needed to be moved up. "I was like this once. I couldn't imagine—I couldn't imagine a lot of things. But the chief thing was being happy… I know it must feel like a bandage coming off to have this out in the open… I also know it's killing you not hearing what I have to say. Even if you say you don't give a damn. Even if you wish you didn't give a damn."

Sarah dropped her hands to her sides. "Follow me."

Sarah led her to the meat department—the little room past the plastic-strip curtain but before the big cooler space: shelves and shelves of boxes and boxes of meat. Pedro was on duty.

Sarah told him to hit the road. "Can you drop a deuce for ten minutes?"

"*Que*? Sarah, we're almost out of baloney. You know how fast baloney sells—"

"You owe me. I covered your shift two weeks ago…"

"Just so I could get fired two weeks later?"

Nina held up her hand. "A hundred dollars for—the deuce."

Pedro pursed his lips. "Sold."

And he was gone.

Sarah sat on a box of cold cuts, twisting her toes inside her shoes. It was always a relief to be off her feet, even in a literal meat locker.

Nina straightened out her hair, stopping with her hand twined in the tips. "Is there anything you'd like to tell me about what happened? Some…feelings you'd like to share?"

Sarah's eye twitched. "What, like I wrote an essay?"

"I thought you might be curious." She held her hair aside now. It bristled through her fingers.

"Curious?"

A single, solitary follicle stayed between Nina's fingers. The rest lay limply against her scalp. She pulled at the strand of hair. Making it taut. "About me. I thought you would have questions."

Sarah felt her jaw going slack. "I do."

Nina pinched her lips together, looking around for somewhere to rest her weight, her attention finally settling on another box. Looking the most ridiculous Sarah had ever seen her, she haphazardly navigated it opposite Sarah's perch, then sat down, trying to remain poised atop a cardboard box of frozen ground beef. "I'm not ashamed. I'll tell you anything."

"Tell me why we have to do this here?"

"We could do it at my home. But if you'd prefer a more neutral setting…"

"A more neutral setting and my shift being over."

Nina sniffed. "I thought a week was a long enough wait. I…rushed into things. If you'd rather wait longer—"

"I don't want you to go," Sarah said quickly, before she could regret it.

"So what *do* you want?" Nina whispered, a conspirator. "For me to come closer?"

The word seemed incredibly small as it slipped from Sarah. "Yes."

Nina stood. She towered over Sarah, but that wasn't what made her feel small. Because after one moment, one breath, Nina was lowering herself back down. Straddling Sarah's joined thighs, bringing her beauty so close to Sarah, so dangerously close. Their bodies slowly merged. Last of all, their breasts brushed together. Sarah felt Nina's nipples against her own, as hard as hers.

"Am I close enough now?" Nina asked, the heat of her breath on Sarah's cheek.

"Not even…a little bit…" Sarah couldn't open her eyes. She just let the other voice, the other her, speak.

With her free hand coiling under Sarah, Nina suddenly pulled them together, crushing Sarah's body to hers. Everywhere on Sarah's skin, she felt Nina's warmth.

"How about now?" Nina demanded, bending her head to Sarah's like a king offering his ring to a subject.

Sarah knew what she had to do. Her body was screaming it at her. Her sex was wet, her skin hot, her inhibitions elsewhere. More by touch than by sight, she found Nina's soft lips. The kiss was slow, unhurried. Not like with Tyrese at all. At first, Nina just brushed her lips against Sarah's, even when Sarah opened her mouth. Then Nina applied pressure, bringing their lips together with greater force so they were crushed together from head to toe, like fire meeting ice, their kiss a way for the steam to escape.

Nina made the kiss harder, harder, *harder*, demanding more from Sarah, forcing her body to respond down to the innermost core. Sarah gave willingly, opened herself as far as she could. Nina plundered her mouth, not letting Sarah up for so much as *air*, and Sarah felt Nina's hands hovering over her body, almost touching but *not*, tracing from her moist cunt to her quivering breasts, finally stopping at her face, holding her still for more of Nina's passion. Hands kneaded Sarah's temples as Nina kissed her, twirled her hair, until Sarah started making *sounds*. Weak, needy, *hungry* sounds deep within her body. She knew Nina could hear them; she smiled against Sarah's mouth and went on kissing her.

It was several long minutes before Nina pulled away slowly, with one last suck at Sarah's swollen bottom lip. Then she licked her own lips.

"Fuck," Sarah mewled, still as water with no ripples and about to come. She was so aroused, so goddamn *horny*, and yet there was a serenity to it, a safety. Nina had her. She was Nina's. Nothing to worry about.

"Do you want me to kiss you again?" Nina asked.

"No, no, I…"

Nina was backing away, giving her space—and just when Sarah didn't think she could be any more grateful to her. She was burning up, on fire, and Nina was all gasoline.

"I have to go. I have to get back to work."

"Sarah, I didn't mean to upset you…"

"*Yes*," Sarah interrupted—she realized it must've been the first time she had talked back to Nina, because she could see the woman's face fall. "You did."

She left before she had to think of whether that was good or bad.

Of course she had a hard time going through with the rest of her shift after that. She got maybe twenty minutes of actual work done, which was still better than Stoner Bill, the manager's nephew. Before she could clock out, her mother texted, asking her to grab toilet paper. Her name tag off, her logo'd shirt inside out, Sarah picked up a pack and waited in line. The things she did for an employee discount.

With her body in stasis, her mind had permission to wander, and it went back to her encounter with Nina like a dog scrambling after table scraps. She thought of how Nina had licked her lips after their kiss as if she could taste Sarah on them and felt an unpleasantly pleasant sparking between her inner thighs. The last thing Sarah needed was to get wet in line at the checkout. She looked over the tabloids, trying to distract herself, but it was all celebrity gossip. She missed the days when there were Bigfoot sightings and UFO abductions instead of Jennifer Aniston baby bumps. Who the hell cared?

That's good, Sarah told herself. *What could be less arousing than the slow death of print media?* She glanced ahead to be sure she wasn't holding things up and caught Beck's eye just as her former friend was looking back from the neighboring line. This was why she hated living in a small town.

"Sarah," Beck said. "Hey."

"Hey," Sarah replied, draining any possible joy from the word. The least gay pronunciation imaginable.

"I was kinda hoping we could talk."

"You have my number."

"I wanted to do this face-to-face."

The cash register drawer dinged open and drawled shut again. Beck was next in line; she broke away from Sarah to quickly exchange pleasantries with the cashier. It set Sarah's teeth on edge. How could she be so phony? Then Beck was facing her again as she took out her credit card.

"I'm really sorry about what happened, I am, and I'm not trying to excuse it, but I think you've got the wrong idea."

"What idea would that be, *Beck*?" Sarah asked, pulling at Beck's attention as she navigated the card reader, which was trying to decide whether it wanted her to slide her card or insert it. And of course Beck was all over it, paying attention to the stupid machine instead of her *friend* Sarah—

"Ty and me. We're not dating, we're not hooking up, we're not anything. It was just a stupid kiss, okay? We do stupid shit all the time!"

"So because we used a dirt bike to spin a merry-go-around, that means you can kiss my boyfriend?"

The cashier cleared his throat, hesitant to interrupt as he handed Beck her bags. She took them but hung around until Sarah completed her transaction.

"I'm just trying to fix things, okay? I don't want you out of my life because of some dumb mistake."

Sarah picked up the toilet paper like a weapon. "Well, I don't want you in my life. You or Tyrese. So don't worry about it, because there's nothing you can say that can fix it. You're a slut."

This was the point in the movie where everyone watching would 'ooh' or clap or cheer, but in real life, they just looked uncomfortable and quietly paid for their items. Sarah walked away.

Beck let her walk for a few moments, then chased after her. They walked almost side by side as the automatic doors parted and room temperature gave way to the evening chill.

"You know what? I don't even think this is about us. I think you just wanted an excuse to ditch us. I think you only hang out with us because it's something to do, but deep down, you think you're better than us. So this is just some great opportunity for you to look down on everyone else, but the truth is, you're here too. And whatever reason you couldn't hack it at college, *you couldn't hack it*."

Sarah jammed the toilet paper into the trunk of her car. "Yeah? How long have you been waiting to tell me that, huh? Tell me how you really feel."

"Yeah, I should've! Maybe I would've been a better friend if I gave you some real talk. Honestly, I have no idea what you're doing here—besides getting your mom a five-percent discount on toilet paper. But if you don't want to figure it out, why should I?" She left.

Sarah slammed the trunk closed. Then she opened it again to slam it back down, harder.

"Yeah, you'd better walk away," she muttered.

Chapter 7

Sarah looked her father in the eye.

"Dad…I'm gay."

As she'd suspected, it was easier telling him than Eileen. And he seemed to be taking it well. He sat right where he was on the pedestal, his notepad still in hand.

Not that she thought Bobby would've had a problem with it if he were still alive.

Eileen certainly didn't hate gay people either. She seemed to find them cute on some level. But it was different when it was your daughter.

Hell, Sarah had nothing against gay people, and it was different when it was *her*. She felt like she'd been drafted into some big, nebulous cause, suddenly weighted down with all this *stuff*…or it'd always been there, and now she'd been forced to acknowledge it, and she both resented that and appreciated finally having a name for it.

Her father hadn't replied, so it was up to her to keep the conversation going. "I know, right? Came as a shock to me too. You know her—Nina Rose. I guess you always liked her… I wonder if you'd like her more as a daughter."

The sculptor had done a good job, and the town had put the statue in a good place—quiet, peaceful, lots of trees around to give him shade as he sat and thought.

She couldn't even remember what his voice sounded like, but sometimes, she could imagine that she felt his presence. That kind of warmth, it took away pain.

"I've never felt this way before. I really want her—I want to be with her. At first, I just liked spending time with her, and I thought it was because she was so smart and cool, but now, all I can think about is…doing stuff. And don't get all judgmental about it, because I'm pretty sure I wouldn't be here if you hadn't… Eww, now I'm thinking about it. Aaand we're both grossed out."

Sarah stood up and set about pacing. "So here's the thing: Should I go to Nina? I haven't been back there since—I mean, I know what'll happen. I feel like if I spend just one more minute with her, I'll explode. And I mean, I'm twenty, and I'm not a virgin, so what's there to wait for? Like anyone would care if they caught us together…"

She started pacing again as if she couldn't control herself, as if her legs were determined to bring her back to that house and she could only divert them. "Do these things ever stay secret? Would I even want that? I mean, maybe someday I'd like to go on a date at a fancy restaurant, hold hands…tell her I love her. Do we ever *get* that? Because people would talk. Wouldn't they?"

With an *ugh*, Sarah dropped herself back down to the bench. She covered her eyes with her hand. "I can't plan for this, okay? I'm not a planner. I just need to know if it'd be worth it. Was it worth it for you, with Mom? I don't know, maybe if you'd never met her, you wouldn't be…"

She took her hand away from her face, listening as a gust of wind blew through the trees. It sounded so peaceful, all those leaves rustling around, but they had to know that sooner or later, the wind would rip them away from where they were and send them down to wither and decay on the ground.

"But then, maybe you were always going to end up like this. Maybe I could go into a coma, drop dead of a brain aneurysm, get hit by a meteor. The only certain thing about death is that you always do it alone."

Sarah put a hand on the statue's knee. As she did, she saw the plaque. It said the statue had been donated to the city by N.R. She let out a soft chuckle and shook her head.

"Okay. I'll go see her in the morning. It'll be worth it just to look at her."

>~~~<

Sarah tied off the boat to Nina's pier. She was dressed in jeans, a denim jacket, and her church blouse, her bra and panties plain Hanes but clean as could be. Not exactly a picture of seduction, but Bathory got cold this time of year, especially this early in the morning, and she wanted to survive the ride over.

She paced on the lawn a moment, trying to think of what to say, then just took the key Nina had given her and unlocked the door. No more waiting. The words would come. They would.

The house was quiet. Barnaby was sleeping near the foot of the stairs, only opening one lazy eye to view her passage and make sure she didn't have any food on her.

She crept through the empty manor, sneaking one moment and almost stampeding the next until she came to Nina's bedroom. She stopped. Raised her hand to knock, then brought it back down. Lower and lower, until she touched the doorknob. It turned.

Inside, the curtains were open, letting in a trickle of light from the sunrise. It ran like wildfire over everything, and Sarah caught just a glimpse of a coiled figure in the king-sized bed before a cloud passed over the sun. The only light now came from behind Sarah, peeking dully over her shoulder from the hallway outside. Afraid it would wake Nina, Sarah slipped inside and shut the door behind her.

The clouds shifted again, and light spread slowly, touching the bed, then the satin sheets, then a pair of arms crossed together, fingers interlocked as if in prayer. The nails were painted as red as fresh apples; the color stood out to Sarah against the white bedsheets and golden light. Nina.

She stepped closer. The curtains rustled as the heater kicked on, making the light shift. She could now see Nina's hair spilling over her pillow, her eyes moving under shut lids. Her lips, pale but still with the washed-out remnants of her lipstick, like dried blood on a vampire's mouth. They moved with each breath, making it seem as if Nina were whispering something. Sarah didn't stop herself. She drew closer and closer, eager to hear.

It was funny how innocent Nina looked as she slept, considering how her sexuality had fixed itself in Sarah's mind. Her face had relaxed somehow; there was something about her that didn't ache. She seemed very young and a little vulnerable lying there.

Sarah bent over her, not quite sure what she was doing even as she did it. Nina's hot breath caressed her cheek as their faces drew closer. And Sarah realized: *I'm going to kiss her.*

Their lips met like—Nina would laugh if she heard Sarah say this—magnets. Like there'd been something keeping them apart and now it'd been removed. Nature was taking its course, and they were kissing. Then Nina awoke and showed Sarah that they hadn't been kissing at all.

She responded enthusiastically, taking it to a whole other level. Sarah felt a tongue in her mouth, stimulating places she didn't know she had, and a hand on the back of her neck, the nails digging into her skin. It tingled; her lips tingled. Her whole damn body tingled.

Sarah only opened her eyes when Nina drew back. Nina stared back at her, Sleeping Beauty awoken by Princess Charming. Her hazel eyes were a deep, rich brown in this light—expensive chocolate, polished leather. The eyes of a Disney character. Sarah giggled a little, pulling back some, working it down to a smile as she bit her lip. She imagined she could still taste Nina, but if she could, Nina tasted vaguely of her own raspberry lip gloss.

"Am I dreaming?" Nina asked her.

"No. I, uh…" Sarah didn't know what to do with her hands. She caught one making for Nina's bare arm, trying to stroke it. "Had to see you."

"See me?" Those big eyes slanted a little. "I don't think those were your *eyes* I felt on my lips."

"Sorry—not, like, *that* sorry." Sarah giggled again. What the hell was wrong with her? Why was she giggling? "I can't stop thinking about you. And I don't want to. Stop. I just want to do more than think."

Oh God. Oh, *God*. Could that sound lamer? Sarah stood up—her butt had parked itself on Nina's mattress—and almost ran out the door. What was she *saying*? This sounded ridiculous, all of it, everything was just—

Nina reached out and took her hand. Immediately, Sarah felt a kind of warmth. Not in her hand. In her breast.

"I feel the same way." Nina's long, bare legs flashed out from under the covers and settled on the floor as she sat up. Sarah could've gasped; they had a golden glow, runner's muscles, and a perfect tan. Her mind blitzed her with images of running her tongue over every languid curve of them.

And Nina felt the same way. Wait, as what? As *her*?

"As me?" Sarah asked, strangling another giggle.

Nina smiled—Sarah had to think it—lovingly.

"Yes, Sarah. As you. You're so beautiful," she said as if sensing Sarah's swirling fears. She stood, seeming to tower over Sarah. A comforting shelter. "And so young, in the best possible way. Full of hope and love. You have so much love to give, don't you, Sarah? And so few are worthy of all that you have to offer."

She was wearing a kimono, covering her from shoulder to floor. Even her feet were covered. It drove Sarah wild, imagining her under that. Was her skin as sweaty as Sarah's? Did she have as many goose pimples? Were her breasts rising and falling with the same panting breaths?

"I'd really like to kiss you again," Sarah blurted out. "Or, uh—" She touched the tips of her pointer fingers together.

"I don't think you're quite ready for that. Maybe we could…watch a movie."

Sarah surged up, meeting her lips to Nina's like a battering ram hitting a gate. She heard Nina actually squeak and finally, *finally*, felt those hands settle around her body. Just on her hips and the small of her back, but it felt like a leg she'd been favoring had finally stopped hurting.

"I need you," Sarah said, shucking off her jacket. Nina watched, her eyes gratifyingly wide, as Sarah stripped off her good blouse. "I've been thinking about this…forever! I need it, okay? I just…" She opened her belt and peeled her jeans down, kicking them off before she let herself think anymore.

Sarah fell silent. She'd never been naked in front of a woman before. Hell, no one had seen her naked other than Tyrese. She was almost ready to take off her bra, her panties, but she couldn't. The realization hit like a bomb: She wanted Nina to do it. She wanted Nina to be the one kissing her, touching her, making love to her, not the other way around. She wanted to be wanted.

She almost cried at the sudden thought that Nina didn't want her, that this was all…letting her down easy.

"You're so warm," Nina said slowly, reaching out reverently to place two fingers on Sarah's stomach. She looked up, for permission, and Sarah gave it. Her fingers brushed over Sarah's skin. Not anywhere…naughty, but not where she was usually touched either. Over her ribs, over her panties; it was like Nina was literally getting a feel for her. "I didn't expect you to be so warm…" Nina looked up at her, her eyes big and dark again. "Are you sure you want this? Do you want me?"

"Yes," Sarah breathed.

Nina sat down and leaned back onto her elbows, splaying herself before Sarah. Her legs were almost bare, and most definitely parted. "Then have me."

"I don't know." Sarah could barely breathe. Her mind was brimming over, all Nina, all the time, a million places to kiss and touch and feel all demanding attention. She thought she'd been turned on before, but nothing could compare to Nina Rose beckoning her on, next to naked. Hers to undress, to make love to… "I don't know what to do."

Nina dropped on her back and crossed her legs. "Well, that part I do have some ideas about." She cocked her head. "Do you know how to touch me?"

Sarah shook her head. It seemed like a major accomplishment.

"I could show you."

Sarah could've fainted.

"Would you like to watch that?"

"I'd like to help." Sarah had no idea where that came from. A moment ago, she'd been sure she'd gone mute. "Just tell me what to do."

Nina reached down and untied the belt of her kimono. "Undress me."

Sarah joined Nina on the bed, hands going to her body as carefully as a surgeon working with a scalpel. Her hands felt like someone else's as they gently grasped either side of the robe, the material as soft as clouds between her fingers, and drew it aside.

This time, Sarah did gasp.

All Nina wore underneath was a nightie, cut high and with a hem that went across mid-thigh. On those terms, it was quite modest. But the material it was made from was far thinner than the kimono, virtually gossamer, almost translucent. With the barest effort, Sarah could see everything underneath—Nina's skin, turned into alabaster by the combination of the moonlight and the tinting fabric. Her nipples, poking through the nightie, a deep, rich red that stood out on the white plain of her body like bonfires. And down below, between her legs—no, that was still hidden, a secret of shadows and fabric.

"Touch me," Nina murmured, eyes closed, head tilted back.

How could she? What if she got it wrong? What if she tickled her or prodded a bruise or—or ripped her nightie?

Sarah stood there, unable to move.

Nina's eyes opened sinuously. They settled on Sarah like a snake eying a bird. "Are you scared?"

"Nervous," Sarah corrected hastily.

"It's okay to be nervous." Nina propped herself up on one perfect arm, a shoulder strap falling down the other. "But you don't have to be scared. You're with me. This is just…a story you haven't told yet. There's no right or wrong thing to do. There's just things to learn." She reached out and took Sarah's hand, a cheeky grin blooming. Sarah couldn't help herself. She smiled back. "Things to learn about you… Things to learn about me…" She brought Sarah's hand to her mouth. Shortish fingernails, no nail polish. She kissed its back. "I want to know everything about you."

She kept kissing Sarah's hand, over the fingers, the knuckles, the thumb, the webbing between fingers. Sarah wondered if Nina could taste how much her fingers had yearned to touch her—smell it like a dab of perfume.

With one last succulent suck on Sarah's finger, Nina stopped playing and moved the hand over her face. Against her cheek, then down her throat. She made Sarah feel her skin. It was warm, and goose-pimpled, like her body was clamoring for attention. Just like Sarah's. Nina fed herself on Sarah's touch, running the hand across her body from shoulder strap to shoulder strap. Her skin was clear, smooth, warm. And human. Not untouchable, not unapproachable. Just a girl.

Then Nina lowered Sarah's hand to her breast.

"Oh!" Sarah said helplessly.

Nina smiled up at her, biting her lip in a show of nervousness. She covered it up quickly. "Do you like them?"

"Yes! Of course I do. They're...wow."

Nina's face settled into smugness. "Yes, I like to think so. Feel them. Take your time. I know you want to."

As if she were tending a flower, Sarah applied the slightest pressure. Nina's breast creased under her touch, filling her hand. It was soft. Impossibly soft, silk layered over silk, warm like it'd spent hours soaking in sunlight. Her nipple was a tiny, perfect core of hardness in Sarah's palm. Sarah rolled her hand over it, amazed at the pebbled surface, the textured feel of it—and the way Nina's eyes closed as she was handled. Everything was so like her own body, only...more so. Finished. Perfected.

"Could you"—Sarah bit her lip—"could you turn around, please?"

Nina's eyes fluttered open. "I get it. Hard to concentrate while I'm looking at you. Easier if we can do this a little blind. Or maybe you're just an ass-woman, eh?"

"No!" Sarah said quickly. "I mean, not that there's anything wrong with your ass..."

"How would you know?" Nina asked, shrugging her kimono off. "Unless you check?"

She turned over. Her bare ass peeked out from beneath her nightie. It was glorious. Tight and sleek, yet...substantial somehow, like a piece of fruit that'd ripened on the vine for the exact right length of time. There was just enough of it, toned and the same gilded color as the rest of her. Sarah could just picture Nina sunbathing nude, making her whole body perfect...

And as she stood there, gaping, Nina rolled her ass at Sarah like a stripper. Her nightie ended up scrunched over the ripe curves of her ass like magic. It nearly gave Sarah a stroke.

Nina worked her way up to her knees, her nightie falling back over her as she did. Internally, Sarah screamed but stopped when Nina reached back to touch her face. Her fingers moved as lightly as feathers. "You know, I've told a lot of people to kiss my ass." The fingers, shy but insistent, ushered Sarah to her knees. "Maybe it's time someone actually does it."

And with a smile fixed on her face, Nina turned back around and presented her ass to a Sarah no longer able to resist. She only had to do as she was told.

Leaning forward, Sarah kissed the flare of Nina's wide hips. Nothing happened. No cops burst in, no laughing pranksters spilled out of a closet, no phone rang to interrupt them. Just a breathy little moan from Nina, barely there at all.

Sarah moved along, pecking at Nina's waist and the small of her back in quick, breathless little snips of passion. Nina moaned again, but impatiently. She looked over her shoulder at Sarah expectantly. And, obeying her gaze, Sarah moved lower. Into the places a bikini would cover.

She made a line right down the curve of Nina's ass, not too deep into unknown territory but decidedly *there*, and kissed her way to the back of Nina's thigh. Then she went back up and kissed the sensitive flesh closer to the crevice. It felt so odd to be touched somewhere she barely even thought of. Was Nina used to the sensation or—

"Good girl," Nina said sweetly, virtually purring. Her body flicked up and down like a cat's. Sarah had to move with her to keep kissing her, and she did. It wasn't just the feel of her ass, the way the flesh seemed more tender there. It was the knowledge that she was doing something she shouldn't, with someone she shouldn't, and getting away with it.

Only now she didn't know what to do with her hands. Should she…touch herself? That kinda took a lot of concentration, at least if you wanted to do it right. Maybe she should touch Nina? But how did you touch a goddess? Wouldn't she smite you?

Sarah moved to the other side of the ass, and as she did, she set her hands on Nina's ankles. As if she were holding her down. As if she could.

"Oh," Nina went. "Mmm."

Sarah had no idea if that was a good "Oh—mmm" or a bad one. Nina had her face buried in the bedspread, expression covered by her own hair. Sarah moved her hands up, feeling the corded muscles in Nina's calves.

"Uh-huh," Nina muttered gently. "Yeah."

Sarah went further, *licking* Nina from thigh to waist as her hands trailed up Nina's thighs. When she looked again, Nina was biting her sheets. That was a good thing, right?

Her hands kept moving, making an executive decision to reach around Nina and dip between her legs. Sarah only realized it when she felt what was there.

"Oh God. Oh God, you're so wet."

"Mmmmm," Nina purred as she all-foured down the bed, her hips wagging from side to side even more than they did when she walked. She turned over, her thighs crossing coquettishly. When Sarah saw her face, she was biting her plump lip. "Taste me."

Panic ran through Sarah like ice water. She couldn't do that—eat a girl out! She'd only ever *seen* that on *The L Word*, during Showtime's free preview week, and if there was more to it than shaking your head over a pair of panties, Sarah didn't know it.

"Sarah, come here," Nina said insistently, uncrossing her legs.

Oh God. Oh Christ. She was *dripping*.

"I…" Sarah began, finding herself crawling onto the bed.

"It's all right," Nina assured her, moving her thigh to bop Sarah's head, her grin infectious. "It won't bite you. I might, so you're far safer down there than up here."

"Well," Sarah said, and didn't have anything after that. "Wuh-wuh-well…"

"Do you stutter?" Nina asked.

"I don't think so…so…"

"Just come down here." Nina moved her hand down over her nightie. The scrunching material obscured and exposed her body in equal measure. "Learn my scent."

"I don't stutter," Sarah said for some reason. She lowered her head, bowing before Nina. Held her breath. Released it and inhaled.

Nina was *fragrant*. Like a kind of rose Sarah had never smelled before, a kind of meal she'd never been served. She was perfume.

"Good work, my dear." Nina moved her legs, steepling them on either side of Sarah's body. The thought stuck in Sarah's head that she was between Nina's legs. "Now how about a kiss?"

"Down there?" Sarah squeaked.

"Well, you can't expect any tongue from me." Nina rolled her eyes. "It's our first date."

"What if I do something wrong?"

"Sarah, I told you…" Nina's wandering hand pulled up her nightie. The other replaced it, running a finger inside her sex. It pulled away, glistening, to touch Sarah's lips. Vacantly, Sarah opened her mouth and sucked on Nina's finger. "There's nothing you can do wrong. Not when I'm this wet."

"Oh Christ, Nina…" Sarah bowed her head once more, mouth open this time. "Christ."

She kissed. She licked. She sucked.

She tasted.

Nina moaned, sighed, breathed, all in musical accompaniment to the love Sarah was making with her tongue. It urged Sarah on…assured her…comforted her…demanded of her. She didn't know how long she stayed, her head nestled in this wonderful woman's thighs, her mouth filled with *Nina*, drinking of the sweetness Nina fed to her in a dream-like procession. Her world was all coos, murmurs, her name screamed like an answer from God. Time had no place in it.

At long last, she felt fingers in her hair, the pain of their tugging a perfect awakening from her enchanted slumber. She was pulled up to face Nina, a new Nina, her Nina. A Nina that was all lust and need and having.

"*I'm coming,*" Nina said hoarsely, and forced Sarah's head back to her sex.

Sarah ate greedily, like a convict eating her last meal, and Nina fed her to the point of gluttony. Dessert was the surge of honey in her mouth, the scream that half of Bathory must've heard. Then Nina's hands went limp in her hair and her legs turned to jelly around Sarah's ears. Nina flopped down on her back, and Sarah laid with her head on Nina's stomach, looking up and watching her come back to herself.

If tasting Nina had gone on for hours, this was over far too soon. Almost immediately, Nina's head came up. She fixed her sights on Sarah. Grabbed her by the bra and pulled their bodies together, kissing Sarah so hard they both tasted Nina on her lips. Then she rolled them around so she was on top.

"Your turn," Nina said, her smile altogether hungry.

Chapter 8

Nina was kissing her. Sarah couldn't think of anything else. Nina was holding her down, cupping her face, invading her mouth with her tongue. Then she felt Nina's legs, twined with her own. Nina's knee, rubbing between her legs.

"Oh God…" Sarah whimpered, breaking her lips away from Nina's.

"Was that too much?" Nina asked.

"No, no—that was a lot, but it wasn't *too* much…"

"Are you sure?" Nina rolled off Sarah, laying abreast of her. "Take a moment. Think. We can stop."

"I don't want to stop," Sarah said, reaching out to take Nina's hand. She gave it a squeeze, but it felt cold. "Why? Do you want to stop?"

"It doesn't matter what I want."

"Of course it does." Sarah sat up a little, rubbing her thumb along Nina's hand. "If you want to stop—"

"I don't want to stop, but I don't want to push you either."

"Trust me, I've been pushing way harder than you have. I've thought about it. I've thought about it…way too much. I don't want to think anymore."

"Could you, though? Just a little more? For me? Be confident that you want this, that you want it with me. I'm— I can be a lot to handle. And this should be special."

"It's not like it's my first time."

"Every time should be special, Sarah."

"It will be special."

Nina rolled on top of Sarah again, her knee landing on Sarah's groin without any weight. "If you're sure."

"I am. If you are. I am too."

Nina smiled down at her and nipped at her ear. "Sweet little Sarah…" Her fingers wiped a smudge of lipstick from the corner of Sarah's mouth. They moved lower, smearing traces of it on Sarah's chin, on her collarbone, between her breasts… "Are you ready to be mine?"

Sarah shivered in anticipation. "I've been yours since I first saw you."

Nina's fingers rolled from Sarah's belly button to the elastic band on her panties. "And I intend to keep you…" She pulled on them.

Sarah felt cool air rush in to touch her groin. She closed her eyes and braced herself.

Nothing but cold air.

She opened her eyes. Nina was eyeing her crotch like an engineer at a construction project. "I've heard of the phrase, 'if there's grass on the field, play ball.' This still seems like a little much." She shot Sarah a look. "When was the last time you managed it?"

"Uh, never?" Sarah pinched her lips together so hard she could hear them in her head. "I shaved my legs. I thought that would be… I have a coupon for a spa."

"Don't be ridiculous," Nina said, petting the fur down there. Sarah couldn't even feel it, her touch was so light, and there was so much…in the way. "I'll take care of it."

><~~~<

And just like that, she was perched at the head of Nina's bath, with Nina crouched in the porcelain tub between her spread legs holding an electric shaver.

Sarah was glad she still had her bra on, if nothing else; her nipples were as hard as stone.

"Now just relax," Nina said, turning the shaver on but holding it clear of them. As if she was letting Sarah get used to the repetitive sound. "Don't move, and if you feel even a little bit uncomfortable, let me know. I'll stop."

"Don't stop!" Sarah said automatically. Even the grating noise of the trimmer was turning her on a little. It sounded like…something else.

Nina smiled lovingly and ran her free hand from Sarah's knee down to…the work area…and then back up the other leg. Sarah obediently spread her legs wider. It was funny how good she'd already become at knowing Nina's mind, her wishes. As if she was born to be Nina's plaything.

"Easy, easy," Nina said.

Sarah wondered if this was Nina's way of making sure she stopped and reconsidered what they were doing, but she couldn't think of anything but how much she wanted Nina. Then the shaver touched her skin, and the vibration ran through her entire body.

"Ohh!"

Nina shut it off. "Sarah? Are you okay?"

"I'm fine." She managed a shaky smile. "It felt good, that's all."

Nina bent to kiss Sarah's knee. "I know it's difficult, but try not to squirt every time I touch you. You might short out the motor."

"Maybe if you weren't wearing a nightgown in a porcelain bathtub."

"There's something wrong with the combination?"

"It's just…fetish-y. You look like you're modeling something. This is all like a magazine cover, not my life."

"Well, I can think of a few things I'm going to do to you that would not be displayed at any reputable magazine stand…"

"Goddamnit!" Sarah said, trembling with lust. "Are we sure you can't get me off really quick? After that, you can shave my head if you like."

"Is that what you really want?" Nina asked, rising on her knees. Making her tall enough to lean forward and rub her face on Sarah's bra—slowly, excruciatingly slowly. "Knowing that this is our first time? And once we're done here, you'll be so sensitive. And when I kiss you down there, I'll taste you and only you?"

Sarah shut her eyes as another tremor went through her. "You talked me into it. But for fuck's sake, *hurry*!"

"Well, if it's for fuck's sake…" Turning the shaver back on, Nina knelt back down and gently, gently, moved in.

Sarah held on to the sides of the tub and tried not to cry out.

A few minutes later, Nina pulled the shaver away to blow some hair from it, leaving Sarah quaking.

"Nina?" Sarah asked, somehow managing not to stutter. She trailed off on the last syllable as Nina made another pass, the shaver throbbing, pulsing at her groin.

Sarah's grip on the tub tightened.

"Almost done," Nina said casually. "I was right, you know. I was right all along. You *are* the most beautiful girl I've ever seen. There." She set the shaver aside.

"You're not even a little bit done!" Sarah insisted, and flowed against Nina like water storming through a broken dam. But in a split-second, Nina had a hand around her throat and was pressing her against the wall behind the tub. Choking her just a little.

It only heightened Sarah's arousal.

"You do…as I say." Nina loosened her grip, turned it into a caress. "We're almost done, my dear."

She reached to the side and turned on the faucet. A slight trickle of warm water poured into the tub, its spray flecking Nina's nightgown. Turning it translucent.

Picking up a washcloth, Nina held it under the stream, getting it nice and wet. Sarah watched her slender fingers as they wrung it out, imagining those fingers on her. Squeezing her, touching her.

Nina draped the washcloth over Sarah's sex, like one of those little modesty towels in an old painting, and then began to roll her fingers over the cloth. Massaging the moisture into Sarah's body. Making the skin there warm and tender. Then she ground the heel of her hand into the washcloth. Sarah had to shove her balled fist into her mouth to keep from screaming Nina's name.

Finally, Nina peeled the washcloth away. The air that rushed in had Sarah whining and whimpering like a puppy that hadn't been fed. Nina smiled up at her and then ran the washcloth over her own lips. She never stopped smiling.

"I think I may have to wring this out again." She dropped it.

But instead of the plunking sound of it hitting the tub, Sarah heard a loud snap, then the death cry of something shrill and shocked. She jumped a little from the suddenness of the noise, and Nina instantly moved to sooth her.

"What was that?" Sarah demanded.

"Mousetrap. They fill up the basement, so I've prepared them accommodations. One just checked in."

"Geez."

"Don't worry about it. That'll scatter them all for a while." Nina picked up a bottle of body wash from the side of the tub and daubed her palm with a bead of soap. Rubbing it between her hands, she worked up a fine lather. "Now comes the tricky part. I know you trust me, Sarah. That's why you came here. But for this, you need to trust me *implicitly*. Trust that I know what I'm doing and that as long as you stay calm and hold still, you're not going to get hurt."

Sarah nodded. "I trust you."

"Good. Just remember. You've seen my crotch. Who do you think took care of that?" Nina kissed Sarah's groin, and heat like a volcano moved up Sarah's body. Then her hands moved in, touching the lather to Sarah.

As if she had all the time in the world, Nina worked the body wash in. And Sarah let it out, moaning and groaning. It was so different, the feel of Nina's fingers against her bare skin, the viscous cool of the lather as Nina spread it everywhere.

"Here's what I think we should do…" Nina began. Then she paused, enjoying the soundtrack as Sarah got used to the sensation Nina was providing.

"Yes?" Sarah was breathing too hard, too fast. She felt like she'd just run a marathon, no air in her lungs. But she couldn't get too excited. Nina might cut her. Worse, Nina might stop.

Nina scrupulously rubbed the lather all over Sarah's inner thighs, taking her time and leaving Sarah simmering. "Now, as long as we're slowing down, we *do* have things to discuss. This is…fun, but fun that can get very intense. And someone like you, someone inexperienced, they might not be ready for that just yet."

Sarah's skin was tender, perfectly receptive to the cool lather Nina now stirred with her finger. The tip of her pointer finger ran over Sarah's labia, letting the lather spread as it wanted to, getting it everywhere.

Sarah felt her tits burning, her nipples like metal in a forge. Getting harder. She pulled down her bra, letting them burst out into the air. The chafing ceased immediately. She could breathe.

"How do I get ready?"

Nina slid her hands off Sarah's sex and casually rinsed them under the faucet. "I'll teach you. I'll show you what your body wants…what it likes…and what other people like. There are some things, my sweet, that everyone likes…"

"Like a bare pussy?" Sarah asked.

"Oh, that's a bit overrated." Nina reached outside the bathtub again and came up with a safety razor. Displaying it to Sarah, she fingered the plastic sheath off the blades. They shined silver.

"So why me?" Sarah asked, meaning *why aren't we fucking*?

"It reminds me of Goya's *La maja desnuda*." Nina took one of Sarah's feet and hoisted it over the side of the tub. "Or maybe I just think it makes you look sexy." She did the same to the other, opening Sarah up in a way she never had been before. "Bare…innocent…ripe for corruption."

Sarah giggled. "I think I'd like that."

"Oh yes…you absolutely will."

Holding the razor with a steady hand, Nina moved it closer and closer to the white film that covered Sarah's groin. Sarah couldn't look away. She couldn't even shut her eyes. Nina sensed her discomfort and paused, kissing Sarah's thigh a few times, rubbing it with her free hand to relax her. Sarah felt her breathing slow. It was like Nina had some power over her, a remote control she could press to turn down the volume.

Her fingers now drew tiny spirals on Sarah's legs, keeping Sarah's breathing deep and even as she touched the razor to Sarah's skin. Just along the bikini line, not quite at Sarah's bush. Letting Sarah get used to the feel of the razor. Its sharpness. Nina's control.

When Nina started in earnest, Sarah couldn't even feel it. The razor gently glided between her legs, replacing tufts of lather with smooth skin. Then, slowly, she began to feel it.

Nina was doing the outer curves of her labia. And it felt amazing. Her skin tingled wherever the razor grazed it. Her nerves, stretched to the breaking point in a subconscious expectation of pain, felt only the exquisite care with which Nina handled the blade. The light, practiced touch with which she groomed Sarah.

"That feels good," Nina purred. It wasn't a question, but Sarah nodded anyway.

The next thing Sarah felt was the razor laid flat against her thigh, pulled away just long enough for Nina to bow her head to Sarah's sex. Mouth open. Tongue out.

The very tip of Nina's tongue hit Sarah's pussy, smooth and bare and sensitive. Sarah yelped and Nina laughed knowingly, holding Sarah still again with a hand flat against her stomach.

"Back to business," Nina said, and dropped her hand down to spread Sarah open. "So you would want that? The game?"

"Yes!" Sarah breathed, nearly choking as Nina made a long stroke over her labia.

"And you'd submit to me?" Nina asked, dipping the razor under the water to clean it off. Taking the opportunity to admire her work thus far. "I'm not a switch, Sarah. If we did this, I would be your top. End of story. Of course, I don't think you'd have too much of a problem with that. You're a natural bottom."

"I haven't—submitted to you—" Sarah was practically dripping on the razor.

"If you haven't yet, you soon will. So, how about it? Would you enjoy being driven to your limit, disciplined by me, obedient to me? Earning the trust that you'll obey my every little whim?"

"Fuck!" Sarah cried, snaring her hands in her hair and nearly pulling her scalp off. It was a good thing she was in a bathtub. When she did orgasm, the drain was going to come in handy.

"Then again…" Nina closed the razor and reached for the showerhead. She turned it on at a gentle spray and rinsed off the lather that had gotten onto her arms. The water splashed against her chest, plastering her transparent nightie to her body. Now Sarah could see all of her.

The sight took her breath away. It was like a vision. Nina's figure was heavenly, curving out almost excessively, but bowing back inward just before her proportions became truly unbelievable. The nightie clung to her like a hazy afterimage on a picture, outlining her wide hips and perfect breasts.

Nina had meant to do that, Sarah realized. Expose herself in that manner. From here on out, there was no going back. Sarah was going to come.

Nina trained the spray on Sarah's chest and watched the residue of the lather disappear from her body. Sarah shook and quivered, the stream of water over her sex its own tantalizing feel. When she closed her eyes, she could still feel Nina watching her bareness.

Sarah was gasping, nearly hyperventilating as Nina moved the stream lower and lower. "Please, please, please…"

Sarah was lost in the feel of the water as it splashed directly against her pussy, in the seductive timbre of Nina's voice as it slipped right into her ear.

"Will you obey me?" Nina knelt between Sarah's thighs, bringing the showerhead closer.

"Yes!"

"Will you learn from me?"

"Yes, yes!"

"Will you come for me?"

"*YES!*"

"Then there's only one thing left to do."

Nina turned off the showerhead. Sarah sobbed in disappointment.

"Make sure I haven't missed a spot." And with that, Nina ran the flat of her tongue all the way up Sarah's newly shaved pussy.

Sarah came as soon as Nina made contact.

She felt like she'd lost control of her body. Instantly, she was shaking and couldn't stop. She coiled her legs inside the tub and slipped down into Nina's arms, hearing gasping cries burst from her mouth. Mostly just gibberish, but she managed to say Nina's name a few times. She was trying to thank her.

"Sorry, sorry, I've never…" Sarah started to say when she could speak again, lying flat alongside Nina at the bottom of the tub. Nina just smiled at her.

"That's all right, Sarah. It allows me to test a theory. How many orgasms can our young vestal have?"

Without allowing Sarah another word, Nina swept her up in her arms and kissed her, thrashing her tongue inside Sarah's mouth, a long and twisting finger inside her cunt. Sarah was totally unprepared. Nina had been absolutely gentle and precise with the razor, but now she was like an animal. Thrusting in and out, her whole hand colliding with Sarah's pussy. The kiss was a constant demand on her lips, not letting Sarah so much as breathe as the finger reignited her sex.

Sarah screamed into Nina's mouth as she came again. Nina started kissing her neck. Added another finger.

"Nina! Nina!" Sarah knew she was begging, but she didn't know what for. Everything Nina had done had left her pussy swollen, sensitive, and in need. Now, like a livewire, it only took one touch and—electricity.

Sarah came again, shaking and screaming, and Nina kissed all along her open mouth. She added another finger. Three perfect fingers, fucking away at Sarah. All it took to bring her completely under control.

"If I keep fucking you, will you just keep coming and coming and coming?"

"For you…for you…" Sarah gasped, her mind shattering in rapture. Her limbs shot out in all directions; her head banged against the floor of the tub as Nina bit down on her lip, the painful hit forcing Sarah to try to hold herself still as three perfect fingers entered her and left her, over and over again, always seeming to know exactly where to go to set her off again.

Sarah screamed wordlessly, overwhelmed as Nina fucked her right through another orgasm. She tore her lip out of Nina's teeth, tasting fresh blood and then being forced to share it as Nina kissed her. She didn't add any more fingers to Sara's agonized ecstasy, but the ones already inside her went faster.

"No more," Sarah muttered as Nina licked at her bloody lip. "I can't—I just can't…"

"Sarah," Nina whispered in her ear, darkly amused. "You *are*."

Sarah looked down to see that Nina was holding her fingers still. Sarah's hips were madly rolling into them, fucking the stiff phallus that Nina provided with her hand. And Sarah couldn't seem to stop herself.

"You're so damn tight," Nina continued, "I'm not sure I could pull my fingers out if I wanted to. I think you may be something of a slut, little one."

Sarah's eyes rolled back in her head as she came again. It hurt a little this time. Good pain. She forced herself to stop nonetheless, half-convinced that if she didn't, she might just fuck Nina forever.

"That's enough," Sarah gasped, gulping in air. She painfully worked herself off Nina's fingers, leaving them dripping wet. "Enough."

"I think not. After all, we still have to moisturize."

Sarah's flesh turned to goose pimples, demanding more, all, everything.

First, Nina picked up the fluffiest towel Sarah had ever seen and patted her dry. The soft down tickled her sex, heightening her sex drive once more and easing her sore body back into overdrive. Sarah panted, not sure if she should thank Nina or beg her for mercy.

When Nina took the towel away, Sarah shook, still not certain what she wanted but aware she hadn't gotten it. Smiling brightly, Nina uncapped a bottle of moisturizing cream and filled her hand.

"I'll come!" Sarah gasped like a warning, as Nina's hand neared her pussy.

"I know you will. I want you to." Nina laid her hand flat against Sarah's groin, letting the cool lotion *touch* Sarah for a moment before beginning to gently, insistently rub. "One more. Just to show you who's boss."

Sarah could only moan as Nina rubbed the lotion into her pussy. She started off slow, almost teasingly, and Sarah thought she couldn't get off from that. Her body disagreed. It heated up, had her toes curling and her fingers turning to fists, and Nina noticed. She smiled and went faster, her hand making a steady circuit of Sarah's groin, circling her thighs and pussy and clit, touching them all in painstaking order. Sarah's hands twitched. Her feet kicked.

"Come for me, Sarah," Nina said with a few little kisses to her cheek. "I know you can. Just once more. You know you want to. Just let it happen."

"I can't—I can't—can't take it!"

"You can and you will." Now Nina was kissing Sarah's barely parted lips, her hand sliding up and down, from Sarah's lower belly all the way to her asshole. The friction it left in its wake heated up with each pass, burning a hole in Sarah's sex. She was going to catch fire.

"Mercy!"

"No."

"Mercy!"

"*Come.*"

It felt too good. Sarah was too close, her pussy was too sensitive, and Nina was too good. She felt herself being lost in Nina's insistent, perfect touch. The heat was rising to close her throat, turn her ears red, and she wasn't sure why she'd ever run away from this.

Nina wasn't bothering to kiss her anymore. Now she just hovered over Sarah, rolling Sarah's cunt in her hand as if it were a stress toy, the slick flesh sliding over, under, around her fingers. Sarah was being manhandled in her most intimate area, a place only one other person had even *seen*, and she loved it. Loved Nina.

"*Love ya!*" Sarah whimpered as Nina ground down on her clit and she came again. This time she actually squirted, a feeling of swelling and building and releasing and gushing and *finishing*.

Then she was done, really done, couldn't move a muscle, just dropped boneless to the floor of the tub. And Nina brought a dripping hand to her mouth and licked the back of it, like a cat about to clean herself.

"Did I say something?" Sarah asked when she could breathe again.

"'Love ya,'" Nina reported, as coy and pleased as she'd been when Sarah had found her body rutting without her like a malfunctioning machine. She took off her waterlogged nightie and tossed it in the sink, then put in the plug and turned the faucet on, filling the tub with warm, soothing water. "Don't worry about it. I found it quite refreshing. Everyone is so self-conscious during sex. It's all 'fuck me' this and 'oh shit' that. The last time I had a really great orgasm, all I could think was 'Jiminy Christmas.' That's the point of sex, after all. You can't think."

Steam filled the air. Sarah could feel her toes again. When the tub filled, Nina turned the water off and maneuvered them around as if it was old hat, positioning them so Sarah was in her lap and held securely in her arms. She kissed the back of Sarah's neck, one of the places that hadn't been touched yet. Sarah knew they had a lot of fun times coming up, finding all of those.

"You make me think a lot," Sarah said.

"Good thoughts, I hope," Nina replied with another kiss. She reached for the bar of soap in its dish. "How about we wash off that dirty little pussy?"

Sarah turned in Nina's arms, scooting over so she could kiss Nina. "I think it'll take more than that to clean me off."

Nina nodded thoughtfully, building up a lather on Sarah's shoulders. "Then I suppose I'll just have to keep fucking you until you're a good girl."

The soap was going lower and lower, making Sarah arch back, so far that she saw the window atop the room.

"What time is it?" she asked.

"Do I *look* like I have a clock on me?" Nina retorted.

"I told my mom I'd help her stock the shelves at her flower shop this afternoon. She got a big shipment in the other— It's not important."

Nina bit her lip. "It's important enough. If you said you'd do something, you should do it."

"*You* said you'd keep *fucking* me until I was a good girl." Sarah tried to make the words sound as delicious as Nina had, but it was impossible. Nina was speaking another language compared to her.

"Next time, Sarah," Nina promised, sealing it with one last kiss. "We can have a nice long soak then. I'll have time to find some bath toys you'll have a lot of fun playing with."

Sarah nearly went cross-eyed at the thought. She forced herself out of the tub and grabbed the towel Nina had used earlier, rubbing herself off. She wondered if she'd be left smelling of Nina. Then she remembered Nina had used it on *her*. More likely she'd end up smelling like pussy. Great.

"Next time, we can dry each other off too," Nina added, still relaxing in the water.

Another shiver of anticipation went through Sarah. She dropped the towel and went to retrieve her clothes. When Sarah came back to check for her bra, which had disappeared somewhere around her third orgasm, the sight of Nina totally bare, hidden only by the barely sudsy water, had her pulse racing again.

But Nina's eyes were distant.

"Sarah," she said, voice lower than before. "Before, when you begged for mercy—you didn't mean that, did you? You didn't really want me to stop?"

"Of course not," Sarah said as she put her clothes back on. "I was just playing along."

"I thought so, but I shouldn't have...been so aggressive. If you wanted me to stop or slow down, you just have to say so."

"Well, I didn't. So what's the problem?"

"And you're not just saying that?" Nina smiled oddly. "Telling me what I want to hear?"

"No. I was playing around, that's all. Do you not want me to tell you no unless I mean it?"

"I..." Nina swallowed. "It might be best if you choose a safe word. So we're clear on what we're doing."

"Okay, I will. Then when I don't use it, you can be sure I want you to keep spanking me as hard as you can."

"Oh?" Nina asked. Her eyes lit up a little. "Is that what you're into?"

"If you wanted to know that," Sarah said, buckling her belt, "you should've let me stay in the tub."

Chapter 9

Sarah needed to decompress. So she went through the motions: She helped Eileen in the flower shop, went home, ate dinner, went to bed, got back up when Eileen woke up, showered, dressed, breakfasted, went to work, and adjusted products on shelves. She just didn't feel like herself anymore. It was like she'd been changed and didn't yet recognize herself. As if she was still getting used to a reflection that had done all those things with Nina.

After work, she got on her bike and rode until her thighs burned, looping around town, seeing how long she could go with her fingers off the handlebars. The sun was hot, and when she needed H2O, she stopped at the first water fountain she saw. Wasn't surprised when she saw her father's statue there.

And there, sitting next to the statue, was Nina. Sarah said her name as she walked the bike over to her, holding on to it like a security blanket.

Nina returned the greeting, dog-earing her place in the notebook she'd been writing in and pulling her headphones down around her neck. "Sarah, hello. Nice wheels." She hesitantly patted the bench between herself and the statue. Sarah could tell she didn't want to impose—was probably worried Sarah was in the middle of some sort of gay panic.

Giving her a reassuring smile, Sarah sat down. "Look who's out and about. They're going to kick you out of Hermits United if you keep this up."

"Hermits United?" Nina asked. "Isn't that a bit of a paradox?"

"It's a *Doctor Who* reference. I assumed someone who never left the house would get it. So, the other night was fun, right?" she said, just to clear the air, and felt the tips of her ears burn. *Fun* suddenly seemed like a very dirty word.

But Nina was relieved, Sarah could tell. "Yes. Very fun."

Sarah nodded. It felt good to have things out in the open. It felt like she'd been longing for so long, wanting for so long, and now she could just admit it. Was this what people talked about, "wanting to shout it from the rooftops"? She didn't need that. She just needed Nina to know.

She looked over at the statue of her dad. Pen in one hand, notebook in the other, lip curled in thought as he prepared to jot down an idea that would never make the page. "He took those damned notebooks with him everywhere. He was bursting with ideas. Just full of them. It was as if he saw something worth writing down in… everything. I've lived here all my life, and the first thing I've seen that's in any way special is you."

Nina took the compliment with a curt nod, her eyes on the statue. "Do you want to talk about him?"

"Why? You probably know more about him than I do. And that's the way he wanted it."

Nina gave an abashed smile. "He talked about you all the time. He didn't want to neglect you, and he certainly didn't want to leave you. Any more than my mother wanted to leave me. One car ride and then…" She looked at the statue. "He's this. The late, great Robert Kay. And I'm not a promising student anymore; I'm his legacy."

"Better than being a disappointment," Sarah quipped.

Nina looked taken aback that Sarah was joking, as if this were her father's grave instead of just a hunk of stone. "No one could be disappointed in you."

"Well, I have some expert people on it."

Nina smiled, but she was a million miles away. "My father didn't care enough to be disappointed. After my mother died…when he had a heart attack, it felt like a formality. Nobody cried at the funeral. They'd cried too much for my mother."

Sarah felt a tension in her jaw. "We don't have to talk about this. It was a long time ago. I'm over it."

"There's only so over it you ever get. These things are like bruises that never heal. You don't feel them for a long time, but then they brush against something and it's back. Like it never left."

"Guess I just don't let it brush against anything." Sarah stood, twinged, suddenly uncomfortable having the statue so close, listening in. "It's a good statue, at least."

"Sarah…"

"Nice little thing for the town to have. It was nice of you to donate it."

Nina reached out and took Sarah's hand before she could bolt. God, Nina was right. But no, it wasn't a bruise; it was an open wound. You took the bandage off for one second and there was blood everywhere.

Sarah squeezed Nina's hand. "You know, I've never seen anything the way he saw the world. But with you… If I had a notebook right now… You make me wish I had a notebook, okay?"

Nina picked up the one in her lap and held it out to Sarah, who took it without thinking.

"Oh, we're being literal now." She paged through to be polite. "What's with all the math?" Looking over the pages and pages of formulae, she couldn't even find X, which was the height of her career in algebra.

"It's…a little hard to explain. Pattern recognition, mostly. Trying to discern a rhythm in what seems like random sound. Loud, random sound."

Sarah eyed the headphones around Nina's throat. "So it's like listening to dubstep?"

"Even harder," Nina told her.

>~~~<

Eileen suggesting a trip to the local theater's Twenty-Four Horrors was just what Sarah needed. It was their annual tradition: The theater showed horror flicks from midnight to midnight, ending in a premiere of the latest scary movie, and for just twenty bucks you could watch as many as you wanted. They'd been going together since Eileen had had to buy Sarah's tickets for her.

The cinema was about the only cool thing about Bathory. It was an old-fashioned movie house with a triangular marquee above the door, one guy with a hat in a booth selling tickets, and popcorn that was popped in a cart and sold in cartons instead of by the tub. Totally vintage. It didn't show movies in 3-D, but nobody liked 3-D anyway.

Tickets in hand, Sarah and Eileen got popcorn, Coke, and Milk Duds so expensive Sarah wouldn't be surprised to find cocaine inside the box. Then it was just waiting in line to get their tickets torn. The guy behind the podium was trying to decide if three acne cases were old enough to see the latest *Final Destination*, so it took a while to get in.

"You have to hold my hand," Eileen warned her as they went past the velvet rope and started the search for seats. "Don't be too cool to hold your mother's hand."

"I'm just slightly not that cool," Sarah promised. "Although I don't know why you see these new Frankenstein movies when they scare you so bad."

"Because the first one just left me with so many questions!"

"Like 'why'd we watch this?'" Sarah teased.

The theater was dark and mostly deserted. A lot of people always showed up for the midnight start, but by noon, most of them headed home, though some had fallen asleep in their seats. Eileen and Sarah showed up in the afternoon, before the rush of the evening shows, when the theater started showing the good stuff—*The Exorcist, Rosemary's Baby*. From noon to six, it was just whatever B-movies the management could find.

They got seated just in time for millionaires to tell them how much the Will Rogers Institute needed working-class charity. Eileen checked her Facebook one last time and turned her phone off. Then some old-timey horror movie trailers—like *Phantom of the Opera* back when people didn't want to bone the Phantom—played to get people in the mood.

She heard a familiar voice—Tyrese was going down the aisle, headed for a seat closer to the screen. The kind Sarah would've sat in if she weren't with her mother, who refused to crane her neck one iota. And with him, Beck. She looked stunning in daisy dukes and a silk print shirt with a grand total of two buttons done up, right where the male population of Bathory would most like them undone. Only a pink hoodie and Tyrese to keep her warm.

In Sarah's tattered leather-studded skirt and similarly holey tee under her well-loved leather jacket, she looked as if she could've been Beck's bodyguard. She whipped out her phone, summoning up Beck's number and sending a frantic text: *WTF are you doing?*

She watched Beck squirm out from under Tyrese's arm—they were sitting together now—to check her phone before the lights went down. *Getting ready to watch a movie, what's your damage?*

With Ty?

Swearing audibly, Beck looked around. Found Sarah behind her, with her mother, and faced front. Hunched over her phone again. *Okay, not exactly how I wanted you to find out...*

Find out what, exactly?

We've decided to give it a try.

So you were going behind my back.

No. U said you were done with us. Yet ur STILL freaking out.

U d freak out too if ur bf cheated on you w ur best friend!

Thot I wasn't ur best friend anymore

Still fucking tacky

The guy took a hint, S. You were spending all your time at Nina Rose's.

Eileen nudged Sarah in the ribs, adding an additional note of panic to the drama that was currently unfolding. Had Eileen been looking at what she'd been texting? Sarah looked over at her. Eileen cleared her throat and nodded to the movie screen. The last annoying "turn off your cell phone pretty pretty please" message was playing. The show was about to start.

Sarah shut off her cell phone. She thought she'd read just about enough anyway.

They were halfway through the 4:00 showing—a horrible Frankenstein reboot that had gained a franchise by dint of being based on a YA novel—when Nina Rose sat down beside them. She was impeccably dressed in a black pantsuit with a tailored white jacket, but when her eyes roamed Sarah's clothing, her smile showed she found it acceptable as well.

"I thought the backs of your heads looked familiar," Nina said, setting a big tub of popcorn on her lap. "But I never saw the two of you as horror fans."

"Oh, I'm not," Eileen protested. "Sarah just can't get enough of watching bimbos in tight shirts get taken out by monsters, apparently."

Sarah clenched her teeth, unable to believe her mother had thrown her under the bus like that.

Nina glanced at the screen. "Well, I'm sure everyone has some eclectic tastes. I know I do."

"We were just watching a movie," Sarah finally stammered. Part of her didn't believe Nina was real. What was her fantasy doing here, watching a movie with her and her *mom*?

"Well, I didn't think you were necking." Nina smiled. "How about a deal? I'll share my popcorn if you promise to go get the refill?"

"Sounds fine to me," Eileen said, already taking a scoop in her hand.

Nina's smile turned on Sarah. "I love making deals with your family."

For ten minutes, Nina just sat there like a good little moviegoer, taking dainty bites of her popcorn. Not even chewing loudly. Sarah was sandwiched in between her mother and Nina, the popcorn now in her lap so everyone could have some. Every time Nina reached for it, Sarah thought the hand would grab her breast, her thigh, her hair to pull her into a kiss, but it never did. Nina was a perfect, infuriating gentlewoman.

Another five minutes and Sarah started to become hyperaware of her own body. It felt different, hotter. As if it was responding to Nina's very presence. Even the slightest sidelong look from Nina was a caress. When Nina gently, stealthily eased her stocking-clad foot out of its sandal, Sarah wondered for the first time what toes would feel like inside her. Then Nina slid her foot sideways and brushed it against Sarah's ankle, right above her shoe.

Sarah moaned. Out loud.

"Sarah?" Eileen asked, turning. "Are you all right?"

"Yeah." Sarah nodded at the screen. "This is just…really scary."

They went back to their silence. After a bare second, Nina's foot ran across Sarah's. It moved from the tip of Sarah's shoe to the loop on the back, never touching so much as her sock. Sarah bit her lip and crushed the popcorn in her hand to dust. Nina moved her foot up, up the back of Sarah's leg. As flexible as Sarah knew Nina to be, she wasn't a contortionist. That was as far as she could go, sitting where she was. But Christ, it was enough.

She got so used to the caress of Nina's foot over the next few minutes that it came as an explosive shock when she felt Nina's hand on her sex.

It wasn't, of course. Nina had just reached down into the popcorn tub, which was now empty, and hit the bottom. But even that contact seemed calculated to make Sarah scream. Which she did. Loudly.

Fortunately, at that point, a seemingly inert Frankenstein had just opened its eyes to the accompaniment of a musical stinger. Everyone chalked it up to just another jumpy teenage girl.

"It's alive, it's alive!" the latest mad doctor cheered.

Just then, the main, heroic, *handsome* Frankenstein blasted it with a bazooka. "Not anymore!"

Eileen turned, sensing something was amiss. But before she could even start, Nina was holding out the popcorn tub to her.

"How about that refill now?" Nina asked. "I always like to have some popcorn during the climax."

"Sure," Eileen said, restraining herself to a don't-embarrass-me look at Sarah.

She took the tub and left the row. Now Sarah and Nina were alone, no one around them for three rows. And Nina barely waited until Eileen was headed up the aisle to say, "Take off your panties."

Sarah winced. Nina had said it low, and that just made it sexier, but if Eileen had heard just one word of that sentence…

Nina dug her nails into Sarah's knee. "*Take them off.*"

Sarah breathed hard for a few moments, wondering how Nina would punish her if she disobeyed. Wondering how long would it be until they fucked again.

"There are people here, people I know…*right there…*"

"Are you saying we shouldn't air our dirty laundry in public?"

Fuck it.

Working fast, and with Eileen not even out of the auditorium yet, Sarah lifted her hips and wiggled her panties down her legs, handing them to Nina, who just tucked them into her purse like a snack for later.

"Now spread your legs," Nina said.

Now Sarah looked at her, looked at her like Nina had just grown a second head. "Are you crazy?" she hissed quietly.

"Spread your legs," Nina said again, looking back at her. Her eyes were dark with lust. "Nice and wide."

"My mother is going to be back any—"

"Judging by the half-empty Big Gulp on the arm of her chair, she'll need to use the restroom. We have quite a few minutes, so the sooner we start, the more chance we'll be done before she gets back. Spread your *fucking* legs." Nina jeeringly emphasized that word, as if she'd bend Sarah over the row in front of them and simply *take* her if Sarah gave her any problems.

Sarah would be a liar if she said that didn't turn her on.

She spread her legs.

"You're such a good girl," Nina said, her voice soothing and warm. She moved her hand on Sarah's knee good-naturedly. And then ran it up her thigh. "Eileen did a good job with you…"

"Could we not talk about her right now?" Sarah muttered.

"What should we talk about? The audience?" Nina's fingers, bastards, began to run back and forth on Sarah's inner thigh. They couldn't just keep going; they had to reverse. "Those people you know? All they'd have to do is turn around to see you with your legs open and my finger shoved up inside you—"

And that was when Nina *did* shove her finger in there. Sarah gasped. It felt good. Too good. She had to force herself not to moan.

"And is that Sheriff Carter?" Nina asked, her finger working steadily inside Sarah. Making her shift in her seat, not sure what she wanted, but knowing she wasn't getting it. "If he saw what I was doing to you, he might slap the handcuffs on both of us. But then, would you enjoy that?"

"Nina…" Sarah moaned at last, softly enough for only Nina to hear. That was what she thought satisfied Nina—having this all to herself, hers and only hers. That's what made her add another finger.

Sarah closed her eyes and prepared to come.

Then Nina took her hand away.

"Goddamnit, Nina!" Sarah started to swear, when she saw the usher walking down the aisle, flashlight in hand. She shut up, closing her eyes, and Nina sat with her hands in her lap.

The usher made his way to the front row, conversed briefly with someone, then left.

Nina looked at Sarah.

Sarah spread her legs, and Nina settled in, resting her head on Sarah's shoulder as she delved into her, two fingers, no waiting.

"Perhaps we should discuss the movie," she said, her breath hitting Sarah's ear.

On the screen, the heroine had gotten her shirt stuck on a Frankenstein's neck bolt and had to strip down to her bra to get free. She was, of course, generously endowed.

"Look at that hot little bitch," Nina hissed in Sarah's ear, her fingers speeding up. "Look at her tits. Look at her ass."

"I'd rather look at you," Sarah moaned, then worried she'd been too loud.

Now the hero had run into the heroine. Since they were probably going to die, of course it seemed like a good time for a sex scene. They kissed. They caressed each other. They gyrated.

"Ooh, is that what you'd like?" Nina asked. "Maybe a big, hard cock filling you up? I have some at home."

"*God!*"

"But do you know what's even bigger?" Nina added another finger, no muss, no fuss, as if she didn't even realize she'd done it.

Sarah started grinding down on her seat, working her hips back and forth as if she was trying to get more *Nina*.

"A fist. Have you ever been fisted, Sarah?" She waited, then said, "Sarah, I asked you a question."

"No!" Sarah said at last, afraid any word she let out of her mouth might be a scream.

"You feel so full. So…loved. I'm going to do that to you, Sarah. And you're going to do it to me. We'll be one big happy family."

"Fucking *please!*" Sarah yelped, just barely cutting herself off before her voice rose.

"Oh, do you want to come? Do you want this over with? Are you not enjoying this?"

Sarah closed her eyes and forced herself to stop rocking back and forth. She knew she wouldn't come unless Nina let her, and she knew that if she moved any more, she'd attract attention. She grabbed the armrests and held on tight, forcing herself to be still as Nina plundered her.

"So what's the matter, Sarah?" Nina asked, filling her voice with concern. "Do you not like being fucked in the middle of a theater where anyone could see you?" Her fingers slowed.

"I love it!" Sarah gasped quickly, opening her eyes to see Nina's smile. The smile she thought only she got—dark and in control.

"That's right," Nina said as she jammed her fingers deep inside. Far enough to make Sarah's breath hitch. "You do."

She drew her fingers out slowly, and then they started again, back and forth, in and out, circling and rubbing, fucking and fucking.

"I really enjoyed our bath the other day," Nina said, her words slick in Sarah's ear. "I especially loved calling you by a few little pet names."

"Me too—" Sarah began, but a wet twist of Nina's fingers had her biting her words before they became moans.

"I want you to call me by a nickname. Mistress. Say 'Mistress' and I'll let you come."

For no reason Sarah could think of, she decided to dig her heels in. She just… relished being disobedient. Making Nina work to bring her to heel. "No…*Nina*."

"That's not what you call me," Nina insisted, her voice hardening with both lust and authority. "When you want to come, you call me Mistress. *Say it*."

"Why? You're going to make me come either way. You can't resist me."

"No, I think you can't resist *this*." Nina drew her fingers out of Sarah just long enough to give her cunt a brisk slap. Sensation filled Sarah, throwing her body around with the scream she had to keep inside. And then Nina was inside her again, thrusting away, pushing her orgasm to the front of her mind. It was filling her up, crushing everything else inside her, and she had to let it out or she'd explode. "Say Mistress," Nina taunted. "Say Mistress."

"*Dontwanna*," Sarah insisted, squeezing her thighs shut on Nina's hand. That only seemed to make her more aroused.

"You can say it now or you can say it in bed, when I bend you over the mattress and fuck you so hard you'll think this was just a bit of light petting, but you are *not* going to come until you say it." Nina straightened up, glancing at the screen, brushing a lock of hair out of her eyes, all while ceaselessly working her hand into Sarah's cunt. "Oh, look. Eileen's back."

Sarah looked over her shoulder. Eileen stood at the back of the auditorium, looking for her and Nina. She had a full tub of popcorn in her hands.

"Stop it, you gotta—"

Nina added her thumb to Sarah's clit. Now Sarah couldn't have asked her to stop if a bomb were about to go off.

"Did you have something to say to me?" Nina asked, looking down casually as if she was checking her watch. "Something that starts with M?"

Eileen saw them. She started down the aisle.

"Mistress," Sarah whimpered under her breath.

"What was that, Sarah dear?" Nina leaned in close. "I couldn't quite hear."

Eileen was almost to them. She paused as she stepped in something sticky.

"Mistress!" Sarah enunciated with all her might, straining to keep the word clear of feeling as she orgasmed, like what she'd said was a magic word. She *clenched* in her seat and felt Nina's hand leave her, and she snapped her legs together like a bear-trap and closed her eyes, the darkness full of colors.

"What was that, sweetie?" Eileen asked, sitting down beside her. She passed the popcorn into Sarah's lap, covering up the wet stain on the front of her skirt. "Everything alright?"

Sarah nodded. "Yeah, I was just getting a little worried. You were taking a long time."

"There was a line at the concession stand. Seems like everyone wanted nachos at the same time." Eileen shook her head. "You look a little pale; are you sure you're not coming down with something?"

Nina reached into the popcorn tub—Sarah could see her fingers were gleaming wet—and had herself a bite. "Mmm! This is delicious, Mrs. Kay! What'd you put on it?"

Eileen shrugged. "Just a little butter."

"Well, you must've gotten just the right amount. It tastes divine." Nina dug into the popcorn again and held out a handful for Sarah. "Here, Sarah, try it!"

Sarah obediently opened her mouth and ate out of Nina's hand. As her mother watched, Sarah found out exactly what she tasted like.

Chapter 10

Being with Nina made Sarah feel as if she wasn't Sarah. That didn't make sense to her until she came across a quote by Gore Vidal.

"Most children tell themselves stories in which they figure as powerful figures, enjoying the pleasures not only of the adult world as they conceive it but of a world of wonders unlike dull reality. Although this sort of Mittyesque daydreaming is supposed to cease in maturity, I suggest that more adults than we suspect are bemusedly wandering about with a full Technicolor extravaganza going on in their heads."

And it felt like her dream-self, beautiful and sexual, *that* was with Nina, while the rest of her lived out her regular life, awkward and plain. As the weeks went by, seeing Nina became a series of prison breaks. Even though she was an adult and didn't have to report her every move to Eileen, pulling one over on her eagle-eyed mother was almost as much fun as being with Nina.

Saturday came like the guards' shift change. Eileen was catching up on her backlog of *Scandal* episodes, and, like potato chips, she couldn't stop with just one. Sarah said she was going to the library, knowing Eileen would soon forget she existed.

Sarah slipped out the window, even though the TV room was nowhere near the stairs, and clambered off the second floor roof to her waiting car. She eased it out of the driveway in neutral before starting the ignition. Maybe Gore was right. Her body really was at the library, studying its little heart out, and this was all a fantasy.

She decided then and there not to wake up.

Nina's manor was as dark and moody as ever, but now Sarah found it comforting; she knew its secret and it knew hers. She took great pleasure in entering Nina's lair with her very own key.

As Sarah crept through the house, she thought of disrobing to surprise Nina, but no, she'd seen enough rom-coms to know how that could go wrong. If Nina was with someone, Sarah would lie and say she was here for work. Anyone would believe that when she had clothes on.

Besides, she was already dressed sexy. Jeans as tight as the skin of a grape. A hoodie with only a spaghetti-strap tank underneath. Keds for that touch of casualness. She might not have passed muster for a rap video, but she could definitely dance with Taylor Swift.

She found Nina in her office, her Aeron chair turned away from her desk and pointed at the window. The computer was powered down. The headphones were disconnected. Nina was all hers.

Sarah slipped out of her sneakers and tip-toed across the floor. She skipped the hardwood floorboards for the white rugs that Nina had arrayed in pleasing symmetry, bare feet sinking into the rich fur. When she reached the desk, like a cat nearing its prey, she pressed herself low to the mahogany. Bringing her knees up onto the desk, she was able to reach around the chair and cover Nina's eyes. "Guess who?"

Nina's face was wet. She turned around, and Sarah saw it was red and puffy as well. Tears had soaked through the wad of tissues she held in her hand. Barnaby was lying at her feet in canine sympathy, trying to soak up the anguish that was spilling out of her.

"I didn't hear you come in," Nina said, in a voice that limped like a wounded animal.

"You're crying!" Sarah instantly pulled another ten tissues from the box on the desk and came around to kneel by Nina's side. She patted Nina's face with them about a dozen times a second. "What's wrong? Something's wrong. Nina…"

"Nothing," Nina said, taking Sarah's hand like a child reaching for a teddy bear. "It's just that sometimes, when everything's all right, it makes you remember when everything wasn't."

Sarah tightened her grip on Nina's hand, welcoming the pressure. "Why are you sad?" she asked, her voice as soft as it had ever been.

Nina demurred, deploying a fresh wave of moist towelettes to wipe down her face. She pushed aside all Sarah's attempts to assist her, not stopping until she was as bare as a marble statue, and in her own way, just as imposing.

Sarah understood. It had been a very personal question.

"I'm sorry," Nina said at last, her voice distilled to completely neutral. "Here you are, on your great love affair, with all your dreams of me, and look how I live up to them. Some temptress. Run off, Sarah. Come back another day; I'll make you swoon and moan and sigh, just as you should."

Sarah grabbed her hand again, rougher this time. Hard enough to hurt. "Look, I'm not gonna pretend it isn't a turn-on that you have a dog collar with my name on it. But that's not the cake, you know. It's just the frosting. And you can't eat a whole thing of frosting. Tried when I was twelve, sick for a week. I like you for you. So if you're feeling like crap, I wanna feel like crap too, even if it's not sexy. And now, I'm going to read your mind with my advanced intellect." Sarah put the first two fingers of either hand on the sides of Nina's head. "You are…feeling shitty because you have a million things to do today and you're behind on all of them."

"I feel shitty because of what happened in the theater."

"What do you mean 'what happened in the theater'? That was your idea—"

"I know it was! And you weren't comfortable with it and I sprung it on you and pushed you."

"It was spontaneous. I liked it. What's the problem?"

"I couldn't stop myself. 'I love you so much, I can't bear to see you constrained.' That's what she used to tell me."

"Who?"

Nina's hands cinched together, orbiting each other like a pair of comets caught in each other's gravity. "I was a couple years older than you are now. Going to a pretty respectable college. There was an adult-art exhibit there. At the time, it was quite enough to scandalize everyone. Curious, I went, almost not believing they would let me in. I was a little disappointed at first. They were just paintings. I couldn't even see why anyone would have a problem. But some—they made you feel things, think things. About pain, about pleasure. One of them just…*held on to me*. It was beautiful. I actually bought it eventually. I keep it in the attic, and sometimes I look at it. When I'm alone."

Her hooded eyes closed.

"It's of this woman. She's not naked, but her clothes are so tight that they're almost a straitjacket. Her hands are behind her back—maybe they're bound, or maybe she was just holding them that way. There's a rope around her neck too. Not a leash or a noose. Silk. To keep her from breathing when she's not supposed to. And there's a blindfold over her eyes. All you can really see is her mouth. It's open and…not quite smiling, but not quite screaming either.

"She looks so beautiful, Sarah. I can't explain it. Maybe the description said she was in pain, maybe the artist intended for her to be in pain, but I could just tell that it was good. She wanted it."

Sarah could picture it, like a quick glimpse of something TV-MA while you were flipping through channels. You hoped no one saw it, you pretended not to see anything, but really, you wanted to *know*. "How long did you look at it?"

"Long enough for the artist to notice. She, uh, brought me a drink. My mouth had gotten dry and I hadn't noticed, but somehow she had. I was in awe of her, how beautiful she was, how confident. She asked me how it made me feel. I said some bullshit about female oppression and power dynamics—she had to tease it out of me. The fact that it made me aroused."

Sarah swallowed. "Did she touch you then?"

"No. Not for a long time. But she told me she had this…collection. And that I could see it, if I wanted. I…" Nina's jaw twitched. The memory seemed powerful. She opened her eyes to look at Sarah, trying to share it, split it between them. "I knew it was wrong. No, not *wrong*… That's what others might call it, but it wasn't wrong. But I knew that a lot of people wouldn't approve. I guess that's why I agreed. And…she did touch me. Just her hand. She just took my hand in hers and squeezed and…" Nina shook her head, breaking eye contact. "It sounds like so little. But she could be overwhelming. I think I'm that way with you. I'm not trying to be. It's just how we mix. Our chemical reaction. When she ran her thumb over the back of my hand, it felt like I'd been alone, without ever realizing it, and now I was finally part of something."

Sarah's phone trilled. She reached into her pocket fast to silence it. Nina didn't even appear to notice.

"The next day I went to her house. I'd wanted to go there all night. I'd lain awake in bed, but I couldn't move. I'd thought about it, but I would picture the stairs creaking, my roommate waking up, and it just— In the morning, it was like no big deal. I told myself I just couldn't sleep. Insomnia or something. But I went to her house."

Nina bit her lip. For a few moments she just breathed, her eyes dashing away from Sarah's. Looking around, like someone might've snuck in just to eavesdrop on them. Sarah looked down at Nina's hands, flat on her thighs. The knuckles were white.

"You couldn't think of anything else?" Sarah asked, almost sullenly.

Nina faced her again. She had a thousand-yard stare, an addict's stare, excited and obscene and rueful, all at once. Regrets, but not over what had happened. Regret that it hadn't happened sooner. Rueful that it hadn't happened more.

"Any*one* else," Nina said. "Her paintings were beautiful, but they weren't really *erotic* unless you knew what to look for. And they spoke to me. I could see what was beneath them. She showed me her private collection." Nina ran her hand over her face. A light glaze of sweat was building. She wiped it away with her sleeve. "She was so gentle. Not that she touched me, not then. But the way she talked to me. And looked at me. I was so used to being judged. The way I dress and the way I talk and act. No one ever really listened to me besides your father. I had to shout just for them to notice, but not with her. She listened."

Sarah breathed at the same time as Nina. "She understood you."

"*She was me*," Nina insisted. "She was a part of me, or I was a part of her." Nina almost stood, bouncing her heels on the floor. Nervous.

"Finish the story," Sarah said.

Nina rested her weight back down. "Have you seen the painting I told you about?"

"No. You know I haven't."

"That kind of art is the sort of thing you can…almost smell on someone. It wasn't *uncouth*; it was hers. Mine. Just beautiful people. Enjoying themselves. I understood that, you'd understand it, but so many people would just see the obscene things. The pain, the bruises, the exposure. But that was just a part of the pictures."

"Just part of life."

"Yes. *Yes*." Nina banged her hand on her thigh. "She took me back upstairs and she showed me some of her photographs in her office. Thirty-five-millimeter stuff. She was a budding photographer too. That's how she put it. Not amateur. Budding. And it wasn't tits and ass; it was sunsets and nature. She made the world look like a fairy tale."

Sarah looked at Nina's hand on her thigh. Tight. Feeling her own skin through the thin fabric. There was something tempting about it. Something curious. Had it touched the artist? Had it entered her? Had she kissed it, sucked on it, run it across the woman's face?

"When was your first kiss?"

"Later. Always later. She made me wait for it—want it. That first day, the sun was setting. She asked me if I'd like to take some pictures in the good light. She let me use her camera. She had on this dress. Alexander McQueen, I think. Red, with this pattern on it. Your eyes follow it, but it never seems to end. She posed for me. Did little dances, made faces. There wasn't anything naughty about it, but we could both feel something. The way I looked at her through the lens—you could see it when the photos developed. How I was in love with her."

Nina's hand moved quickly, wiping a tear from under her eye like it'd been stinging her there. And for a moment, Sarah couldn't imagine how it could hurt to be in love. Then she thought of how she'd been feeling lately. The agony of its sweetness.

"I came back later, to see the photos. She'd had one framed, and she gave it to me. She looks like a goddess in it." Her hand seemed to inch toward Sarah, although maybe that was just a trick of the light. "She asked if she could photograph me this time. I agreed. Some of the pictures were—a little embarrassing. I was flirting with her. I tugged on my shirt, flipped my hair, you know. She didn't say anything about it, but I could tell she liked it. So I went back to her house again, and this time, she said she had a photo shoot in mind. We'd go to this spot she'd found and use her new camera. And she wanted to get me some special clothes. She took me to a boutique, and we tried things on. Things I still have."

"With your painting," Sarah said. "And your picture of her."

"There's one—the dress I wore that day. I feel like if I go for too long without feeling it on my skin, then…it'll just disappear."

"Where'd you go? On your photo shoot?"

"There was this lagoon. She actually got me to go in with my new dress on." Nina smiled at the memory—not a tease, not a grin. An effervescent joy. Sarah tried to remember seeing that before. It seemed almost too private. "I had to lift it up and wade in up to my knees, but the pictures she took… It was how she saw me, and I could touch it, I could hold it in my hand."

"She kept taking pictures of you."

"Yes." Nina moved with blinding speed, moving her hand from her thigh to Sarah's wrist. It felt right, the pressure she was putting on it. It felt real. "You don't know the way people looked at me. Different. Strange. When she photographed me, I looked beautiful."

"You are beautiful."

"Not like this. This was…" Nina's eyes were misty as she reached down into a desk drawer, brought out an envelope, and pressed it into Sarah's hand.

Sarah opened the envelope. It wasn't sealed, and she could imagine Nina paging through it again and again. She took the pictures out, a thick stack of them. The first few were just of Nina in an old-fashioned waitress outfit, demure despite the way it fit her buxom body. Maybe it was the way she was shy, a little awkward, unused to being photographed. Sarah moved the photos from the front of the stack to the back as she went, the little sound filling up the space. Louder than either of them breathing.

Nina got used to the camera quick. She struck poses, girlish things, doing a little rock-star hand gesture, grabbing herself, playing her leg like a guitar. Sarah could imagine someone behind the camera, smiling beatifically at the antics, laughingly urging her along.

Then some photos in black-and-white. More professional than the casual shots from earlier, some monkeying around with the format. Nina wore a man's suit now, tailored to fit her femininity. She was more serious, though it alternated with shots of her cracking up, gesturing at the woman behind the camera. *C'mon? Lighten up? Play with me? Let me have the camera?* Who knew? In one photo, she jokingly choked herself with her own necktie. In the next, the tie led off the photo's borders, held by the photographer. She was so *young*.

Sarah looked up. Nina was staring at her. *Dining* on every little face she made, every furrow in her brow, every squint and every wide eye. As if she was waiting for something.

Sarah flipped to the next photo, still looking at Nina as if asking a question, then her eyes dropped back down. It was the lagoon. The dress was amazing, shades of red and black, sleek and flattering, with leather forming a kind of jacket to top off its tight curves. The kind of thing Nina would still wear now.

In the first picture, even Nina herself seemed to be marveling at how well it suited her. Her face was set in an impressed grin. But in the next few, a change had come over her. Some coaching from her lover—something she'd said or done. Now Nina looked godlike. Unapproachable. Impervious. Ethereal. Wading into the water, she was a mermaid visiting home.

There was one picture done on a timer, or taken by someone else, from a fair distance away. Nina and a woman, sitting in the hatchback of a Kia. She was drying off Nina's bare feet with a towel, playing with her toes, a set of knee-highs next to them. Nina was laughing. The woman was grinning. They looked like two people talking without words.

She was beautiful. They both were.

After that, the photographs moved inside. A house. At first, the natural light of the windows. Nina in jeans and a tank-top, her bra visible, her trousers riding low. It wasn't very revealing but felt more explicit than before. Intimate. Sarah instinctively looked up to see if anyone had seen her looking at this and caught Nina still watching her. Tongue traveling her lips.

That just forced her attention back to the photographs. Now they were away from the windows, or at night, or in rooms with no windows. The look was different, some calculated lighting done by the artist. It threw sharp shadows across Nina's body, camouflaging her. She wore the shadows, and lingerie. Camisoles. Babydolls.

Corsets. Kimonos. A dozen other things Sarah didn't know the name of. There was an insane variety of bras and panties, and they all suited Nina to a tee. She had a "body made for sin," as Eileen would say.

Then Nina was wearing nothing at all. The camera was close to her. Consuming her. It caught her face. Her hands. Her legs. Her breasts, covered by her arm. Her sex, hidden by her fingers. Her ass, gloriously unhidden.

Her lips, parted.

"She did it herself first," Nina said. Sarah would've thought that would shock her, but it seemed perfectly all right. Like the photos were speaking to her out loud. "I was uncomfortable, so she took her clothes off. I still remember... She was wearing a red bra and red panties. They were so damn sexy. I thought about her wearing those all the time, under all those stylish suits. That's what made me do it. Realizing that I was naked all the time too. With her, I mean."

Sarah went to the next photo, the last photo. It was a self-portrait. The artist in a bodice, a choker, gloves, boots. All black, all leather. Her back to the camera. She held a riding crop. The kind you'd use to control an animal.

"That's when you kissed her," Sarah said softly. She would've.

"No." Gently, Nina pulled the pictures out of Sarah's slack hands. She put them back in the envelope. "It wasn't until graduation that I really..." Nina's hands tightened on the envelope, a note of possessiveness. The paper crinkled as she tucked it away. "She photographed me when I was on stage. It seemed so innocent; everyone was taking pictures. But when I had her eyes on me, I couldn't breathe. I could barely speak, barely accept my diploma. Sweat ran down my body. I felt it over my breasts. Between my legs. Everyone else went out partying, but I saw her car at the curve. She looked at me. She just—" Nina held up her hand. It was shaking, but she still managed to crook her finger. "So I went with her."

"Did you know what was going to happen?" Sarah asked, not sure how she knew. But she did.

"Part of me." Nina half smiled. "I felt...wonderfully *alone* with her. Alone together. All my friends had booze and dancing, but I had her. I was special. We went back to her place. She popped a bottle of champagne, showed me how to drink it. How first you smell, then you toast, then you drink. Slowly. Not like cheap beer. Then she took me to a room with this amazing mirror—it looked like something Marie Antoinette would own. I looked at that, and I think I saw myself as she saw me. I'd never really looked at myself that way before. As a woman."

"What'd she say to you?" Sarah had to know. Had to.

Nina closed her eyes, remembering. She wouldn't share it. It was too private. Hers and hers alone.

"I watched in the mirror," she finally said. "Like it was happening to someone else. I had to keep telling myself it was happening to me. That it was really happening, and that it was happening to me. She took my clothes off. I had all this time to stop her, but I just kept wanting it more and more. As she took my shirt off. My skirt. My bra. Then she kissed me."

"What was it like?"

"I can't describe something like that. It was…perfect. I took my panties off for her. Then she held me from behind, with an arm around my throat as if she couldn't bear to let me go. But her other hand… Sarah, her other hand… I saw it in the mirror."

"Was she gentle?" Sarah asked. People were always gentle in the books.

Nina smiled, her teeth showing. "No. She was rough with me. She knew I wouldn't break. I had bruises the next day. Sore spots to make me remember. I had to stop dressing like such a slut so no one would realize. But I wasn't a slut anymore, or a party girl, or whatever you want to call it. I was hers. And nothing we ever did could be bad or dirty. Afterward, I felt like I'd lost my virginity all over again. But it wasn't a disappointment this time; it was how it was supposed to feel. This time my world really had changed. Like I want it to change for you. We all deal with our issues in our own way. My parents died, I shut down, and then I found Emmaline. For a while, it felt as if she was building me back up. And I still think of how good it was, in the beginning, but…I'm sorry. I'm so sorry. You never have to do anything you don't want to do. Ever."

Sarah caressed Nina's face as if she could sift through the flickers of emotion Nina was displaying and get to what she really felt. "Can you tell me what's going on, please? Every time you let me in, it's like you push me away again."

"I can't talk about it. I just can't. But it's not you."

Barnaby rose up to rest his head on her thigh, and Nina enthusiastically rubbed behind his ears. Sarah joined in, running her hand down the dog's broad back.

"Maybe we should take a break from the kinky stuff for a while, if it's bothering you so much. Just some nice, normal kissing and cuddling and heavy petting…"

Nina frowned at her. "I could do with a little more than that."

"Okay, we'll go to third base—well, I guess that's lesbian fourth base. We'll, you know, we'll take things slow. Like you wanted to."

"I don't know what I want." Nina sighed, slipping back into her darkness. "I see you and I want you and you enjoy it…"

"But?" Sarah prodded.

"I want to know you're okay. And I can never know that. Not really." Nina reached up to tap Sarah's forehead. "Not in here."

"You could always trust me," Sarah suggested.

"You're not the one I don't trust."

She kissed Sarah's cheek, and of all the ways Nina had touched her, that was the one that made her blush. Nina smiled and played at Sarah's hair. "Would you mind if I tried something with this? I just want to see how beautiful I can make you."

Sarah smirked and threw her arms wide. "I'm your canvas!"

"You're my everything."

Sarah made a show of hugging herself and vibrating. "Flirting! Nice. Normal."

As Nina drew her toward the master bedroom, Sarah noticed something without quite noticing it. It just pegged her as wrong, and it would take time, and distance from Nina, to realize just what it was that had disturbed her.

The thing she'd seen was the door to the basement.

It was ajar.

>~~~<

"Thank you for being my guinea pig."

"I really hope this isn't how you always intend to use me for stress relief. A girl gets bored not being sexualized…"

Not that having Nina brush her hair wasn't doing *something* for Sarah. There was a weird bit of intimacy to it, especially with Nina's indomitable sex drive put on hold, at least for the moment. She had no complaints about how thoroughly Nina desired to, and had, ravished her, but it was nice to just luxuriate in the other woman's presence, feel the charisma of her, the affection that boiled off her. It made Sarah wonder where all that beautiful, terrible love had gone before she came along.

"Eyes shut," Nina said, and Sarah put an exaggeratedly naughty look on her face as she closed her eyes. It was just for Nina to apply hairspray, though; with all Sarah's hair on one side, grips holding it in place at the back, the combing portion of the evening was over. Shame. "So, what do you want to be when you grow up?"

Sarah smiled a bit dismally. "Like, if a genie let me wish for a full-ride scholarship and a job opening in my chosen field not taken up by some can't-let-it-go Baby Boomer?"

"Yes." Nina wrapped Sarah's hair around her thumb and, holding it secure with her other hand, twisted it around conically.

"I'd want to be the person who gives out those big checks from the Publisher's Clearing House."

"Hold still," Nina cautioned, now staking pins into and around the twist, holding it in place.

"I'd try to pick out people who really needed it. It'd still be random, but out of a hundred people who were dirt poor, not anyone living in San Francisco."

Nina had left some hair loose at Sarah's crown. With the French twist in place, she took the loose part and gently pulled it back, gathering up the ends. "They don't have poor people in San Francisco?"

"Oh no, the rent is obscene. What about you? What's your passion?"

Nina was lost in concentration, coiling the ends of Sarah's hair just a little off-kilter above the main twist. "Breeding."

Sarah paused. "That could pose a problem to our relationship."

"Horses."

"Okay, I know you're kinky, but that's still going a little—"

Nina slapped at her playfully. "*With other horses.*" Then, shaking her head, she reset the spiral and started pinning it into place. "I own a stable outside of town. I'm pretty hands-on with it. I was driving there the day we met."

"Wow. Never pictured you for a horse girl."

"Don't be jealous. You're a much better ride. I've actually made a fair bit of change racing some of them."

Nina took up a bristle brush, neatening out the style, and held up the hairspray bottle with her other hand. Sarah dutifully shut her eyes and mouth. She could only imagine the look of concentration on Nina's face. From the sensations, Nina was using the brush as delicately as a scalpel.

It struck her again how rarely Nina spent affection. Maybe Sarah was her only outlet, a way of processing emotion that she hadn't mastered yet. Maybe there was a reason Sarah had had to make the first move.

Nina stopped—a clatter as she set down her tools, a gentle touch on Sarah's shoulder to tell her to open her eyes. Then Sarah checked her reflection in Nina's vanity, Nina holding a hand mirror behind her so she could see it from the back too.

It was such a *look* that the rest of her almost felt unworthy in comparison. All her wild, unmanageable hair now gathered up, formed not only into a chignon, but one that spiraled in on itself, twisting down into a tight little knot of elegant concentration. It brought out something in her face—a seriousness, a maturity. She liked the effect; she just wasn't sure it was her.

"It's pretty intense," Sarah teased.

"I thought you liked intense," Nina teased right back. "And I certainly like it on you."

"It's nice," Sarah agreed. And she figured out what she wanted to ask. Just not how to ask it.

It was one of those answers without a right question.

"Have you ever been in love with someone?" Sarah didn't dare look at Nina. The vertigo-inducing spiral of her new hairstyle was much easier to hold her eyes on. "Really, really loved them?"

Nina turned away, and her shadow slashed over Sarah. But a moment later she was behind her again, hands on Sarah's shoulders. A perfect picture in the three reflections of the vanity. "You," she said glibly.

"Stop it."

"Why?"

"You don't just love someone after a few days, a few weeks. It takes time and stuff. That's why they always have montages in romantic movies."

"It doesn't take time at all. That's something adults imagine to explain why they don't feel it; they say it just takes time." Nina's voice grew wistful, even as her hands seemed to work mindlessly, massaging Sarah's shoulders. It was hard not to just dissolve into that idle, soothing touch. "They say that seeing and just knowing is something that only happens in fairy tales. But when I first saw Emmaline—everything else was just me second-guessing myself."

Sarah cleared her throat. "So what happened between you two, in the end?"

Nina smiled, a little sadly. "It's complicated. You don't want to hear about it."

"I don't?"

"No. Please believe me, Sarah. Having you makes me feel like that wrong is finally being put right."

When Nina touched her cheek, Sarah melted like her hand was a match being touched to ice. Then Nina knelt beside her, resting her temple against Sarah's, their faces merging in the mirror, and Sarah felt just perfect—perfectly connected to Nina, building a barrier with her against all pain and doubt. They stayed like that for a few minutes, Nina's hands rubbing up and down Sarah's arms as if they weren't sure where else to go. It was the kind of thing Sarah would've thought of as sexual in the past, but now it was just intimate.

"Hey, what were you working on, anyway?" Sarah asked. "I noticed the headphones. Same problem as in the park?"

"Yes."

"*Which is?*"

"Later," Nina said.

"Later?" Sarah asked.

Nina's hand trailed down to Sarah's hip and pulled her close.

"Later," Sarah agreed.

>~~~<

"Was that okay?" Sarah asked afterward, the taste of Nina still thick in her mouth. It hadn't been the wild bout of passion she'd expected when she came over; more peaceful, more serene. Nina had been hesitant to do much more than lie in bed with her, holding her and kissing her, but things had soon heated up to the point where Nina had laid back, spread her legs, and allowed Sarah to show off what she'd been reading on WikiHow.

"Very good," Nina replied, tugging on a lock of Sarah's hair until she joined her up on the pillow. "I noticed you tried a few new things…"

"Yeah." Sarah blushed. "Did you like any of 'em?"

"I liked *you*. You don't have to do tricks for me. Just do what comes naturally. Trust your instincts. If you want something…interesting, I could give you a few pointers."

"I'm listening…" Sarah said, flirting with all her might.

"Not tonight, little one. I just want to sleep."

Sarah's mind whirled, something in those words sinking into her. She wanted to be there for Nina in a way she couldn't explain, give her something—she didn't know what. "Can I stay with you?"

"To sleep?"

"I'm told that in some parts of the country, it's customary for two people who are fucking to sleep in the same bed."

"Mm," Nina said achingly. "It's been a while for me."

"I want as much time with you as I can get."

Nina smirked and opened her arms, ushering Sarah down to her chest. Sarah fit against her like a blanket. There was a tension in Nina, a stiffness, and she held Sarah loosely. But after a few minutes, Sarah felt Nina's body lengthen, her breathing slow, her skin warm to match Sarah's heat.

"Sarah?" Nina began. "How long have you wanted me? Us?"

"It feels like a long time," Sarah said. She spoke carefully, sounding each word out in her head before she spoke. Nina was too important to let just anything pop out. "Like I was waiting for you before we ever met, and then the more I saw you, the more I knew you were missing from me. Like…" She trailed off.

"Like what?" Nina pressed.

"Like when you download a new app on your phone and you're like, 'This is amazing, how did I ever get by without it?'" Sarah shrugged apologetically. "Sorry. I'm dumb."

"It's all right. It's the twenty-first century. I suppose I'll have to get used to being compared to an app."

"No, you're the phone," Sarah said. "And there's all this cool stuff in you, like… showing me how to do a French twist…and that's the app. So, you're more like one of those claw machines, full of all this neat stuff, only your claw actually works." She groaned and buried her head in Nina's armpit. "Please shut me up! I'm being an idiot."

"I like you being an idiot. It's very becoming." Nina kissed the top of Sarah's head. "And now you have me."

"Mmmm…" Sarah could do no more than moan at that.

"All your wanting…all your desire…all the fantasies and secret dreams and imagined plans… Now I'm yours."

Sarah perched her head on Nina's shoulder. She couldn't imagine herself more content. "Yours," she repeated drowsily. "Wait, what's with the headphones? Seriously; you promised."

"It's a signal I'm trying to piece together."

"From?"

Nina pointed upward.

"The attic?"

"Space."

Sarah's eyes, which had been drifting closed, shot open. "Aliens?"

"Or a pulsar, a supernova. It could even be a double-blind. I could be poring over something out of a busted MP3 player so the government knows I can tell the difference."

"But it could be an alien."

Nina was blasé. "So could most SoundCloud rappers. I mean, have you seen them?"

"No wonder you're stressed. I am going to have to fuck you much harder." Sarah slipped her arm snugly around Nina's waist, but softly; they'd pick this up in the morning.

"It's probably just a pulsar. But you have to do what you think is best." Nina returned to the idea she'd been circling. "You can touch me…kiss me…do anything you like with me."

"Go out on a date." Sarah was half-asleep but lucid still. Hanging onto Nina's words as she held on to the woman herself. "A real date. Like having dinner where the waiters have French accents. Or going to the movies, but without my mom. Unless you're into that. Please don't be into that."

"Uh, no. Not so much. But everything else sounds fine."

"Then we're dating?" Sarah asked, opening one eye hopefully.

"Yes, I think so. Or if this is a sewing circle, we're doing a very bad job."

"Either way, I get socks out of it… I mean, I could get you to buy me socks…" Sarah yawned. "Am I talking about socks? Oh, God, promise you're not listening to me…"

"I don't think we're that far along in the relationship yet."

Sarah drifted off to sleep as Nina stroked her back.

>~~~<

Sarah spoke into the phone as if she weren't slanted across Nina's lap, skin-to-skin under the sheets. "Mom, I told you last night. I got dizzy while I was working and had to lie down. I think it was an allergic reaction or something. Nina let me stay in the guest bedroom; she said I shouldn't be driving in my condition and honestly, she was probably right. … Oh, you want to talk to her?"

As Sarah handed over the phone, Nina brought her hand to Sarah's breast and squeezed it with the lazy ownership of a woman toying with her own hair. Equal parts mortified and thrilled, Sarah flushed as her nipple sprang to life and met Nina's palm.

"I'm sorry for all the trouble, Mrs. Kay," Nina was saying into the phone. "… Yes, I completely understand if you want to come over. I'll set an extra place for you at the breakfast table. … Yes, I think she's definitely feeling better." Sarah took Nina's hand and brought it to her other breast. Nina squeezed tighter. "Yes, I'll expect you in an hour. Good day, Mrs. Kay."

She hung up and dropped the cell phone on Sarah's hip.

"I do hope she calls back. I noticed you have it set to vibrate."

Sarah shivered delightedly and got another kiss from Nina, then kicked the sheets off. "I have time for a shower. Think you could fluff my clothes in the dryer a little?"

"Certainly. And then we could make an apple pie. I'm sure Eileen would love a slice."

Sarah smiled. "You really get off on doing this under her nose, don't you?"

Nina picked up her own phone from the bedside table and hid herself behind it. "I know I shouldn't… Too kinky?"

"Did I complain?"

"You like me too much to complain," Nina said, almost accusatorially.

"Call my mom back. Ask her if I love her, then ask her how much I complain. I'm very multitalented."

"There is a simple solution. You could tell her about us. Since we're not a sewing circle."

"I don't think she'd understand. The woman part, that'd be fine. She loves Ellen… But…"

"Which woman it is, yes. That's the hard part." Nina got up, taking a moment to stretch in the morning sun—a moment Sarah greatly enjoyed—then took up her kimono from the foot of the bed and hung it over her arm.

"It's not you, exactly," Sarah said. "She's angry at my dad for leaving her. Only she can't be angry at him, so she's angry at you. And that way she can still love him. She goes to visit him. She thinks I don't know, but I can always tell. She cries those nights."

"I'm sorry," Nina said reflexively.

"No, it's good… I mean, there's goodness in it…somewhere. That you can love someone so much that it still hurts a little, no matter how long you live. It's a win, you know? You won just finding that in the first place."

"Some days I wish I had never met Emmeline." The sentence came off Nina like a loose tooth after a fight. Not in any measured tone; her words *stung* with feeling.

"But you still love her, right? So my mom, she'll still love him, even if she has to let go of this feud."

Nina said nothing. She seemed in another time, another place. "I'm sorry I still love her. It's not fair to you. I try really hard—"

"I like you exactly the way you are. And anything that made you the way you are… Nina, you're amazing. I like how amazing you are."

"I appreciate that, but do you think we could—" Nina suddenly sounded short of breath. "Do you think we could call a time-out on this? You have your shower, and I have breakfast to make. I think we should… Yes. I think we have too much to do to stand around talking."

Sarah wanted to stay with her, comfort her, but she didn't know how. All the reassurances and affection she could muster had been dashed against Nina's troubled mind like hailstones breaking against the street. She squeezed Nina's shoulder, more for her own sake than the other woman's, and then left her alone.

>~~~<

After a brisk shower, Sarah went to the laundry room and quickly changed from the towel into her revitalized clothes, their warmth reminding her of Nina's oh-so-recent touch.

In the kitchen, she found Nina in her version of relaxed housekeeping clothes: jeans, a semitranslucent top, and a cooking apron that hid just how translucent her top really was. She was kneading dough when Sarah came in, a big mug of coffee next to her area of the countertop. "Find me some plastic wrap, slave," Nina said teasingly before picking up the dough and casually slamming it down. "If you wanna help."

Sarah automatically scanned the cabinets for a clue as to where the plastic wrap was before looking back at Nina. "Where?"

"Far cabinet."

Sarah found it hiding behind the Tupperware. Nina split the ball of dough in half and stuck one into the plastic wrap, then held it out to Sarah. "Put that in the fridge, please?"

With a goofy salute, Sarah did so, then turned back around to ask what her reward would be when the intercom buzzed.

"That will be her," Nina said. "Go on."

As irritating as the interruption was, Sarah just counted her blessings that Nina had been able to surface so quickly from her black mood, or at least put it on the backburner to be dealt with later. That was a skill she herself had never mastered.

She got the door, holding Barnaby back by the collar, but it hardly mattered. Eileen barreled inside and immediately planted a hand on Sarah's forehead to feel its warmth.

"Ma!" Sarah growled, unable to stop some of her frustration from leaking through.

"Oh, don't you look pinkish," Eileen said. She looked past Sarah to Nina, who whistled to call Barnaby back before he could give the stranger a going-over. "I'll get her home. Thank you so much for looking after her, Ms. Rose."

"My pleasure. Your daughter is a very charming young woman. I could get used to spending time with her. We were about to bake a pie," she chimed, smiling so disarmingly it was a wonder her jaw didn't unhinge. "I had hoped to have it done soon enough for Sarah to take home with her. I don't know how much dessert you let this one eat, but according to her, I have the finest pie she's ever tasted."

Sarah felt herself turning so red that, if the lights were turned off, they could have read a newspaper with her.

"She's definitely coming down with something," Eileen said, one eye trained on Sarah no matter how much Nina swirled around her. "Baking... Aren't you worried you'll catch what she has?"

"Oh, I'd be far more worried about her catching something from us," Nina said. As sweetly as ever.

Eileen's preternaturally smooth brow crinkled slightly; she clearly didn't know what that meant and neither, quite frankly, did Sarah.

"Well, we should get going," Eileen said after a moment.

"It's like being a child again," Nina said, subtly leaning in their way...and then back out again. "Asking if Sarah can come out to play."

Before Nina allowed them to leave—the whole thing had the feel of an audience with the queen—she brought Sarah close for a hug. "Get well soon," she said, her hand cinched in the small of Sarah's back. With one little twitch, it could be down her pants, on the curve of her ass. And then she'd be Nina's, right in front of her mother; she'd do anything asked of her.

But Nina released her, like a little fish into a big pond. "Run along now."

Sarah did, walking briskly to catch up with her mother. Eileen was running *toward* their home, while Sarah was fleeing *away* from Nina and all the wonderful, terrible things she made Sarah feel.

She'd learned two things in her night with Nina. First, that Nina held undeniable power over her.

Second, that Sarah couldn't bring herself to care.

Chapter 11

It took a few more weeks of dating, but Sarah got comfortable enough with the butterflies in her stomach that she could talk about it with a friend—at least, a friend who was hundreds of miles away. She *wanted* to share the news about Nina, but she *needed* to talk about the seismic shift in how she thought of herself and what she really wanted.

"She just, she knows so much, she knows what she wants, and she knows her value. She has all this experience, but at the same time, it's like it's new to her? Like I'm new to her? So it doesn't matter as much that I have no idea what I'm doing, because she has no idea what *I'm* doing either, you know? We're both figuring it out. But she has a much better wardrobe than I do."

Jonesy didn't answer. Sarah turned onto her side, looking at her phone where it lay on the nightstand, doing the speaker-phone thing. "Jonesy? You there?"

"Yeah, I'm just trying to picture Nina Rose going from, like, the Phantom of the Opera to your sugar momma."

"She's not my sugar momma."

"I mean, I know about the older-man thing, but I just never really heard about women finding older women attractive. I guess I get it, though. Have you always been into MILFs?"

Sarah reached over to pick up the phone. "It's not like that," she said, bringing it close to her mouth. "She was born in the same decade as me, so shut up."

"Oh, wow, when did you decide to look that up?"

"Seriously, shut up."

"Okay, okay. At least she isn't your professor or something. Just your boss," Jonesy finished airily.

"Well, not anymore. It seemed weird when we decided to make it official." Sarah rolled onto her back, dropping the phone onto her chest. She idly tapped her hands on her belly, trying to irritate Jonesy with the slaps.

"That's probably smart." A deep sigh traveled from cell phone tower to cell phone tower. "So how are things with, you know, Tyrese and Beck?"

Sarah suppressed a growl. "I wouldn't know. It's really not any of my business at this point."

"They're your friends. You've moved on, they've hooked up... Do we all really still have to be bitter about it?"

"Yes! If your boyfriend cheated on you, I would back you up!"

"Maybe I wouldn't want you to. I mean, I don't know, isn't life a little short to have a civil war every time two of my friends break up?"

"He cheated on me!"

"Ty says he didn't."

"Well, he's a liar and Beck's a whore." Sarah heard a floorboard creaking somewhere in the house. She lifted her head, wondering if her mother was coming. The last thing she needed was for Eileen to hear her bitchfest. She picked up her mobile and turned off the speakerphone, putting it to her ear. "You still there?"

"Yeah, yeah... Are you listening to yourself, though? A month ago you would've kicked someone's ass if you caught them talking about your friends like that."

"Things change."

"It's just weird to me. You come back to Bathory for your mom, only you don't get along with her—"

"I love my mom!"

"Then you're staying for your friends, only now you're alienated from all of them. I guess you're staying for Nina Rose now..."

"What are you even getting at, huh?"

"It's like you just keep coming up with excuses to stay and then you sabotage them."

"I didn't sabotage anything. Tyrese cheated on me!"

"All I know is, a year ago he was crazy in love with you and now—"

"So, what, so I pushed him away?"

"I don't know. I don't know. I'm not even in the same zip code."

Someone knocked at Sarah's bedroom door.

"Just a minute!" Sarah yelled, pushing the phone against her breast. She quickly put it back to her ear. "I've gotta go. Think you can hold off psychoanalyzing me for a while?"

She didn't wait for an answer, jabbing the disconnect button as Eileen opened the door. Only it seemed more as if she got the door for Nina, since no one could open a door in that woman's presence without seeming like they were getting it for her.

Eileen was wearing a smart business suit instead of her usual flower-print blouse, but as stylish as it was, she couldn't hold a candle to Nina in a pantsuit with a black vest and white blouse, holding Barnaby by his leash with the élan of a woman who had sent her dog to obedience school.

"You have a visitor," Eileen said as Nina came in holding a picnic basket with a towel-covered pie pan on top.

"Apparently," Nina said innocently, crouching down to unsnap Barnaby's leash, "your mother just got called in to develop the floral centerpiece for a town-hall luncheon. And I stopped by to see if you'd like to join us for a picnic."

Eileen gave them a strange look, her eyes quickly darting back to follow Barnaby anxiously as he shuffled around the room, sniffing over the carpet like a very hairy vacuum cleaner. He came to a sit at her feet, his big tail thwacking solidly from one side of his butt to the other, and Eileen gave him a few quick pats.

Distractedly, she said, "Sarah was the fussiest eater growing up. She wouldn't eat anything I'd put in her mouth!"

"That won't be a problem for me, I'm sure. Good luck with the contract, Mrs. Kay."

"Thanks." Eileen checked her watch. "Oh, I'm late! My purse…" Eileen looked around frantically. "Ah." Apparently remembering where it was, she left the room, then shouted back through the house, "Bye, girls!" And with that, Eileen was out the door.

Nina stood up, idly strolling over to the bed. Sarah suddenly felt like a maiden being paid a visit by Count Dracula. "I thought you were going to stop teasing my mom."

"I thought you were going to tell her about us."

"She's going to have an aneurism when she finds out and gets all your little jokes."

Nina waved a dismissive hand. "We can leave this for another time. For now, you should thank me."

Sarah's mouth went familiarly dry. "How?"

Nina pulled back the covers. "Get dressed. We're having a picnic."

>~~~<

The park was only a couple blocks from home, something Sarah was sure Eileen had taken into account when buying the place. With the sun setting, the streets were mostly empty and the mossy woods were abandoned, as people had fled in anticipation of an evening chill. But it hadn't shown up yet, a warm front keeping things crisp and cozy, as if Nina were holding back the night with sheer force of personality. After tying Barnaby's leash to a nearby tree, they spread out a blanket, sat down on the banks of a lake full of swans, and poured each other apple cider. Barnaby sagged down to the ground to pant animatedly. Nina toasted them both, and Sarah giggled.

"I've often eaten in silence," Nina said, opening an array of Tupperware containers and spreading out dinner for them. "But it's amazing how much more companionable that silence is when you have someone to share it with."

"So I'm just here to look pretty in the sunset?" Sarah held out her hand, turned golden by the dying light.

"Nonsense. You'll also be enjoying my delicious cooking." Nina reached out and undid the top button of the blouse Sarah had thrown on, but Sarah got the impression it was purely an aesthetic consideration—a brushstroke on the painting she was making of the two of them. Nevertheless, she warmed.

"Everything about you is delicious."

Nina took a big bite of a cupcake. "Have you given our relationship any thought?"

"I'm twenty. I try not to think about everything. It gives the other kids a bad reputation."

Nina smiled chidingly. "I mean, are you—comfortable with where we're at? Sure about what we're doing?"

"I'm *very* sure. I've had time to sleep on it and everything. In fact, I thought a little about those pictures you showed me."

"Oh?" Nina wiped her chin with the back of her hand, the gesture slow and deliberate. Above her hand, her eyes were locked on Sarah. "And you want to try it?"

Sarah busied herself with her own cupcake, unwrapping it from its little cupcake skirt. "I don't know, it's just, that stuff is really, really—" She almost said "wrong." Instead she said, "naughty."

"Is there something wrong with how things are now?"

"No, no, nothing *wrong*. But you do want more, right?"

"I want—"

"Yeah, I know, you want me to be safe and happy and all of that." Sarah smiled easily. "But that's not all you want."

"I want you; the rest is just details."

"But a part of you wants *that*. I mean, you don't just stop wanting it, do you?"

Nina was quiet for a moment. "There's want and then there's priority. The two are linked, but not the same."

"God, no wonder you're such a good codebreaker. You have to listen to yourself all the time."

Nina looked stung. "I'm sorry, I didn't mean to be—"

"No, don't, I didn't mean that. I get it. You want *me* to want it."

"That's *not* it," Nina insisted. "I mean…" She looked heavenward. "There's a difference. There is such a difference, and I keep thinking you know, but then you act like you don't—"

"So tell me. Just tell me. What is it you want?"

Nina took a deep breath. Took a long drink of cider. "To be perfectly frank: yes. I am interested in…certain scenarios. Not nice. Not normal. But I don't want them if *you* don't want them. I don't want you to do anything if it's to make me happy, only if it's what you want. That's very important to me, Sarah. Only what we both want."

Sarah reached into her pocket and took out a much-folded piece of paper. "I've been reading up about BDSM. Lots of people complaining about *Fifty Shades of Grey*."

"Yes, I assume they would."

"Because it's bad?"

"Because it's the internet. And because it's bad."

Sarah unfolded the paper. "I made a list of things I might be interested in. So just look it over, underline the things you're interested in, and that's what we'll do. Only things we're both interested in."

Nina took the paper and read through it quickly, her rapidly scanning eyes betraying excitement, even a sense of relief. "Number twelve… You're *certain*?"

"That's the first thing that jumps out at you? Twelve?"

"Oh, I know it's not the most extreme, but it's not the most common either."

"Well, I don't know if it'll make me squirt, but I figure it's worth a shot. You only live once, right?"

"I'm going to be very amused if this turns out to be a fetish for you."

>~~~<

Sarah was nervous. Of course she was nervous. She was about to feel pain. Not even pain like a doctor's shot or something, but pain for pleasure. Nina's pleasure. But of course, that was the important word here. Not *pain* but *Nina*, especially *Nina's pleasure*. And, if Nina was right, if she could cultivate it like some rare flower in unforgiving terrain—Sarah's pleasure too.

So there she was, bent over the bed, undressed from the waist down, her ass upturned for Nina's artistic inspection. Nina so close that Sarah could feel her breath between her cheeks like a light promise. She was scared, but somehow excited in her fear. It was as if she was on a roller coaster. Climbing up, up, up.

Nina's hand approached her sex, and Sarah thought she might melt before it got there. "I just thought of something…" Nina spoke haltingly; her hand stopped, quivering, before it could touch Sarah. "I've been 'just thinking' of something for days now."

Sarah submerged a grumble; Nina couldn't have picked a better time. But she got it. It was like a blockage, something that didn't come into focus until you actually tried to go through it. And before you could, you had to get it out.

"I'm all ears," she said, looking back at Nina as best she could while in this unforgiving position.

It was like Nina was hiding behind her own body. "You trust me, don't you?"

"With all of me," Sarah said firmly. She didn't want to sound as if she was pleading.

She could sense Nina's smile. The hand dipped closer. "So you know I won't think less of you if you use the safe word. I won't be disappointed one bit. I'll be proud of you for knowing your limits and stopping me before I hurt you. I never want to hurt you, Sarah. Not for real. I couldn't bear it."

"You won't. I know how you feel about me. You can't love someone and hurt them."

Nina's smile was achingly perfect. That was the look of a woman in love, Sarah thought. It had to be. It was so beautiful. "You're so young, Sarah, that you make me feel old. Remember, this isn't about me. We're not doing this to please me. We're doing it together. Partners."

Sarah had thought it would be odd to feel pain and know it was meant with love. But how much odder would it be to not be able to feel love at all? "Partners." The word flew out of her mouth. Then she giggled. *Damnit.* She couldn't help feeling like a schoolgirl. "That always seemed like such a weird way to put it. But now I kinda like it."

"I like it too." Nina darkened, brow furrowing. "Part of me almost doesn't want to share this with you. It'd be so much simpler if you just didn't want this than if you're willing to try. There've been other girls, but they were…arrangements. There was fondness, affection, but we always understood there was a limit on it. With you—I feel like I'm someone else. Someone I can't control."

Sarah's mind was racing—no, exploding. She'd never even imagined this. She'd gone into this thinking she might have a fling. And that could have been enough, more than enough. But when Nina talked like this, she wanted more. Always more.

But just like that, Nina was solid, impenetrable. "I'm going to use you," Nina said as she dipped her head, her face just briefly touching Sarah's flesh. Her nose, her lips, her cheek—Sarah felt them where she was naked and couldn't believe the simple intimacy of that. Her heart was racing, and she'd barely been touched. "Like a good hunter doesn't waste any meat from their kill. All this virgin flesh—all this unmarked skin—I'm going to take it and I'm going to make it feel things it's never felt before. Every inch. Every nerve. When I'm done, you'll be painted red."

"I've been spanked before," Sarah said. She didn't know why.

"With a belt?" Nina asked with a little kiss at Sarah's tailbone.

"No. My parents threatened me with that, but they never actually did it."

"Mmmmm." Nina rested her chin on Sarah's bottom. "But then, you've never been so bad."

She reached down and hooked her fingers in her studded leather belt. Sarah heard the buckle rattling as the belt worked its way through Nina's pant loops. She looked up, as carefully as she could, to see Nina folding the belt up. She brought it down on her other hand; it sounded like a crack of thunder.

"Now, Sarah," Nina began, and Sarah could barely think to listen with the belt smacking into her palm. Thunder rumbling in distant clouds. "Remember. The safe word is 'Fermi.' You can cry out all you like, say 'stop' or 'no' or whatever you need to say, but unless you say 'Fermi,' I'll keep going. Do you understand?"

"Yes."

"What makes me stop?"

"Fermi."

"What doesn't make me stop?"

"No. Stop. Don't."

Nina smiled, and as beautiful as Nina's smile usually was, it looked even better when Sarah had made her smile. Sarah turned away, looking straight ahead, pleased with herself. The belt stopped against Nina's hand.

"You have been naughty," Nina said. It sounded like disapproval. Really, it was glowing praise. "And naughty girls get punished. It's the only way they learn."

Sarah felt tension kinking up her body. She couldn't stop it. Her body knew what was coming, and it didn't trust Nina the way her heart did. She closed her eyes. She let herself tremble. She felt small, and frail, and she let herself feel that way. Nina wasn't just a lover, not in Sarah's present state. Now, towering over Sarah, she was a goddess, and that was both a danger and a comfort.

"Your lesson is going to be how to take ten strokes," Nina said.

The leather belt keened through the air, and when it struck Sarah's ass, the impact sizzled across both her cheeks like acid. Sarah had never felt a pleasure as intense as Nina bringing her to climax; she'd never felt a pain as bad as this either. She let out an agonized cry, not even able to think of holding it in, and Nina let her scream. Then she crisscrossed the welt her first blow had raised. Sarah's mouth was wrenched open by the howl that came from her. She instinctively tried to scramble to her feet, to flee, but Nina was upon her, pinning her down on the bed, and Sarah had the oddest feeling of being *held* as Nina trapped her.

"Let it out," Nina said. Sarah could feel the belt dangling from Nina's hand, flickering between them, brushing against her skin. "Is that all there is? Or is there more?"

Sarah sucked in air to replace what she'd screamed out. She didn't realize she was crying until she felt the tears on her cheeks. She sniffled. Then she felt Nina massaging the stiffened muscles of her neck, soothingly, possessively.

"Do you want to keep going?" Nina asked, her voice less firm but not any softer. "This has to be what you want, Sarah. I can't want it for you."

"Keep going," Sarah said. She looked back at Nina, still crying, feeling flushed and a little shamed and strong somewhere. "I was bad. Make me a good girl, Nina. Please."

When Nina spoke, it was through an audibly dry mouth. "Eight more now." It took a moment for Sarah to realize that what she was feeling wasn't just lust but pride in arousing Nina so.

She didn't tense this time. Thunder cracked, and she felt it traced in fire across her ass. Twice, one after the other. Sarah gritted her teeth, limiting her response to a long groan. She was graffitied with crimson, marked with it from the swell of her buttocks to the tender skin just below her waist. The pain robbed her of control; she tensed again, bracing for the whoosh of the belt moving through the air, even the sound stinging. Instead, she felt Nina's finger like a feather, floating down the vale between her buttocks, where the belt had barely touched her, the delicate touch somehow stronger than the pain around it. Sarah had never felt anything like what was now filling her.

"Nina," she whispered, not as if it was a question but as if it was an answer. The finger went between her legs. It lost itself inside her, in the dampness, in the softness. Sarah bit her lip as if she had forgotten what pain was. "Oh, stop, oh, *oh*!"

She didn't know why she said it. It felt better than the whipping, but it *wasn't* the whipping, and she had been feeling the whipping so *much*—but just because she'd said it didn't mean she meant it. The word 'Fermi' echoed through her like a physical tremble, but she didn't let it reach her lips.

Nina's other hand clutched at her throat, pulled her upright. Sarah was spun around, the pain of Nina's grip rebounding off everything she was feeling in her cunt.

Nina looked at her for barely a second, then kissed her, and Sarah felt everything fall away. There was still a muted throb along the curve of her ass, though. As if she needed more to remind her whose she was.

Compared to this, Nina had been treating her like a porcelain doll. Always kissing her as if she was afraid Sarah would break. She was as slow to stop as Sarah would've been.

"There'll be more of that when we're finished," she said, and her tongue traveled from Sarah's chin to the tip of her nose, making Sarah think of it elsewhere. "But first, let's see how badly you want it. Do you know how we'll find out?"

"How?" Sarah barely whispered.

Nina threw Sarah back on the bed. Face down. "You're going to tell me. Do you want it, Sarah? Do you want it badly?"

"So much. So badly."

"How badly?" Nina teased, and just the sound, just the thought of the wicked smile she must've been wearing… *Yours, yours, yours*, the pain on her backside pulsed. "Bad enough for another six lashes?"

Sarah nodded frantically.

"Answer me!" Nina demanded.

"Yes!"

Sarah heard the belt, felt it, not as pain but as pressure—she was half numbed to it and half feeling it more vividly, spreading beyond the skin and into the muscle, biting down on her cunt like a fire burning hotter. She barely noticed the pleasure among the pain, just the throbbing, how insistent it was.

"Bad enough for another five lashes?" Nina asked smugly. She already knew the answer.

Sarah nodded again. Speech was eluding her, like the belt was bringing her down to a wordlessly primitive level. "It almost feels…good," she said, when she got her mouth open.

Barely understanding where she was or what was happening to her, Sarah pushed her ass out, knowing she would feel more. The belt flew. Sarah hissed and mewled, but it was what she wanted.

"Another four lashes?" Nina asked as if she was taking a survey.

"I want you to fuck me," Sarah sobbed, burying her face in the bedspread. "Please fuck me…"

"Then let me hear you beg for it."

"I am begging!"

"Not for me. For the belt."

Sarah hissed in a breath. "I want the belt. Give it to me. Please."

She convulsed as Nina did 'it' again, such a little thing, barely the twitch of a muscle, but there was so much of it. The whistle through the air, and then that *feeling*. "Three more, Sarah. Just three more."

It happened once, then again. Sarah didn't know what she was feeling, how there could be so much of it inside her. The horrible liveliness of the welts raised on her ass had spread all over her body. She could feel everything, pulled tight, wickedly alive with sensation, her clit especially tingling with need.

"Harder…" Sarah begged quaveringly, like the words were being shaken out of her vibrating body. Her cunt spasmed along with the rest of her, and she ground it into the bed. "I can take it."

"One more lash?" Nina asked, her voice heavier. *She's looking at me*, Sarah thought. *She likes looking at me…*

"Yes! Please! *Please*!"

"One more lash from who?"

"From you, from my mistress, from my queen, Nina—"

Her breathing almost as harsh as Sarah's, Nina swung the whip up, between Sarah's legs.

For just a moment, Sarah knew it was coming. She felt the air part before it, like a little pleasing breeze. Then it hit, and it was horrible and wonderful and a snake biting her and a finger penetrating her and every muscle in her body was tensed and everything hurt and everything felt good and she was coming, her fingers digging into the bedspread like claws and rending it. She didn't hear any of it, not even her own scream, as she was consumed by the purest orgasm of her young life.

Afterward—what felt like a long time afterward—she lay still, knowing what she was expected to say as if it was written inside her, spelled out with everything she was feeling. "Thank you, mistress. Thank you for whipping me. Thank you, thank you…"

"You're very welcome," Nina answered sweetly.

Sarah couldn't move, couldn't speak now that she'd said what she had to say. She could only breathe and feel. Nina picked her up, one arm under her knees and the other beneath her shoulder blades, lifting her as if she weighed nothing. Sarah cooed as she went boneless. She seemed to be all sensation, every little feeling heightened and pure.

"Wrap your arms around my neck," Nina said, and Sarah did. Nina carried her to the pillows with gentle, stately steps that made Sarah feel safe.

"Are you tired?" Nina asked, her voice even more sugary than before.

"A little." Sarah wasn't…*sleepy*. It was more as if she was wrung out, permanently out of breath. Maybe sleep would help, but she also felt as if she was on a caffeine high. Like if Nina wanted her to, she could just nestle between her legs and drink forever.

"Quite an ordeal, wasn't it?" Nina rocked Sarah in her arms with all the care she'd show a newborn baby. "A trial by fire. But I knew you could do it, Sarah, and you've impressed me very much. I think you're ready for a great many things."

"I want to. I want to do everything with you."

"You will, my sweet. You will. I'll take such good care of you, my Sarah. Mine. And I'll be your Nina."

Sarah tried not to yawn, but she was so tired, and being carried by Nina was relaxing her so much. Nina laughed softly and lowered Sarah to the bed.

"Don't leave me," Sarah pleaded. She wanted more. Not more sex or more touching—more Nina.

"I won't, baby. I'm going to stay right here with you." Nina held on to Sarah's right hand as she circled the bed. She petted its knuckles. "You've had a very intense experience. It's time to sleep on it. But I know how…frenzied…events have left you. So I'm going to help you calm down. I'm going to get you nice and relaxed."

Nina started by undressing. Her slender fingers undid each of the buttons on her vest in turn, and Sarah felt a pulse of excitement, seeing them in action. She remembered them inside her, between her lips, the taste they'd carried...

Nina teased her vest open and spoke softly, as if she was reading a bedtime story. "You'll never get to sleep in the state you're in. And you need sleep, Sarah. So you must relax. Breathe deeply and relax. Breathe...and relax..."

Sarah felt herself comply hypnotically. Her whole body was in tune with Nina. Her racing heart slowed, and her hot blood cooled... Her flesh itself was obedient to Nina. She lay on her side, staring up at Nina as the woman handed her vest off. Nina gave her a loving look as she bent over her to brush some hair from Sarah's eyes and toy with it.

"Would you like it if I held you until you fall asleep?"

"Yes, mistress."

"You don't have to call me *mistress* when you're not being punished. We're friends, after all. And I like the way you say my name."

"Nina..."

She finished undressing and got into the center of the bed, with Sarah on her right. She ran her fingers over Sarah, and warmth drenched her body, like her nerves were spigots slowly being closed off, her body going gently numb.

She could've spent days like that—Nina felt warmer and softer the longer she touched Sarah—but it must've been only minutes before a crash of thunder seemed to shake the house. Sarah reflexively jolted, and Nina petted her hair with a soothing nonchalance.

"It's just a little—" she began, then said, "Oh no" as a stampede of scrambling clicks and paddings traveled the house.

Barnaby threw himself through the ajar bedroom door just as another lightning bolt blushed the room a jagged blue. He whined and spun in a circle, scratching at the carpet as if he was trying to dig it up.

Nina sat up to point a chilling finger at him. "Barnaby, *no*. Sarah, I am so sorry..."

The thunder came again, and Barnaby barked animatedly, forcing out great belches of woofs at the loud noise before heaving himself onto the bed like a beached whale. Two massive forepaws and the great bulk of his doggy head shifted the stance of the mattress like a bowling ball had been set down on the bedsprings. With a wary little whine, Barnaby propelled himself the rest of the way onto the bed, knocking the mattress several inches out of alignment with the bedframe before he was successfully standing on top of the sheets in all his ursine splendor.

By now, sheets of rain had started coming down, painting the light through the windows with their teary streaks. It gurgled down the gutters, and Barnaby huffed impatiently, somewhere in his doggy brain associating the peaceable but *intent* sound with the lightning and thunder of his phobia. Nina sat up further, the sheet spilling down to bare a dark-tipped breast lowering to her belly as she reached out to ruffle Barnaby's head.

"You big chicken," she said with the elaborate weariness of someone who could not be truly angry with their pet, no matter what the offense. "You couldn't let me be a sultry temptress for five minutes…"

Sarah snuggled against Nina as she settled back against the pillows, patting her warm thigh, part of her still unbelieving even now that she could touch Nina so intimately and it just *was*. She felt as if she was being allowed to pet a tiger. "Hey, lay off him. I'm very tempted just to lie in bed forever cuddling with you and your enormous coward dog…"

Appearing to notice Sarah then, Barnaby settled his weight onto a protesting Nina and brought his huge head around to sniff at her. He took particular interest in Sarah's hair, wheezing at it like a lazy bloodhound, then he licked her from chin to temple with one swipe of a tongue about the size of a shower loofah.

"Barnaby, get *down*!" Nina ordered firmly, hauling on his collar. Complaining with heaving-sigh insolence, Barnaby let himself be dragged to the confines of one side of the bed. "That's my job. You don't even brush your teeth."

"Really? I never would've noticed," Sarah said, wiping her face off with her hand and her hand off with the bedspread. Nina stared at this process. "He's your dog."

With a little grumble, Barnaby set his steam-shovel head down on Nina's thigh. Sarah reached down and flicked his ear as she cuddled up with Nina from the other side.

There was a bolt of lightning, a gong of thunder, and Barnaby whined under his breath. Sarah reached down further, now resting her head on Nina's sternum so she could pet the nape of Barnaby's neck. He lolled out a happy tongue.

"Don't spoil him," Nina said, setting both hands beneath her head. "He's not scared anymore; he's just milking it."

"He is too scared," Sarah said, scratching him behind the ears. "You're just a total wimp, aren't you? An absolute wuss, yes, you are! Yes, you are!"

"Sarah." Nina eyed Sarah's nails flashing through Barnaby's fur. "You are making me positively jealous."

>~~~<

Eileen was in the kitchen when Sara got home that night, chopping vegetables, the noise so jarring that Sarah almost couldn't believe she was hearing it on such a special night.

"How was dinner at Nina's?" Eileen asked. Her knife kept slapping against the cutting board, crisply cutting whatever was in between. "If you're not full, I'm making enough for two."

Sarah sat. "I'm pretty full. But I can have that for lunch tomorrow."

Eileen smiled ruefully. "You're not going to *Nina's* for lunch too?"

"Would it matter if I did?"

Eileen paused. No, it was more as if she just stopped, the way a watch would stop when it finally wound down. And Sarah thought she could see her winding herself back up again. Starting to move once more, but slower than before. Older.

"She likes the company, you know. Having me around. And I like spending time with her. She's a really nice person. You'd like her too if you got to know her."

"I know I haven't been the best mother," Eileen interrupted. "But did I ever do anything to make me deserve being lied to?"

"I'm not lying!" Sarah protested instantly, shrilly.

"Do you think I'm an idiot? Do you think that I would think it's normal that a thirty-year-old woman would suddenly want to be *besties* with some *girl*—"

"She's not thirty," Sarah said, teeth gritted. "And I am not some girl. Not to her."

Eileen put her hands on her hips. The knife pointed down her leg. Dripping. "Then say it. Please. Just say it."

"I'm dating Nina Rose." Sarah didn't think she had ever said that before. She virtually vomited it out; it had the half-horrid flavor of a nauseous purge, and then there was only the relief of being empty of it. It had no more power, no more fear—she'd said it.

Eileen walked to the sink, turned it on, rinsed off the knife before setting it on the drying rack. She left the water running. Steepled her arms on the counter and held herself over the sink and its babble of tap water.

Sarah almost couldn't catch her breath, staring at her mother's rigid back. "Don't freak out," she said, her voice higher and tighter than even the admission had been.

"I'm not freaking out," Eileen said.

"It's not like, you know, she seduced me. I'm twenty years old. I want to be with her."

"You don't know what you want."

"I do now."

"For how long? The next five minutes?"

Sarah scoffed, shaking her head. "What would be so wrong with that? I'd rather be happy with her for five minutes than—not. Not being happy. I wasn't happy, Mom, did you know that? Have you even noticed that she's made me *happy*—"

"Of course I noticed!" Eileen shut the water off. The wedding ring on her finger clicked against the faucet. "I just thought it was *you*, not some woman…"

"Isn't that how it's supposed to work?" Sarah ran her hands through her hair. "Isn't that how it was for you and Dad?"

Eileen turned around, sagging against the sink as if she was about to be washed down it. "I didn't need your father to be happy. I was a whole person before I ever met him. You, you're…"

"A child?" Sarah offered.

"Adults don't sneak around and *lie*—"

"That hasn't been my experience," Sarah interrupted. "And I told you, I didn't want you to freak out—"

"I'm not freaking out!" Eileen shouted it this time.

Then she slowly started to laugh.

Sarah walked back into the living room and collapsed onto the couch. She heard Eileen's slippers slap against the tile as she came to the island and leaned against it.

"I wish I could take this better than I am," Eileen said.

"And I wish I'd just told you. But I didn't want to talk about it. It was my secret. It made me special."

"You've been special for a lot longer than that woman…" Eileen broke off, forestalling another protest from Sarah, who thought she could hear Eileen's bones creaking as she came around the island and sat down on the back of the couch. "I want to meet her. *Really* meet her. No more games. God knows I didn't tell my parents anything, but if she's so important to you—a part of your life."

"She is," Sarah said quickly. "And she'd love to meet you, all 'official' and everything…"

"I take it you've been seeing each other for a while?"

"A little while, yeah." Talking about Nina, her nerves came rushing back. Even with the secret out, she felt as if she was in a minefield. One false move and she'd give Eileen the wrong idea, set her on her warpath again.

"You're not her gardener anymore?"

"I mean, she doesn't pay me…" Sarah laughed oddly. "Obviously. A lot of times we do it together, actually. I show her how to trim things and—"

"And the money for rent?"

"I'm taking it out of what I make at the supermarket."

"Oh," Eileen said. "I thought maybe you were saving that."

"What do I have to save for?" Sarah asked.

"Going back to college. Have you thought about that?"

If she was in a minefield, *that one* was poking up out of the dirt. "I don't just want to be some kept woman. I want Nina to be proud of me… I can see myself going back to school, doing the long-distance thing with her, but I would want it to be for something important, something I'm passionate about. Right now, what I'm passionate about is her."

"You could be hermits together," Eileen said half-jokingly. The other half was very much not a joke.

"She's not a hermit. She's been—getting out there. Like at the movie theater."

"I suppose that must've been nice. You two watching a movie together."

"Mom, c'mon."

"No! No." Eileen held up a hand. "I think I'm being very reasonable, but please don't treat me like I'm overreacting about you getting a tattoo or something."

"I don't think you're overreacting," Sarah said, trying to be placating.

"It's a lot to take in all at once."

"I know," Sarah said.

"Did she tell you that I blame her for your father's death?"

"No," Sarah said.

"I don't," Eileen said. "But he was so proud of her. He sacrificed for her… He sacrificed *you* for her. He was certain, *certain* that she was going to change the world. That woman has a big house. She has a lot of time to read books in that library of hers. And clearly she has a lot of money. But I don't think she's ever done anything to make this world a better place. She's never gone anywhere, and she's never been anything but *comfortable*. I can see why you like her so much."

Chapter 12

Sarah felt like a second moon, heading up the path to Nina's manor, her white dress reflecting the setting sun's light. The wind pulled at its hem, swirling crisp dead leaves at her white pumps, skeletal fingers of the fallen husks touching her calves as she held the skirt of the gown aloft with one hand. In her other hand, she held a bouquet. Smelled it as she approached the front door. She didn't think about how deeply Eileen had scored her with what she'd said the last time they'd spoken. She was determined to be happy and carefree and not in pain. She deserved that, didn't she? Not being in pain, not being in mourning, being *happy*. If Eileen couldn't manage that, Sarah could.

She didn't even have to knock. Nina opened the door, light from inside streaming out, silhouetting her in black. She wore a Jean-Paul Gaultier dress—black leather, sleek and pristine, buckles in back. The whole effect was fetishistic and ladylike all at once.

"Whoa," Sarah said. "Little on the nose, isn't it?"

Nina frowned and indicated the short sleeves. "I didn't wear opera gloves, did I?"

"You just know how much I like your biceps. These are for you." Sarah held out the red roses, suddenly feeling a little awkward. She'd never presented anyone with flowers before. It felt wrong to be shoving them out at full extension. Maybe if she tipped them a little, more offered them up than—

Too late, Nina had taken them. "They're lovely."

"I thought about getting white, but—" Sarah gestured to herself. "Seemed like a little much."

"Quite right. And they do match." Nina plucked one rose from the group. She flicked the bulb at Sarah, petals and thorns rustling almost imperceptibly over Sarah's cheek. "After all, not all of you is white."

"I'll put them in water," Sarah said, taking the bouquet back save for the flower Nina had plucked. It gave her a charge to be so slightly submissive—she wondered if that was what Eileen was always talking about with her easy-to-please stuff.

In the kitchen, Sarah took an empty vase, started filling it with water. Behind her, she heard Nina closing the front door and locking it. The click of her high heels on the tile floor. And then there was Nina in the kitchen doorway, looking like a supermodel using Bathory as her own personal runway.

"What shall we do?" Nina asked silkily, striding into the kitchen with slow, bold steps. "We could cuddle up on the couch and watch some TV. Or listen to an album. We could skip straight to dinner if you like." Her words were reassuring, but her voice said she knew Sarah had no intention of doing any of that.

"I'm not that hungry," Sarah said, teasing Nina right back. She set the vase on the kitchen island, shuffling its flowers around into a more OCD-compliant arrangement. There was a big heart-shaped box beside it on the counter. Sarah laid a finger down on it. "This mine?"

"Mmm," Nina said in confirmation.

Next to the heart was another package the shape of a shoebox but half the size. Sarah thought she knew what was in it. She teasingly rested her fingers on it. "This too?"

"Yes."

Sarah opened the first box. Chocolates. She picked one from the box and popped it into her mouth. It was sweet as sin; she kissed Nina, sharing the taste with her. Nina's arms wrapped possessively around Sarah's back, holding her still as Nina surged against her, backing her into the counter and practically breaking her spine against it. Just like that, Sarah was bent under Nina, her body thrilling with the feeling of being taken so...elegantly.

"I still intend to cook for you," Nina said certainly. "But...perhaps breakfast?"

"Or a midnight snack." And Sarah automatically started to worry about her mother.

"What's wrong?" Nina asked.

"Nothing. Well, something... I don't want to ruin tonight."

Nina sidled off Sarah, leaning against the counter next to her. "There is no tonight if you're not happy. Come now, you're altogether too annoyingly well-adjusted. I can spoil you any night; I can only console you *now*."

"I told my mom about us last night."

"Oh," Nina said.

Sarah shoved off from the counter and stood there, flexing her tense muscles again. Every time she thought about her mother, it felt as if she developed another kink. "Yeah. Oh."

"How'd she take it?"

"She said it didn't change anything." Sarah smiled weakly. "Do they ever really mean that?"

"Life is change," Nina answered.

"Sounds like a no."

"Really? I thought it sounded a lot wiser and more sensitive than 'no.'" Nina reached out to take Sarah's hand, petting it with one solitary finger. "Change doesn't have to be bad. She loved the woman she thought you were. This is the real you. She'll love that person more because she's real, not less."

"And how long will that take?"

Nina gave Sarah's hand a squeeze. "Just know that I'll be waiting right here with you."

"That sounded a lot wiser and more sensitive than 'I don't know.' She wants to meet you, by the way." Sarah made finger quotes. "'Really' meet you."

"I'll consult my attorney. In the meantime, I have another present for you," Nina huffed out. Sarah got the impression she'd meant to flirt her way around the revelation, but Sarah had just sapped too much of her willpower. "Look by the heart."

Sarah practically branded Nina with another kiss before tearing herself away to pick up the other box.

"What is it?" Sarah asked teasingly.

"There seems an obvious way to find out."

Sarah opened it. Inside was something black and smooth that reminded her for a moment of a remote control.

"That isn't chocolate."

"It is black, though."

"I was, uh…kinda hoping you were gonna be my sex toy," Sarah joked.

"Always," Nina replied. She picked the dildo up and showed Sarah the base. "You'll notice the slots where it attaches—very firmly, I might add. I couldn't fit the harness inside, but I have it…"

"This is…" Sarah stared at the dildo, suddenly picturing *all of it* inside her. "Yours?"

"Yes, dear. Unless it doesn't meet with your approval. I realize it's a bit on the longish side, but trust me, you'll have no problem taking it. Not with me."

Sarah was speechless. Smiling with pride, Nina laid the dildo against Sarah's belly—letting her feel its heft, its cool satiny surface, through the thin fabric of her dress.

"And guess what I have on?" Nina teased. She pulled up the skirt of her dress just far enough to reveal a leather strap curving around her thigh.

Sarah bit her lip. "I want to go to bed," she said almost petulantly.

Nina nodded. She took another chocolate from the box and carried it with her to the bedroom. After she pushed Sarah down on the bed, she maneuvered the chocolate to Sarah's mouth. Sarah obligingly ate it and stuck out her tongue to suck Nina's fingers clean after she'd been fed. Then those saliva-slick fingers pushed her face to the side, pressing her cheek firmly into the mattress before releasing. The message was clear: *don't move*.

Sarah could barely whimper, barely breathe, as she watched Nina undress out of the corner of her eye. First, Nina put her foot up on the bed. Her boots were strikingly tall; they took time to unzip. First one, then the other, then Nina stepping out of them, revealing stockings that made it look like soft shadows were covering her legs and nothing else.

"You look so wonderful," Nina said, eyeing Sarah's dress, its folds and its expanses. As if she weren't the one who looked like…everything.

Nina put one foot up on the bed again, closer to Sarah this time. If she wanted, Sarah could grab hold, pull Nina to her, thrust against those amazing thighs. But she was paralyzed, unable to do more than watch as Nina rolled those sheer stockings down her legs. One by one. Then her dress—each buckle getting its own consummate attention from Nina, fondly touched and undone, until Nina could shrug the dress off and all that was left was her slip, practically sheer.

"Would you like to help me?" Nina asked teasingly.

Sarah shook her head. She wanted to rip Nina's clothes off. She wanted to keep watching. It was confusing, but in a good way.

Nina kept smiling at Sarah as she pulled the slip over her head, somehow not moving a hair out of place. Her breasts in their lace bra were perfect as always. Everything about Nina was. Intimidatingly perfect, untouchably perfect. Even now, Sarah felt as if she was contemplating vandalism imagining sex with her. And Eileen thought Nina was going to corrupt *her*…how? She had innocence to be marred, maybe, in theory, but Nina was perfection, and how could Sarah possibly add to that?

How could she try?

Sarah's mouth hung open slightly as she watched Nina attach the strap-on—quickly, professionally, with a craftsman's love for her tools.

"Would you like to ready it?" Nina asked, producing a bottle of K-Y from the nightstand. For some reason, the fact that Nina had *lube* in her *nightstand* made Sarah giggly.

She nodded; she had to be part of this. She couldn't just be a tiny participant in her own…usage. She held out her hand, and Nina squirted a thick blob of lube into it, then canted her hips to present the cock. Sarah took hold of it before she could even think, rubbing her hands over every nook and cranny, practically grinding the lube into the thing. It was hard to ignore the heft of the dildo, its weight—a real, tangible thing that would be inside her, that would enter her…that Nina would use to fuck her. But that was good; it was good to get used to it. She was prepared for it now. She was.

"You're doing very well, my love," Nina said, setting her hand on Sarah's shoulder.

"Uh?" Sarah replied eloquently.

The hand rubbed and soothed like Nina was petting a kitten. "One can barely tell how nervous you are. It's all right to be nervous, Sarah. I was too."

"You're not nervous now."

"I am." Nina's hand moved to Sarah's wrists, stopping them so Sarah was just… gently *holding* the dildo. "I'm nervous I'll hurt you. That I won't make you feel good. Or that I'll ruin this for you somehow."

Sarah looked up at her with a tiny but bold smile. "You always make me feel good."

Nina smiled right back at her. "Lie down."

Sarah lay back. Now Nina wasn't just taller; she was towering above Sarah. Her cock was towering above Sarah. "Do you want to take your clothes off?" Nina asked as she removed her bra at just the right time to take Sarah's mind off what was going to happen. "Or shall I?"

"I'll do it."

Sarah reached behind herself, patting ineffectually at the back of her neck where the zipper hid. The dress seemed even harder to get off than it had been to get on, which was just *bonkers*.

Nina looked down at her dildo and idly rubbed a glob of K-Y into the black material with a single outstretched finger. Sarah almost tore her dress as she wrestled the zipper down her back, pulled her arms free, slid the gown over her legs. She lay there, kicking it off her feet, feeling like her panties were on display. Like they had their own website. Like they were on the big TV at a football stadium.

"You're very brave." Nina reached for her.

Sarah rolled out of bed, frantically clasping her hands together in front of her groin. "Uh, uh, Nina, can you sit?"

"Certainly." Nina seated herself on the bed. She was now at eye level with Sarah's panties,

"And, uh, lie down. On your back."

Nina gave her a dazzling smile as she complied. "As you wish."

"I'm just gonna…" Sarah tucked a loose strand of hair behind her ear. "I'm just gonna sit on you, okay? I mean ride you. I mean, lower myself onto you—your thing. Dildo."

Nina nodded. Now that she was on her back, the dildo stood up like a totem pole. "I think I get the gist of your plan."

"Okay. All right." Sarah peeled her panties down her legs and came up with her hands knotted in front of her crotch. "Do we have time for a drink first?"

"Sarah," Nina said fondly. "It's all right. Come here. Just give me your hand."

And when Nina held out her hand, with those long slender fingers that had brought Sarah so much pleasure, Sarah couldn't help but obey. She took Nina's hand. Felt those long fingers take hers in a sure, strong grasp and slowly pull her in. She got onto the bed on her knees, shuffling forward to straddle Nina, all the way until the dildo was flush against her crotch.

"Are you ready?" Nina asked, and Sarah couldn't answer. With her free hand, Nina petted Sarah's hip lovingly. "Look at your little pink pussy, Sarah. It's so wet, it's shimmering. You're ready for this, Sarah. I promise that you are. Come on now. You know what to do."

Sarah lifted herself up. She held herself over Nina, her perfection, her dildo, and was very glad that she was still wearing her bra. At least she was a little covered. At least Nina couldn't see *all* her sweat and goose pimples and underarm hair. God, would she ever feel as secure as Nina, or did Nina feel as if she did, even when *she* looked like *that*?

Sarah's thighs were beginning to burn. She'd held herself above Nina so long, with Nina just waiting patiently, petting her skin and looking so supportive, so *proud* that she'd gotten this far. Sarah couldn't disappoint her. Couldn't disappoint herself. She made herself go lower…lower…her eyes closing, then opening, then looking away, then looking into Nina's eyes with all their warmth and intimacy.

She felt the tip of Nina's dildo push against her groin. Gasped as it caught and slid inside, not much wider than a few fingers, but somehow painful, *cold*…

"Stop," Nina ordered, using her commanding voice for the first time that night. Sarah obeyed instantly, freezing in place, and Nina…giggled. "I was about to tell you *not* to tense up. You have to relax, Sarah. You just have to relax."

She kept stroking Sarah's hip, now running her hand from Sarah's splayed leg up to her ribs. Her other hand went to Sarah's face, holding her cheek in her palm as if she was touching a diamond. She brushed her thumb over Sarah's lips. She wound her fingers in Sarah's hair.

Sarah looked down at Nina's face. Her smile was a different kind of perfect—full of love and acceptance and respect and kindness. Why couldn't anyone else make Sarah feel the way Nina did? Warm. Loved. Home. Sarah reached down and dared to touch Nina's cheek the same way Nina had hers.

"I love you so much, Nina."

Nina kissed her wrist, right on its throbbing pulse. "Do you want to stop?"

"No. I never want to stop."

"Then *wait*," Nina said, pulling Sarah down gently, away from the dildo, leaving it poised in the air as Sarah came down on Nina's body instead. Arms wrapped around Sarah, hands on her back, lips on her lips. Nina was everywhere.

Sarah gasped as she felt Nina's finger where the dildo had been, so soft and warm, small—just the right fit. As Nina added a second finger, sought out her G-spot, she realized Nina no longer intended to *use* the implement still strapped around her waist.

"I can take it," Sarah said.

"I know you can," Nina replied. "But that can wait. Right now I just want you to feel good. I want you to clench on *me* when I make you come—not some *thing*."

Sarah managed a shaky smile; there were three fingers now, slipping into her as easily and as gently as she'd touch herself. "Then I guess I'll just come for you."

"I guess you will," Nina purred.

>~~~<

In the dark, the bedroom was almost threatening. None of the familiar posters of Sarah's room giving her eyes something to do before they shut. Just the strange bulk of the fireplace casting an alien silhouette in the moonlight. She was breathing hard, her vision blurred, exacerbating the disconnect. Beside her, Nina was undoing the strap-on. She set it on the nightstand. In the moonlight, it was blacker than black. True darkness.

Sarah caught her breath at the same time Nina threw an arm across her, loosely pulling her close. The room settled.

"Are you all right?" Nina asked, resting her forehead against Sarah's cheek.

"All right?" Sarah giggled. "I think I'm still coming."

Nina smiled, clearly pleased with herself, then sobered again. "No, really. You can tell me if anything's wrong, or if you don't feel comfortable, or just if there's something you don't understand—"

Sarah turned just far enough to kiss her. "I'm fine. I feel fine. No regrets."

"Good. That's good, when it comes to regrets. Neither of us should have them." Nina pushed on Sarah's chin, turning her away again, and then buried her face in the back of Sarah's neck, smelling her hair with a contented sigh. "I don't want to give your mother the wrong idea about us. We're *not* doing something shameful, so let me make an honest woman out of you. Invite me to dinner. Let me talk to your mother with everything out in the open."

"Do lesbians hate their mothers-in-law, or is that just a guy thing?"

"I don't know. I guess we'll find out." Nina ran her hand back over Sarah's arm. "I kinda like finding out things with you."

"Me too," Sarah said, then twisted in Nina's grasp, breaking free, rolling atop Nina.

"What are you doing?" Nina asked, somewhat amused, somewhat bewildered.

Sarah kissed her way down Nina's body, her mouth lingering on every curve, every mole, every scar. A supplicant approaching a temple on her knees. "Showing you how much I love you." She parted Nina's legs, shifting them up onto her shoulders.

Chapter 13

Someone rang the doorbell, its few melodious chimes echoing through the house.

"That'll be her," Sarah said to her mom. "Can you get it? I'm gonna wash up real quick."

She could faintly hear Eileen opening the door and exchanging pleasantries with Nina as she splashed cold water on her face and ran a wet washcloth hurriedly over her upper body, then put on a fresh shirt. She didn't hear anything as she dabbed herself off with a towel, and when she went downstairs, Nina was sitting awkwardly at the table while Eileen ferried food out from the kitchen.

Taking Sarah's advice, Nina had dressed down to avoid lording herself over anyone, though her "dressed down" looked as if she was attending an awards show. White tank top, white chinos, a red chiffon blouse that translucently veiled her toned arms. Sarah touched Nina's shoulder as she passed her to sit down, and the thin material felt almost as smooth as her skin itself.

It was the first time in a while that Sarah and her mother had sat down together at the dinner table, much less had a third place setting.

"This is really good, Mom," Sarah said, though she didn't think she could taste anything with how loudly quiet everything was.

"Thank you," Eileen replied by rote. Her eyes were fixed on Nina.

"Yes, it is," Nina agreed. "Did you use cumin?"

"Yes," Eileen said.

"I thought so. It's a very popular ingredient these days."

"Is it?" Eileen asked. "I've always had it in my recipe."

Nina paused before taking another bite. "I guess you're ahead of the curve."

"Well, Sarah always seemed to like it." Eileen set down her spoon. It chimed against her plate. "May I say something to clear the air?"

"You don't have to," Sarah said quickly, but Eileen ignored her.

"I'm aware of how it looks, me having reservations about your relationship. But it has nothing to do with you and Sarah being lesbians. I'm very supportive of gay rights. I hardly ever even go to Chick-Fil-A."

Sarah turned to Nina. "It's a restaurant that has some anti-gay policies…" she explained.

"I know what it is. They have good sandwiches."

"Yes, they do!" Sarah agreed extravagantly. "Good fries too. It's like, ahhhh, how can you know so much about food and so little about sexuality!"

"So I guess what you're saying," Nina's eyes flicked from Sarah to Eileen, directing her response to the latter, "is that you don't have a problem with my sexuality, just me as a person."

"You could say that," Eileen replied.

"Or you could not," Sarah said, and hastily drank some water.

"I feel you're taking advantage of Sarah," Eileen continued.

"I don't see how that could be the case," Nina replied. "She's a grown woman. She's capable of making her own choices. And I think more than capable of telling the difference between someone who wants to manipulate her and someone who genuinely cares for her."

Her voice had a barbed edge there, making Sarah wonder if she was accusing her mother of something.

"I didn't say you were knowingly manipulating her. But I think she associates you with her father and being with you stirs up buried emotions that she doesn't know how to deal with—"

Sarah interrupted, "Mom, who are you to talk about buried emotions? Nina makes me happy, and it's like you resent her for that."

"No, why should I resent her?" Eileen asked. "Just because she gets you to make an effort, gets you emotionally involved…"

"What am I supposed to do, keep mourning Dad for the rest of my life?"

"No, you're supposed to move on, you're supposed to be happy—"

"I am!"

"*How?*" Eileen's questions were now a demand. "I had this happy little girl, we both did, and I couldn't wait to see her grow up and become a young woman…and then your father died and there was this haze over everything. Maybe I thought it was just me and I… I didn't do enough, was too caught up in my own pain to see what you were going through. But when you went away, I thought you could leave it all behind, leave it here. And then you came back, and you were just a sad woman who'd lost her father, living with a sad woman who's lost her husband. And now Nina's here, and suddenly, you're all better, and yes, I wish I'd been the one to help you. I was supposed to be the one to help you. But what I really wish is that I could know this is real and not just something for you to lose yourself in."

Nina spoke next, softly. "I knew your husband very well, Mrs. Kay. He would've wanted me to do whatever I could to help you get by without him. But I didn't. I locked myself away, and I felt sorry for myself. I used every setback as an excuse to hide. And now I'm upsetting you. I'm sorry for that. But I do care a great deal for your daughter, and I don't want that to be a source of misgivings for you."

"Nothing in life is a guarantee, Mom," Sarah said. "Maybe it's not real, maybe it won't last, but I think the only way any of us can move on is to at least try to be happy."

"I am happy. I'm happy you're happy," Eileen clarified. The strength went out of her arms. Her hands were already settled on the table, and now the fingers went limp. "I never thought that would mean I'd lose you…"

"You're not. How could you? You're always gonna be my mom."

"I would never dream of taking her away from you, Mrs. Kay," Nina said.

"You're not taking her. She's leaving me." Eileen held up a dissuading hand before Sarah could protest. "It's all right. It's what's supposed to happen. I didn't think it would be this hard for me, but—even when I could feel your father gone from me like something had been cut out of my body, I still had you. And now I'm making you miserable, pushing you away, fighting with your girlfriend… I'm sorry, Sarah, I'm so sorry…"

Sarah got up, went to Eileen, and found that her mother's body fit into her arms like a small old woman. Not the towering crane she'd remembered from childhood, the authoritarian, the healer, the teacher, but someone wounded. Someone in pain.

She felt an acute sense of shame as she realized she'd become blind to how sad her mother had been once the initial mourning was over. The outward signs, all the tears and puffy cheeks… Eileen had tried to shield Sarah from that, to be a better mother to her. As if Sarah had only lost a father and Eileen hadn't lost a husband. And Sarah had played along.

"I'm not leaving. I'm never leaving," she said. "I'll just be with you differently."

The small figure in her arms trembled and was still. "I think I need a moment. Could you please excuse me?"

Outside, it seemed like impossibly good weather for the scabs that had been ripped off. The sun was still out. Birds were humming. The swing hanging from a branch of the elm tree in the front yard drew Sarah's eye, the plank of pine wood dutifully shifting as the wind caught it and pushed it on its ancient rope. She sat on it, her weight solidifying the swing's position, while Nina leaned against the trunk of the tree. After a few moments of silence, Nina reached out with her foot to give the plank underneath Sarah a tap. It spun lazily.

"What are you thinking?" Nina asked.

"Oh, just that I'm an asshole…" Sarah smiled ruefully at Nina. "I spent all this time thinking of how unfair my mom was to me and never thought of how fair I was being to her."

"You were a child who lost her father," Nina pointed out. "No one could expect you to be mature about that."

"And now? I'm trying to think of when I stopped being a good daughter…"

"Well, it's never too late," Nina reasoned. "I'll completely understand if you want to spend more time with her. I know what good company you are."

"I could probably stand to let my mom know that too." Sarah shook her head. "I thought she was doing so well. I knew Dad dying hit her hard, knew she visited him and was sad sometimes, but I guess I still thought…"

Nina came away from the tree, crouching beside Sarah and steadying her swaying perch by grabbing hold of the rope. "We never get over things like that. We forget for a while, but then they come back to us in a smell, a song, a dream… And it hurts again. But that's the natural order of things. Love becomes pain becomes wistfulness. And becomes love again, when it's done hurting."

Sarah looked at her. She put her hand on Nina's where it was holding the rope, her fingers trailing over the unflinching grip. Nina held on to her like a drowning man would hold on to a life preserver. "I never thanked you."

"For what?"

"Giving me back my good memories of him and not just the loss. It used to hurt to think about him. Now I can remember all the good he did."

"You mean me?" Nina teased.

"And me. I kinda ended up a smart cookie, through no fault of my own. I mean—" Sarah's voice lightened. "Soul-sucking ennui aside, I was doing pretty well with my grades for a hot minute there."

"You do seem smarter than the average bear," Nina opined. "Maybe you could be my lab assistant."

"Like you need one."

"I need you."

Sarah ran her thumb over Nina's knuckles. They felt hard as walnuts, their grip intense. "There are probably people like us all over. Hurting, but quietly, unobtrusively. With no idea how happy they can be. I wish I could do for them what you did for me."

"Is this your way of asking for an open relationship?"

"Not like that. I mean showing people there's more to life than just…" She gestured straight ahead of her. "What you're going through. Finding people like my mom and helping them heal. I don't think she had anyone to really talk to when my dad died. Maybe if she did, things would be better between us."

"Hey." Nina gave the rope a shake. "She's still here. There's nothing so broken it can't be fixed."

"I have no idea what to say to her. She's my mother and I don't know how to talk to her."

"Would it be easier without me? Because I could go."

"No—we could use a referee." Sarah smiled slightly. "Maybe I should become a therapist. Seems like the world could use some."

"Or a social worker," Nina suggested. "Though you'd have to be careful. With your brains, you'll start there and end up as mayor."

Sarah stood, blowing out a deep breath. "You know any good stories about my dad?"

"One or two."

"Well, I'm ready to hear them."

"And your mother?"

"I think she is too. If we open a bottle of wine first."

"I'd be interested to find out if they teach that in therapist school."

Eileen was feeling more personable when they went back inside—all cried out. She acquiesced to passing the bottle around as Nina told them stories, though Sarah mostly abstained, nursing a single glass. She followed up Nina's story with one of her own, unable to remember the last time she'd summoned up the memory of her father so vividly—the way he talked, how he chose his words, the look in his eyes, whether approving or disapproving. Eileen talked about how they'd met, long before Sarah was born. Then they were all talked out, and together they put away the leftovers and washed the dishes, but with a silence that was permissive instead of oppressive. The thoughts each held in the quiet were there because they were delicate and fragile, not because they hurt.

Finally, Sarah asked if Eileen would be okay if she went home with Nina. Eileen just nodded and told them to drive safely, but it felt weird, her mom knowing she wouldn't be returning to her childhood bed that night.

Back at Nina's, they watched TV in the living room, the gentle prattle and low-grade dramatics preparing them for bed. After the episode was over, they went to the bedroom, undressed, washed up, brushed teeth. Nothing anywhere near as intense as what they usually did together but intimate all the same. Sarah tried to think if she and Nina had ever slept together without having sex. Even if it wasn't a first, it felt like one. They climbed into bed, Sarah on one side, Nina on the other. It didn't quite feel like home, but it felt like Nina. That was enough.

Distantly, Sarah heard something shrill and grating—sounding like a broken klaxon under the floorboards. She quirked her ears, trying to identify what it was. Whatever it was, it was *loud*...

"Nina, what's that sound?"

"Rat fight, I'm afraid."

"What?" Sarah asked.

"Two rats fighting in the basement. You can see why I put out traps."

It didn't sound like a rat fight, but Sarah played along. "How long do these things last?"

"Until one's dead or one surrenders. Whichever comes first."

"Kinda scary. Glad I have a big strong career woman to hold me close. Hint, hint."

"I didn't know how to ask." Nina smiled in the dark. Sarah counted it as a triumph.

Sarah turned onto her side, regretting that now she couldn't look at Nina but eager to feel her pressed against her back—married to her from head to toe—those smoothly muscular arms wrapped around Sarah almost protectively. Just like in all the books, all the movies, all the TV shows. Spooning: what you did when you were in love.

Nina's voice was in her ear, soft and lovingly gentle. "It's been a long time since I've held someone like this. Like it means something, I should say." She ran her lips along Sarah's ear, her cheek, her hairline—as if she was tasting her. Sarah felt her delight in the simple nearness. "I think I've just had everything work out well for me. It's something of a new experience. I half thought your mother would make some ultimatum or say something horrible or make *me* say something horrible, and that would be it, you'd be gone. But here you are. Mine."

"Bull." Sarah grinned. "You're mine."

The next thing Sarah felt was a soulful kiss on the back of her neck. Then a strong hand gripped Sarah's face and turned her to Nina's lips, her tongue, her passion. Sarah felt a moan rise from her.

Nina stopped, kissing her jawline instead, tiny little pecks that cooled Sarah down instead of heating her up. "Since I'm yours, would you like me to keep kissing you?"

"Yes, please."

Nina smiled, albeit with a distinct lack of humor. "I saw it from her perspective, you know. Her only daughter with no education, no career, just a…sugar momma. And the only thing that I could think to say in my defense was that I love you, Sarah Kay. And I want you in my life not because of the sex, not because of the way you look, but because of the way you make me feel and how you let me make you feel. Am I making any sense?"

Sarah turned to her, smiling broadly. "You're telling me that you love me. Nina, I've known for ages. I love you too."

Nina took a deep breath, as if recovering from some great exertion. "Believe it or not, there's something else I'd like to talk about, besides how lucky I am. Sarah, do you ever think about the future?"

"Donald Trump is president. I try not to."

"I was thinking about you—if you really want to do charity work or social work or counseling. Or anything, anything at all. I want to support you."

Sarah's brow furrowed. "I don't need your money…"

Nina, noticing Sarah's concern, reassured her with a small kiss and a running of her hands over Sarah's arms. "That's not the kind of support I meant, dear. I mean, if you have to go away, I'll understand. You have so much more to offer this world than giving orgasms to an older woman."

Sarah smiled. "I don't know. I can think of a lot of people that need to get laid."

"Not me—after the last few weeks, I may need to convalesce."

"Uh-uh. No rest for the wicked," Sarah insisted, giving Nina a quick kiss and a slow caress. As unexpectedly cute as she found the idea of simply sleeping with Nina and not making love to her first, some ideas just weren't practical.

"Well, I always did want to die in bed…"

Sarah licked her palm before reaching down to find Nina warming, as soft as ever. Her lover's face instantly flickered with pleasure as Sarah massaged her into readiness, a long, slow smile blooming on her lips. Sarah could *see* her becoming aroused as well as feeling it, and the combination was absolutely irresistible. "Do you really think I'd be good at it, though? Helping people? Being some kind of healer?"

"I know you will be. You healed me." Nina reached down to grab Sarah's forearm, pausing their lovemaking to look Sarah in the eye. "You saved me. And…" With one supple motion, Sarah was on her back and Nina was over her, her hand between Sarah's legs, all warmth and tightness and softness and need, waiting for her. "I should be the one to thank you for that."

>~~~<

Sarah jerked upright. That was a voice. A woman's voice. She'd only heard it because the window was open a crack; it seemed to be coming from the other wing of the house, carried to her by a chance breeze.

It sounded like someone was in pain.

Padding out of bed, uncomfortably sensitive to the feel of cool air against her bare skin, Sarah pulled on one of Nina's nightgowns. Her mother's daughter, she felt her racing heartbeat slow a whole measure, being all wrapped up in white. She moved to leave the room, eased the knob around, and cracked the door. There was no one in the hallway, but she heard another sound carrying. This one…closer. Dangerous, somehow.

"Hello?" Sarah called softly, not that she was sure what the point of calling out to someone was when she was whispering. Just in case there was a really polite burglar out there with really good hearing, she supposed. It certainly wasn't for Barnaby's sake. He was sleeping at the foot of the bed as if he was in a coma.

She slipped out the door, something oversensitive sending a twinge through her body. Fuck, this was too much.

"Please!" The voice again, the woman again. "Oh please!" It definitely sounded as if she was in pain.

Gathering her courage and trying to ignore her unease, Sarah crept through the house, toward the woman crying out in agony.

The door to the basement was open.

She stood in the doorway. A bare lightbulb lit up the base of the stairs and nothing else. Sarah went down the steps. They creaked under her.

On the last step, the wood gave way to a cement floor. She patted the wall where a light switch would be. Threw them all. More lights came on.

Well, there were rat traps.

Then there were the pictures. The ones Nina had shown her in the office were just the beginning. There were some of Nina and her mistress together—maybe taken by automatic timer, maybe by a third party, Sarah didn't know, didn't care. There were others of *her* alone, and here Sarah did care, *felt herself* caring, a pang in her heart as she realized Nina had taken them. Had been in love.

On the shelves and tables, under glass, were the random sort of things that could only be memories. Seashells. A saddle for a horse. Handcuffs. No rhyme or reason to it. Except that they'd been *hers*.

And there was Nina, dressed in jeans and an old T-shirt, rubber gloves over her hands and earbuds in as she pried open sprung rat traps and transferred the corpses into a big black garbage bag.

"Nice tunes," Sarah said, as the woman's cry of pain merged into a driving techno beat.

"Mmm?" Nina hummed, coming about. She saw Sarah and peeled her gloves off, then took out one earbud. "Sarah, I was hoping to get this done before you woke up. Bit of a nasty chore."

"I heard your music," Sarah said.

"Oh?" Nina reached down to her pocketed phone and found that the aux cord of her earbuds was dangling at her waist. "Oh! Sorry. I didn't mean to wake you. Marshall sent me a demo track from his brother's CD—or whatever they use now—and I figured it couldn't make this job any worse. It's something called pulsecore, and I'm sure children like it very much."

Sarah sat down on the bottom step. "Generation below me. Those guys are *freaks*." She looked around. It was as Nina had described it. Cracks in the walls, water damage…but hardly a disaster area. Unless, of course, you counted the mementos of Nina's old relationship. "Bad breakup?"

"Yes. It's funny. I used to just let the rats have this room because I couldn't bear to come down here, but now—no point in wasting space, is there? If I took down the photos, this would make quite a coffee klatch."

"Or a game room," Sarah said, standing up, pointing around. "TV there, speakers there and there, couch and easy chairs and maybe a little nacho station there. Minifridge. You close the door, I bet you could screen a Michael Bay movie in here, wouldn't bother anyone on, oh, the second floor." She crossed her arms, suddenly anxious. "It's what I would do."

Nina wasn't listening to her. She was looking at the pictures. The memories. Not fondly, but with a thousand-yard stare. As if she was looking over a battlefield she had fought in, finding no more barbed wire or craters, just green grass and sunlight. Trying to square what she was seeing with what she had *felt*.

"I should throw them away. As long as I'm down here."

"You don't have to," Sarah said. "I'm fine with there having been other women in your life…"

"It wasn't like that. They're not those kinds of memories… Are you ever curious about Emmaline and me?"

Sarah shrugged. "It seems a little like you don't want to talk about it."

"I don't. But…"

"You can tell me anything. Or not. But either way, I'll understand."

Nina's mouth gaped open a moment, as if testing the size of something fitting through it. She closed her mouth, rolled her tongue through it, until it finally opened again. "The thing I worry most about is hurting you. That I'll take advantage of you somehow, that I won't even realize I'm doing it until it's too late. And you'll hate me."

"I could never hate you, Nina."

"Let me finish," Nina insisted, but she held out a hand to put on Sarah's shoulder. "You're right. It's silly of me. Because I've been hurt, but it wasn't an accident. It wasn't. I told you about Emmaline and how good it could be with her, but there was this other side. Thinking about it is almost like having two sets of memories; I remember it, and it's like I just woke up from a dream. When we were first dating, we were very into the scene. Other people with our interests. Emmaline was older than me, more experienced, so she showed me around. Taught me. And for a while, it was wonderful. I was learning, I was getting better at anticipating her needs, and she seemed to know everything about me. It was like we were bonded somewhere deep inside. Or maybe it just seems that way now because it changed so much.

"I would set hard limits, and she would push against them. Things I didn't want to do. Wasn't comfortable with. I would say my safe word and she wouldn't hear. She'd want sessions when I didn't, and…and slowly I realized that every time I displeased her—really displeased her—that was when she would hurt me. There was no aftercare. Sometimes it was as if she wouldn't even look at me unless she wanted… Finally, I'd had enough. Bad breakup, if you can still call it that. She would say things, do things, and I just wanted her to stop. And this whole community, which was so welcoming, so supportive… They didn't want drama. Couldn't believe she'd do anything bad when she was so nice. I was on the outside looking in, just like that. I came here, and it felt safe, and didn't stop feeling safe, but everything else felt so twisted and off. Not like this place. Then you came along, and I thought I was ready. But I keep worrying I'm her. I keep worrying you're me."

"You're nothing like her," Sarah said.

"That's only half of it. Because I tell myself that: Emmaline *was* doing it on purpose. It *was* abuse. And I don't want to hurt you. I don't ever want to hurt you. I just want to love you. I want to *be* in love with you, but it feels like I don't know how. I keep thinking it'll click. Something one of us does or says will make it so that I don't feel that way anymore. But I keep feeling everything's jagged. Sharp edges. I don't think I'm ever going to be fixed, Sarah. I've tried. I should've told you before you came out to your mother. I'm sorry. I wanted to give it more time… I'm broken. You should know you're getting damaged goods."

Sarah was quiet for a long time. Nina was quieter.

"I still miss my dad," Sarah said. "It might be days, weeks, months, but I miss him over and over again. You think while I wait to stop missing him, you can wait to stop hurting?"

"Maybe," Nina said. "With company." She shook her head. "I don't want to keep you here…hoard you like a dragon's gold…"

"You don't need to. I'm yours, wherever I go."

Nina smiled slightly. "What happened to me being yours?"

"Yeah, who was I kidding?" Sarah's lips twitched almost like a grin as she pressed her head against Nina's. "You don't have to worry about me. You aren't keeping me prisoner. You never have. You set me free."

"So…you're going?" Nina sounded exquisitely unsure of how to feel about that. Barely even able to say it out loud.

"Yes. I think I should go back to college. But that's all I'm doing. I'm not leaving you, I'm not falling out of love with you, I'm not changing anything. I'm just… doing like you showed me. Figuring out what I want and going after it."

Nina smiled proudly, and the grin almost reached her sad eyes. "Sarah Kay: social worker. It has a nice ring to it."

"It does," Sarah agreed. "But that's not all I'm going after."

"Oh?"

"You, dum-dum." Sarah gave Nina another kiss to show her just how sincere she was. "If you think a couple hundred miles is going to stop me from romancing you, you're dead wrong. I'm just gonna up my game. You're going to be getting romantic letters and sexy phone calls, and there's this thing called Snapchat, I don't know if you know it, but it's going to come in very handy."

"I'll look into it," Nina promised.

Sarah took her hands, squeezing them tightly. "Hey. I know what the answer's going to be, but I'm going to ask: Are you cool with this? Because if you need me, I will always be there for you. If that means school has to wait a year—"

Nina's head gave a convulsive shake. "Don't you dare tempt me. You've gone and made me too good a person, Sarah. I can't be selfish and keep you all to myself. Go back to school, my love. Show everyone else how wonderful you are. I already know."

Epilogue

Between her part-time job and student loans, Sarah could afford an apartment off-campus. After her bedroom in Eileen's place, it seemed shockingly big, especially with most of her possessions still at home. It all seemed dizzyingly fast for her, even though she'd had months to get used to the idea. Who was she without her mother, without her friends, without Nina? Well, lonely, for one.

She cut open the single box of books she'd brought—enough to last her a semester, counting the one million on her Kindle—and ruffled around. Her nightstand had a little shelf built into it, the perfect place to show off…the entire run of R.L. Stine's *Fear Street*.

I really should not have grabbed a box at random.

Her phone rang. Sarah picked it up, checking the caller ID and letting out a little squeal when she saw who it was, then letting all *that* die down before she answered. "Nina. Hi. You know my mom called three hours before you did?"

"Really?" Nina's voice was as droll as ever, no actual surprise in her surprise. "I'm surprised she let you end the call so soon."

"I think she had to take a roast out of the oven."

"She really is quite a good cook." For a moment, Nina just let the call hang in the air, and Sarah felt herself simpering. Hearing Nina talk was like having the woman tongue her ear, bite down on her lobe, start promising things that Sarah would be happy to hold her to. And Nina knew it. "So, what're you wearing?"

Sarah smirked. There was no way her voice could be as sexy as Nina's. But maybe, to Nina… "Blouse. Pants. Underwear. I was just feeling sexy."

"And what's your apartment like?" Nina asked, something slyly insinuating even in that innocent question.

Sarah looked around, lowering her voice to three-dollars-a-minute sultry. "One bedroom, one bathroom, one…other room. Where I change underwear."

"Go to the front door," Nina said seriously.

Breathing a short sigh through her nostrils, Sarah walked on her bare feet to the door. "Do not tell me…"

"Open it."

Sarah opened the door. There was no one there. She looked to either side in the hallway. Nobody.

"There's no one here."

"That's good," Nina replied. "Then you shouldn't have any problem taking your shirt off."

Sarah froze. Nina's brusque come-on sounded *good*, so good it took Sarah a split second to remember where she was and that stripping while on the phone with Nina wouldn't result in the same quality time as stripping in person. "What, with the door open?"

"Why not?" Nina asked her. The lilt in her voice was like a perfectly raised eyebrow—Sarah could just picture it—suggesting all kinds of rewards the next time they met in person. Maybe this long-distance thing could work out after all.

Taking one last look around the hallway, Sarah stripped her shirt off before putting the phone to her ear again. She shivered as the air touched her bare skin, a lot cooler than it had been when it was just blowing against her hands and face. "There. I did it."

"You wouldn't be lying to me, would you, Sarah?"

Sarah smiled despite herself. She felt sexy, with the thought of Nina on the other end of the phone, picturing her. She could almost feel Nina's eyes on her, and her hand flexed convulsively on the phone. She could feel her nipples puckering inside her bra. "When have you ever known me to be modest? Can I close the door now? I'm letting a draft in."

"No, leave it open, I think." Nina's voice was becoming a little husky. Still poised, still in control, but Sarah could imagine her lips parting, or her legs spreading… "Go back into the living room."

Sarah stepped backward, the open door becoming more intimidating as it shrank in her view. She couldn't just slam it shut anymore. If someone were to walk by, they'd be able to get a good look at her tetons. "It's really more of a game room," Sarah quipped, trying to put away the thought of Nina *enjoying herself* to this call. She was still half sure it was crazy—that the proper place to have a sexy phone call was in the bathroom, door locked, shower running just in case the FBI was eavesdropping.

"And take your pants off," Nina breathed. She was definitely panting a little. She didn't even pant when she picked Sarah up and carried her to bed—another mental image Sarah wasn't sure she should be entertaining with the door open.

"Do you have any particularly clever response if I do a 'buy me a drink first' joke?"

"No, I think that's perfectly clever on its own," Nina said. Her voice sounded harsh, close to the phone's mouthpiece. Maybe she was holding it in place with her shoulder. Maybe her hands were doing other things. "This is taking a while, Sarah. From what I recall, it's not *that* hard to get your pants off…"

Sarah undid the button, unzipped the zipper, and shuffled her shorts down her legs. Adrenaline was flooding into her as she stared at the door. Was that a footstep she heard? No—just more creaking in the old building's bones.

"You're lucky I'm wearing clean underwear, or there's no way I'd be doing this."

"I'm not sure I'm the lucky one when it comes to you wearing clean underwear." Nina was virtually purring now, a slight elevation in her voice prickling Sarah's ears, making her wonder what Nina was wearing—if anything. "Why don't you go into the bedroom?"

Sarah bit her lip. If Nina was in there, sprawled out on the bed in expensive lingerie, this would be worth all the anxiety in the world. If she wasn't wearing any lingerie, Sarah would try to contain her disappointment.

There was no one there when she opened the door, just her lonely, empty bed.

"Door open? Good." Now Nina sounded dryly amused and heatedly aroused, all at once. "Take off your bra."

Sarah squeezed her thighs together. Shit, she was getting wet. If she didn't stop now, she'd be humping her pillow when some well-meaning neighbor walked in to make sure she hadn't had a stroke. "Okay, Nina, if we're going R-rated, then I really have to ask for an explanation here."

"You love me and want to make me happy?" Nina teased.

"I would like something more—"

Sarah heard footsteps coming down the hallway. She hid behind the bedroom door and watched, eyes starkly focused, as someone walked by the front door in a blur. Thankfully, they didn't slow down or investigate the open door, even with her shirt laying just inside the apartment. This was crazy, this was so damn crazy…

"Sarah," Nina said firmly, "take your bra off." And she moaned, like just saying the words was turning her on as much as it was Sarah. So how could Sarah not join her, share this with her, especially when it felt so good?

"Okay, okay..." Sarah hurriedly opened the hook on her bra and threw it down inside the doorway. She backed a few more steps into the bedroom, protectively clasping her arms in front of her chest.

"Now get onto the bed."

Sarah crossed the room and sat down on it, grabbing up a pillow to hide behind, even though there was now a wall between her and the front door. All she could think of was how whoever it had been that'd walked by could turn around at any moment and catch her, they could be setting down their mail in their own apartment right now and looping back to see what was wrong. And all the thought did was arouse her.

"And why don't you take your panties off too?" Nina's voice a whisper, as if she was right beside Sarah, saying her naughty words right into Sarah's ear. "It must be maddening to be almost completely naked except for those little cotton things..."

"Hey, you're not funny," Sarah said into the phone, her thighs shaking, her fingers twitching—Nina just had to give the order and she'd touch herself, she'd come for Nina, she'd do anything for Nina... "You're a witch."

"I know, dear."

Sarah heard the front door close. *Please let that be the wind, please, please... Wait...*

"Nina?" Sarah called. "Is that you?"

Footsteps clicked through her game room. High heels on hardwood. She looked at her phone. The call had ended. Whoever was in the apartment with her had stopped just before the bedroom door, not yet coming into sight.

"Are you going to take those panties off?" Nina asked her. "Or am I going to have to do it for you?"

Sarah flopped back on the bed in relief. "What are you *doing* here?"

"Painting very badly," Nina answered, coming over to the bed to rip away the pillow. "Which I'm sure I can do here as well as anywhere else. Also making sure you eat more than ramen for the next few years."

"But I thought you couldn't leave."

Nina laughed. "Leave? I'm not a ghost, Sarah. The house is just a very large part of my holdings, and it's very hard to sell. You know someone was murdered in it once?" She shook her head. "But I fully intend to return to it, hopefully dragging a cute graduate behind me. And I believe I told you to take your panties off." She hefted the pillow threateningly. "Don't disobey me, girl."

Sarah skimmed the panties down her legs, then fixedly crossed them just to pay Nina back for giving her a minor heart condition. "What happened to being a hermit?"

"I figure anyone can be a hermit when they're alone. Being a hermit in an apartment building, that takes skill. Besides, your complex allows pets."

Sarah closed her eyes. "Do not *tell me*—"

"He's waiting in the car," Nina said. "And I've left him alone long enough. Hold that pose. I will be right back."

She left the front door open.

###

About Georgette Kaplan

It was never easy for Georgette Kaplan. She was born a poor child in Mississippi, where she still remembers sitting on the porch with her family, singing and dancing around her. After learning she was adopted, at the age of 21 she hitchhiked to St. Louis, where she worked at a gas station and in a traveling carnival. After a shooting incident at the gas station, she decided to quit and pursue her lifelong dream of a career in writing. She now lives back in Mississippi with her life partner Marie.

CONNECT WITH GEORGETTE

Tumblr: georgettekaplan.tumblr.com
E-Mail: kaplangeorgette@gmail.com

Other Books from Ylva Publishing

www.ylva-publishing.com

Scissor Link

(The Scissor Link Series – Book 1)

Georgette Kaplan

ISBN: 978-3-95533-678-3
Length: 197 pages (72,000 words)

Wendy is in love with Janet Lace. Janet is beautiful, she's intelligent, and she is also Wendy's boss.

Still, a little fantasy never hurt anyone. Or so Wendy thought until Janet got a look at the e-mail she sent. The one about exactly what Wendy would like to do to Janet.

But when Wendy gets called into the boss's office, it might just be her fantasy coming true. If it doesn't get her fired first.

In Fashion

Jodiy Klaire

ISBN: 978-3-96324-090-4
Length: 220 pages (68,000 words)

Celebrity Darcy knows all about perfection. She's famous for stripping bare and restyling women on her UK TV show, Style Surgeon. Fans hang off her #EmbraceDesigner tweets and there's no challenge she can't meet. That is, until security guard Kate struts into her changing room. Suddenly Darcy's the one who feels exposed.

A lesbian romance about facing and embracing your own unique design.

One Way or Another

(The Window Shopping Collection)

A.L. Brooks

ISBN: 978-3-96324-094-2

Length: 186 pages (63,000 words)

Corporate lawyer Sarah is living a simple life: No ties, no hassles, no love. Demure teacher Bethany just wants to be swept off her feet.

A chance meeting outside a London sex shop draws the unlikely pair together. But how can two people so different even connect, let alone fall in love? Can Ms. Wrong ever be right?

A fun, sexy, lesbian romance about finding not what we want, but what we need.

Major Surgery

Lola Keeley

ISBN: 978-3-96324-145-1

Length: 198 pages (69,000 words)

Surgeon and department head Veronica has life perfectly ordered...until the arrival of a new Head of Trauma. Cassie is a brash ex-army surgeon, all action and sharp edges, not interested in rules or playing nice with icy Veronica. However when they're forced to work together to uncover a scandal, things get a little heated in surprising ways.

A lesbian romance about cutting to the heart of matters.

The Woman at the Edge of Town
© 2019 by Georgette Kaplan

ISBN: 978-3-96324-186-4

Also available as e-book.

Published by Ylva Publishing, legal entity of Ylva Verlag, e.Kfr.

Ylva Verlag, e.Kfr.
Owner: Astrid Ohletz
Am Kirschgarten 2
65830 Kriftel
Germany

www.ylva-publishing.com

First edition: 2019

No part of this book may be reproduced, scanned, or distributed in any printed or electronic form without permission. Please do not participate in or encourage piracy of copyrighted materials in violation of the author's rights. Thank you for respecting the hard work of this author.

This is a work of fiction. Names, characters, places, and incidents either are a product of the author's imagination or are used fictitiously, and any resemblance to locales, events, business establishments, or actual persons—living or dead—is entirely coincidental.

Credits
Edited by Alissa McGowan and Michelle Aguilar
Cover Design by Streetlight Graphics

www.ingramcontent.com/pod-product-compliance
Ingram Content Group UK Ltd.
Pitfield, Milton Keynes, MK11 3LW, UK
UKHW041428180426
11947UKWH00007B/351